BOYSTOWN

Season Three

Jake Biondi

Share your comments and feedback with the author!

www.JakeBiondi.com

"Like" BOYSTOWN on Facebook:

www.facebook.com/biondiboystownseries

Follow BOYSTOWN on Twitter: @boystown_series

Cover Design: Michael Vargas

Cover Models: Robert Axel, Kevin Benoit,

Brennen Scott Cooper, Pablo Hernandez, Brad Jan,

David Clark Partridge, Justin Rambo, Aaron Savvy,

Cory Zwierzynski

Episode #21

Some people are at their best when things are at their worst. Chaos had erupted in the Ritz Carleton party room when images of Derek Mancini and Cole O'Brien appeared on the large video screen as Derek and his wife Joyelle were concluding their toast honoring fiancés Emmett Mancini and Max Taylor. The New Year's Eve engagement party was designed to be a memorable celebration of Emmett's and Max's love and commitment. But Rachel Carson had other ways of making the evening a memorable one.

Joyelle Mancini had dedicated hours to creating a special video for her toast to Emmett and Max. Carefully gathering photos of the fiancés, Joyelle produced a sweet tribute to the engaged couple that she planned to show to all the party guests after Derek finished his portion of their toast. However, Rachel had managed to switch the DVD so that what the guests ultimately viewed was footage of Derek in Cole's hospital room. Partygoers as well as Joyelle watched in shock as they witnessed Derek confessing his love for Cole while Cole lay unconscious in his hospital bed after being shot.

Upon seeing the video, Joyelle ran from the room. Derek rushed after her and several others followed them, leaving the room in a complete state of chaos while Emmett and Max stood on the small stage in front of the room at a loss for what to do.

Tyler Bennett rushed through the crowd and hopped up onto the stage next to Max. He picked the microphone that Derek had dropped up from the floor and began to address the party guests.

"Ladies and gentlemen, can I please have your attention?" The crowd eventually quieted and focused its attention on Tyler. "I'm Tyler Bennett, one of the co-hosts of tonight's party celebrating the engagement of Max and Emmett. I want to thank you all for coming and joining in this special evening." Tyler turned to Max and Emmett. "Maybe with a little applause we could urge the happy couple to say a few words?" Tyler clapped and soon the rest of the party guests joined in.

As Max reluctantly took the microphone from Tyler, two hotel security guards entered the room and hastily made their way to the front. When Max was about to speak, one of the guards reached out and took the microphone from Max's hand.

"Everyone, can I please have your attention?" The puzzled guests focused their attention on the man. "We have had an incident on the ground level that necessitates us evacuating the hotel. I would ask you all to please remain calm; you are in no danger. Please gather your belongings and my colleagues at the door will escort you safely out of the hotel." Guests loudly reacted to this announcement and the guard tried to reassure them. "Everyone please remain calm. There is no imminent danger. My colleagues are at the doors ready to escort you safely from the hotel."

Guests rushed toward the exit as Keith Colgan pushed against them trying to get to the stage. Tyler, Emmett, and Max hopped down from the stage with the assistance of the security guard and Keith approached them.

"What the hell is going on?"

"We have no idea," Emmett said. "But it sounds like we need to get out of here."

"What about Michael? And Derek and Joyelle?"

"They must be outside already," Max said. "They said the entire building is being evacuated."

"We better go," Emmett added.

"What about that video?" Keith asked.

Max looked directly at Keith. "Really?"

"Now's not the time, Keith," Emmett said. "We need to find the others."

As Keith followed Max and Emmett out of the party room, Jesse Morgan was on his knees in front of Ben Donovan in a room on the hotel's fourteenth floor. Having peeled Ben's costume all the way off of him, Jesse was sucking Ben. Digging his fingers into the wall behind him, Ben tried to resist Jesse's advances. He fixed his eyes on the ceiling as Jesse continued.

"I don't...want...this..." Ben mumbled as Jesse reached up to caress his chest. Ben moaned loudly and then, in one violent motion, he leaned forward, pulled Jesse up from his knees, and threw him against the wall, pinning him there. Holding Jesse's wrists high above his head against the wall, Ben looked angrily into Jesse's eyes. Breathing hard, the two stood staring at one another.

After a moment, Ben threw his body up against Jesse and kissed him hard on the mouth. Jesse struggled to get free as Ben forced his tongue down Jesse's throat. His hard dick pressed up against Jesse's hips as Jesse's cock grew erect beneath his tight briefs. Ben forced his mouth under Jesse's chin, roughly kissing his neck and shoulders.

When Ben loosened his hold on Jesse's wrists, Jesse lowered his hands to Ben's back.

Their mouths found each other and their rage calmed as they wrapped their bodies around each other. Jesse ran his hands down Ben's back and cupped his hot ass while Ben pulled off Jesse's briefs. He wrapped one leg around Jesse as his muscled arms pressed against Jesse's sides. Pressed against each other, Ben and Jesse kissed passionately.

Smiling oddly, Ben slowly knelt down in front of Jesse, who quickly pushed him backwards against the bed and reached down to grab his underwear off the floor. As he tried to pull it back on, Ben lunged at Jesse and grabbed him around the waist.

"Let go of me!" Jesse yelled.

"Oh, no," Ben said. "Not this time."

Ben lifted Jesse off the ground and threw him onto the bed. He attempted to climb on top of Jesse, who used his legs to push Ben backwards. Regaining his balance, Ben leapt forward onto Jesse. When Jesse tried to resist, Ben pinned him down. His legs on Jesse's chest, Ben used his weight to keep Jesse in place as he reached over to grab the sash from his costume that was lying nearby on the bed.

"Let me go!" Jesse demanded.

Ben didn't respond. Instead, he tied the sash tightly around one of Jesse's wrists, ran it through the bed's headboard, and tied the other end to Jesse's other wrist. Jesse continued to struggle but there was no getting free. With his arms tied above his head and the weight of Ben's body on top of him, Jesse lost control of the situation.

Ben looked down into Jesse's wide eyes. "You denied me this once before." Ben grabbed Jesse's ankles and pulled them over his shoulders. "You won't this time." Keeping hold of Jesse's ankles, Ben leaned forward and kissed Jesse's neck and ears. When Jesse turned his head away, Ben let go of one Jesse's ankles and firmly grabbed his face, turning it back toward him. He pressed his lips against Jesse's; the kiss was deep and violent.

Ben repositioned his hands on Jesse's thighs, spreading them apart. "Stop, fucker," Jesse pleaded. Ben ignored him and began to suck Jesse's cock.

With Jesse's dick hard, Ben put his hands on the back of Jesse's knees and pushed his legs up toward his head. Jesse tried to kick as Ben pressed his hard dick against him. Kissing the insides of Jesse's calves and thighs, Ben pressed the enlarged head of his penis against Jesse.

Jesse yelled. "Don't!"

"You're mine," Ben sneered. "Always have been and always will be."

"No!"

With one powerful thrust, Ben shoved himself into Jesse, who winced as Ben tore into him. He tried to get his arms free of the sash as Ben pounded him. His thrusts became quicker and deeper. When Ben looked into Jesse's eyes, he saw Jesse's rage and smiled. Then he forced another kiss onto Jesse's lips and released his cum into Jesse.

Jesse's eyes filled with tears. "I...hate...you."

Still inside Jesse, Ben grinned and replied, "You love this."

When Ben leaned forward to kiss Jesse again, Jesse spit in his face. Ben wiped the saliva from his cheeks and then positioned his hands around Jesse's throat. He strangled Jesse and watched the boy gasp for breath. Suddenly, he let go of Jesse and kissed him again.

Just then, the door to the room opened. Both Jesse and Ben turned toward it and saw Logan Pryce and Jacqueline Donovan standing in the doorway.

"Oh, my God," Jacqueline gasped as she turned her head away from the bed.

"Logan," Jesse said, his eyes still teary.

"Oh, my God," Jacqueline repeated as if she were having trouble breathing.

Logan didn't say a word. Instead, he put his arm around Jacqueline and turned her away from the bed to escort her from the room.

"Logan, wait..." Jesse begged.

"Baby," Ben said, hopping off the bed.

"Oh, my God," Jacqueline said a third time, Logan ushering her back into the hallway.

A member of the hotel staff approached them. "Excuse me," he said to them. "But we are evacuating the hotel."

"Evacuating? Why?" Logan asked, his arms still holding Jacqueline tightly.

"There was an incident on the first floor. Evacuating is just a precaution. Please exit that way," the man said, pointing to the exit sign down the hall.

Pulling his costume pants on, Ben rushed into the hallway and stopped at the sight of the hotel staff member. Logan and Jacqueline were already headed down the hall to the exit.

"Sir, we need to evacuate the floor," the man told Ben. "Please head in that direction." The man moved on to the next room and knocked on the door. Ben looked

10

down the hallway for Jacqueline and Logan but they were gone.

He stepped back into the room and looked at Jesse, still tied to the bed. As he walked past one of the cameras that Jesse had carefully set up in the room earlier in the day, he pulled it off the shelf.

"I'm sure you're going to want to watch this over and over again," Ben declared. "I don't blame you; it was pretty hot."

"My mother will want nothing to do with you now."

Ben threw the camera at Jesse. "She's carrying my child. We are tied together forever. Even this little stunt of yours can't change that."

"You'll never know that kid," Jesse said. "And more important, he will never know his asshole father."

"The same way you never knew your asshole father?" Ben walked closer to the bed. "Think what you want, Jesse. But I assure you -- I will be a part of my child's life. One way or another." Ben paused. "Besides, when I explain what happened here, your mother will forgive me. She will never forgive you."

"You two are finished," Jesse said. "Now untie me so we can get out of here."

Ben smiled. "Looks like the only two who are finished are you and Logan." Ben pulled on his costume shirt. He leaned over and put his face near Jesse's. "Even you have to admit what just happened was pretty damn hot." Ben kissed Jesse's chest.

"You fucker," Jesse said, struggling to free his arms.

Ben picked up the camera and its attachment. "And this is just the proof I need to convince your mother I'm innocent in all of this." Ben turned around and left the room, closing the door behind him.

"Untie me!" Jesse yelled toward the closed door. "Somebody help me!"

When Logan and Jacqueline emerged from the hotel, the sidewalk was crowded with people rushing in every direction. Sirens from emergency vehicles echoed off nearby Michigan Avenue buildings and police officers on the sidewalk directed people to cross the street to safety. While Logan and Jacqueline followed some people across the street, Keith, Emmett, and Max hurried over to meet them.

"There you are," Keith said. "Are you okay?"

"We're fine," Logan said. "Does anyone know what's going on?"

"They said there was an explosion of some kind," Emmett replied.

Jacqueline looked up from the ground toward Emmett. "An explosion? Was anyone hurt?"

Max shook his head. "We have no idea. Everyone is rushing in every direction."

"Have you seen any of the others?" Keith asked. "Jesse? Derek? Michael?"

Logan sighed. "We saw Jesse."

Jacqueline put her hands to her face as she started to cry. "I have to get out of here." Jacqueline rushed down the sidewalk.

"What's the matter?" Max asked.

"I need to go after her," Logan said, following after Jacqueline.

"What was that all about?" Keith asked.

"Not sure," Emmett said, checking his phone again. "Derek isn't answering my calls or texts. I'm worried about him. He ran out of that room like a crazy person."

Max added, "And Joyelle, too."

"Well that video was pretty startling," Keith added. "Derek telling Cole that he loves him? Joyelle looked devastated."

"Not now, Keith," Max said. "We need to find the others. Haven't you heard from Michael? He ran out right behind them."

Keith removed his phone from his pocket and showed it to Max. "Nothing."

"Why don't you ask one of those police officers?" Emmett asked. "They may know where Michael is."

"Sure," Keith replied as he headed toward a nearby cop.

"What should we do?" Emmett asked Max. "Head home and wait? Follow Logan?" Max put his arm around Emmett. "Max, I'm scared."

Max kissed the top of Emmett's head. "It'll be okay." Max tightened his arm around Emmett as they both scanned the crowds of people for a familiar face.

From the crowd emerged Brian, the Whiskey and Cherries pianist who had performed at the engagement party. "There you are," he said as he hugged Emmett and then Max. "I've been looking everywhere for you. Is everyone okay?"

"We don't know," Max said. "We haven't been able to reach some of them."

"What about Danielle and Meredith?" Emmett asked.

"They are fine," Brian said. "I put them in a cab home, but I wanted to check on you two before I left."

"Thank you," Emmett said, giving Brian another hug. "Go on and head out. I'll keep you posted on the others; I promise."

"Okay, thanks," Brian said. "What a night."

"Thanks again for everything, Brian," Max added. "You guys were great."

Brian smiled back at Max and Emmett before heading through the crowded street in search of a cab. Emmett and Max lost sight of Brian as David Young approached them from a different direction.

"Emmett!" David yelled as he pushed his way to Emmett and Max. David's hair was messed up and he was covered in dust and debris.

"David," Emmett said. "My God, are you okay? What happened to you?"

David tried to catch his breath. "I ran through the police line looking for Cole. He went racing out of the hotel after Derek and Joyelle."

"Did you find him? How is he?" Max asked.

"No." David paused a moment. "Guys, it's bad. The limo you came in exploded."

"What?"

"I couldn't get close enough to see what was going on. There's smoke and shit everywhere. I tried to get to the car, but the police pulled me away."

"Did you see anyone? Derek? Justin?"

David shook his head. "There was too much smoke. And it's crazy in the area. Police. Firemen."

"I knew it was something terrible," Emmett mumbled.

"Ambulances just arrived," David added. "And Tyler, too. They let him in because he's a nurse...to help with triage."

"We've got to get in there," Emmett said, looking at Max.

"Come with me," David said. "Maybe because you're family, they'll tell you more." David grabbed Emmett's hand and pulled him into the crowd; Max followed close behind.

As the thick smoke in the driveway area of the Ritz Carlton dissipated, policemen scrambled to identify and

16

rescue survivors. Flashing lights and sirens penetrated the area as ambulances worked their way through the crowded street.

Officer Michael Martinez slowly pushed himself up from the ground, coughing violently from the thick smoke. Blood from the gash on his forehead dripped over his eyes, blurring his view of the debris around him. He wiped the blood from his face and reached out to the cement pylon next to him to stabilize himself and regain his balance. Once standing, he tried to catch his breath and wiped more blood from his face.

Michael heard the yells from someone nearby. "Help! Somebody help!" He turned to his left, then his right, trying to determine the source of the yelling. Then as the dust cleared a bit, he saw a figure kneeling on the ground near him. He stumbled in that direction, trying to avoid tripping over debris in his path.

He approached the figure on the ground and he saw that it was Derek Mancini. "Derek?"

"Michael," Derek said, waving for Michael to come closer to him. "Hurry. They're trapped under the car door." Arriving to Derek's location, Michael saw that Derek, too, was covered in blood. "Hurry!"

Michael bent down next to Derek; he saw that the limousine's huge back door had been blown off the car, pinning two people beneath it. "They're trapped," Derek cried as Michael noticed two sets of bloody legs beneath the car.

"Come on," Michael directed Derek. "Grab that side!" Michael positioned himself on one side of the car door as Derek reached the other. "We can do this." Both Michael and Derek worked to get a solid grip on their sides of the door. "On three!"

Michael counted to three and then Derek and he struggled to lift the door off those trapped beneath it. Suddenly, Tyler rushed over and assisted them.

"Be careful," Michael instructed as they slowly managed to lift the door. Groaning occasionally, Derek. Tyler, and Michael pulled the door and dropped it to the side of the people underneath it. Then they returned to them.

"Joyelle! Joyelle!" Derek called to his unconscious wife.

"Oh, God," Tyler said, bending over Joyelle's body.

Michael checked Cole's O'Brien's neck for a pulse. "He's alive," Michael told Derek. "But his pulse is slow."

Derek was focused on his wife. "Joyelle. Joyelle, please wake up." Two paramedics rushed over to them. "Please help her. She's pregnant." The paramedics stooped down to examine Joyelle.

A third paramedic ran over to Michael for his assistance. "Over here! Hurry!" Getting up from Derek's side, Michael followed the paramedics to two other bodies lying one on top of the other. With the assistance of the paramedic, Michael carefully rolled the top body over and onto the ground.

"He's not breathing," Michael told the paramedic as he looked down at the bruised face of Gino Ciancio. The paramedic quickly knelt down next to Gino as Michael looked at the other person on the ground.

Justin Mancini had been lying on the ground beneath Gino and, with Gino's body moved to the side, began to moan softly. His body trembled and his arms stretched out above him as if they were trying to grab the air around him. "Help me, help me," Justin cried out. "I can't see. I can't see anything." Michael looked toward the paramedic and then back down at Justin.

As the paramedics worked to assist the victims, fireworks exploded high above the city. Their vibrant colors and patterns welcomed the new year to Chicago. Reflections and sounds from the fireworks bounced off nearby buildings, including the hotel in which Ben and Jacqueline were staying for their holiday visit.

Ben rushed into his hotel room. He turned the lights on and scanned the room. "Jacqueline? Jacqueline?" He quickly checked the bathroom, which was dark and empty, and then returned to the main part of the suite.

There was no sign of Jacqueline anywhere. He opened the closet and saw that all of her clothes were gone. Then he turned around and noticed that only his suitcase was on the couch; Jacqueline's was gone.

"No!" Ben yelled as he pulled all the empty hangers from the closet and threw them on the bed. "Damn you, Jesse!"

While Ben raged over Jacqueline's disappearance, across the hall in another hotel suite, Marco Ciancio kissed Rachel Carson. Their naked bodies intertwined, Marco and Rachel kissed each other deeply. She dug her fingers into his back as he worked his tongue along her jaw line and down to her breast.

Then he sat up somewhat and ran his hand down the side of her body, over her stomach and between her legs.

Rachel moaned with pleasure and he smiled as he watched her body squirm beneath him.

Raising her hands to his head, Rachel pushed Marco down between her legs. She held his head in position with one hand, grinding her hips up toward his mouth. With her other hand, she reached over and grabbed the condom from the night stand. Quickly and with precision, she poked her fingernail into it, causing a small tear. Then she returned the condom to the night stand.

Moving his mouth up her body, Marco reached over to the night stand and picked up the condom. Quickly pulling it on, Marco wasted little time pushing into Rachel. He pumped her quickly, rhythmically, as he looked into her eyes with confidence. Rachel clung to his hips as he worked himself deeper inside of her. Leaning forward with one final, powerful thrust, Marco filled the torn condom.

Eventually, Marco rolled over onto his back. Rachel turned and put her head on his chest as he reached over to grab their half-filled champagne glasses from the night stand.

"We did it," Marco said, passing a glass to Rachel. "A triumph for the Ciancios. I just wish I could reach my brother; he isn't answering his phone." Marco took a sip of his champagne. "This is a night the Mancinis will never forget. The beginning of the end."

"The end of all of them," Rachel added, smiling.

Marco touched his glass to Rachel's. "Happy new year."

Rachel smiled. "It's going to be a great one."

Marco and Rachel drank from their glasses as the fireworks continued to explode outside the hotel window. Some people are at their best when things are at their worst.

Episode #22

The past has a way of working itself into the present. As Derek Mancini knelt next to his wife Joyelle in the back of the ambulance, images from the past invaded his mind. He recalled the stormy night that he first met Cole O'Brien in Boston, a one-night fling that turned into so much more. He recalled the Christmas party at which Joyelle stunned him with the news that she was pregnant, only later to find out she was, in fact, carrying twins. He recalled his promise to Cole that he would find a way for them to be together permanently. And he recalled the look on Joyelle's face as she watched him confess his love for Cole in the video that played at the engagement party earlier in the evening.

The paramedic sitting with Derek startled him from his daydream by asking, "Sir, are you okay?"

"Me?" Derek refocused on the man sitting nearby. "Oh, yes. I'm sorry -- just worried about my wife."

"I understand," the paramedic replied. "Everything will be okay. We'll be at the hospital very soon."

Derek forced a smile and then looked down at Joyelle, whose bruised face was covered with an oxygen mask. "Hang on, Joy," Derek whispered to her. "Hang on."

As the ambulance raced to get Joyelle to St. Joseph Hospital, Keith Colgan was following Michael Martinez toward the hospital's emergency room entrance. Michael was a few steps ahead and Keith rushed to catch up to him and grab his arm.

"Michael, please," Keith said as Michael turned around to face him. Keith looked at Michael's blood-stained forehead and cheeks. "Let a doctor check you out."

Michael put his hands on Keith's shoulders. "I'm fine, Keith. I promise you."

"Fine? You're covered in blood."

Michael smiled. "That's part of my job. Your boyfriend's a stud, remember?" Michael winked and Keith wrapped his arms around him in a warm hug.

"You're a hero."

"A hero? Naw." Michael paused. "But that Cole O'Brien sure is. He jumped on top of Joyelle to try to protect her when that bomb exploded. It's the second time that I know of that he's risked his own life to save someone else."

"I just don't want anything to happen to you."

Michael laughed. "Me? Never. I have more lives than a cat. Now, I have to get in there to help the others." Michael released himself from Keith's embrace, kissed him on the forehead, and turned to enter the hospital. "Don't worry so much."

Keith let out a sigh as he watched Michael go inside the hospital. He stood for a moment in the cold night air until Emmett Mancini and Max Taylor rushed up behind him.

"Have you seen anyone?" Emmett asked as he came face to face with Keith.

"Michael just went inside, but I haven't seen the others," Keith replied. "There are ambulances arriving left and right."

"We should get inside then," Max added. "And find out what's going on."

"Wait," Keith said abruptly. "Before we go inside. I just want to say...I'm sorry this is all happening on the night of your engagement party. You both deserve better."

Emmett forced a smile. "Thank you."

"We all deserve better," Max said. "No one deserves what happened tonight. Especially not Joyelle."

"Let's pray they're all okay," Emmett said. "Come on, let's get inside." Emmett turned and headed through the glass doors; Max and Keith follow him.

At the same time in the Napa Valley, Carlo Ciancio sat in his leather chair near the roaring flame in the fireplace. A sparkling Christmas tree standing proudly behind him, Carlo had his cell phone in one hand and a glass of champagne in the other. While he listened to the person on the other end of his phone call, he raised the champagne glass to his lips and took a sip. Then it was his turn to speak.

"I wish you a happy new year as well, my friend. I am sorry to intrude on your evening, but you must get on this first thing in the morning. And I'll have my boys on it with you as well -- once I can finally reach them. Apparently, they are partying a bit too much in Chicago, because they are not answering their phones."

Carlo paused a moment as the person responded. Then Carlo added, "Excellent, my friend. I knew I could count on you. Buon anno."

Carlo ended the call and tossed his cell phone onto the nearby table. Then he stood up from the chair and stepped over to the Christmas tree. He touched an ornament that his wife had given him long ago and then sipped his champagne again.

"If there is a fourth Mancini son out there, I intend to find him before they do." He smiled and then let out a soft laugh. "It's going to be a great year."

While Carlo pondered his next move, Cole O'Brien struggled with one of the nurses in the emergency room. She was trying to clean a cut on his forehead, but he was agitated and arguing with her.

"I'm okay; just let me go," Cole said.

"Sir, you are not okay. I need to tend to these bruises," the nurse said sternly. "Now please, relax."

"If I let you do your work, will you let me go then?"

"Once the doctor has checked you out."

"I told you," Cole said, rolling his eyes, "I'm fine. I need to see how my friend is."

"I'll be right back," the nurse said. "Please stay put."

"I'll make sure he does," David Young said as he walked over to Cole's bed and sat down beside him.

"You shouldn't be here," the nurse said. "But if you're going to keep this one from rushing off, you can stay."

David smiled. "I'll do my best. Thank you."

As the nurse walked away, David pulled his chair closer to the bed and took Cole's hand. "Hey, how are you?"

"I'm fine," Cole said. "I wish everyone would just let me out of here."

"So you can find Derek?"

Cole pulled his hand from David's and looked at him directly. "Maybe. What difference does it make?"

"After that video of you two tonight? I think it makes a pretty big difference." David paused a moment. "And I don't think it would be wise of you to go rushing after him here in the hospital. Where his wife works."

"How are they?"

"I don't know. I came here to see how you are. You are my concern."

"Well, thank you, but I'm fine."

"Your head doesn't look fine," David said.

"I've survived worse, remember? That's how you and I first met."

David smiled. "I remember. You're a super hero."

"Not quite."

"Well, Derek is going to need to be. To survive that video. If he survives the explosion."

"David, I had nothing to do with that video," Cole said. "It was just as surprising to me."

"I understand," David said. Then he asked, "Do you remember what you were doing just before the video was shown?"

Cole forced a smile. "Yes. I was drunk, but not *that* drunk."

"Good," David said, chuckling. "Because I enjoyed--" Before he could finish his statement, the nurse returned to the area. David stood up from his chair. "I kept him from running for you."

"Thank you," the nurse said. "Dr. MacMahon will be here to see you in just a moment."

"Great," Cole said. "Then I can get out of here."

"I'll be in the waiting area," David said.

"Thank you again," the nurse added.

David smiled and headed out into the waiting room. After passing through the doors and entering the room, he was greeted by Tyler Bennett.

"Tyler!"

"Have you heard anything? From anyone?" Tyler asked his roommate.

"I just saw Cole. He seems like he's okay. But I haven't heard about any of the others."

"Well, I'm going to see what I can find out. Derek and Joyelle must have arrived by now."

"That would be great."

"Is there any news?" Max asked as Emmett and he rushed in from the other hallway.

"Tyler is going to try to find out something," David said.

"I'll be right back," Tyler said as he disappeared behind the nurse's station.

"I just saw Cole. He seems to be okay; the doctor is with him now," David explained.

"Well, that's some good news," Emmett said.

"Yes, now maybe he can explain that horrible video to us," Keith said as he entered the room behind Max and Emmett.

"For God's sake, Keith, not now," Max said, rolling his eyes. "There are a few more important things going on here."

"He's quite the hero," Keith continued. "At least according to Michael. He said Cole jumped on Joyelle to protect her. And her babies."

"Then we all owe him a great deal of gratitude, don't we?" David asked. "Especially if Joyelle and the twins are okay."

"That's right," Max added.

"What about Justin?"

"What about him?" Keith asked.

"He's my brother, Keith," Emmett said. "I need to know he's okay."

"Of course," Keith sighed.

"I'm sure Tyler will be able to get us some information soon," David said.

"Michael is checking on things, too," Keith added.

From the doorway behind them, Tyler returned to the room carrying a stack of scrubs. "Here you go. I thought you might want to change out of those costumes into these. They are hardly fashionable, but they are comfortable and clean."

"Thank you," David said, taking the scrubs from Tyler.

Tyler smiled. "One size fits all."

"Have you found out anything?" Max asked.

"I'm on my way," Tyler said. "There's a bathroom right through there," he added, pointing to his right.

"Can you find out if my brother Justin is here?" Emmett asked.

"Sure. I'll be back as quickly as I can."

As Tyler left the room once more, David handed the others the scrubs. When he tried to hand Keith a set, Keith put his hand up.

"We ask for information and he brings us a bunch of rags. What the hell?"

"He's just trying to help," Max said. "As most of us are."

"Except for me, of course," Keith added sarcastically.

"Okay, guys," Emmett interrupted. "Let's just all take a breath and change out of these costumes. By the time we do, maybe we'll have some information."

David smiled. "Good idea."

While the men changed into the scrubs, Jesse Morgan was stepping out of the shower in his apartment. While drying off and staring at himself in the mirror, he reflected on the events of the night: his plan that had gone all wrong, the looks on Logan's and his mother's faces when they saw him in bed with Ben, and the pain of Ben forcing his way inside of him. But most of all he revisited the agony in Logan's eyes, a hurt he wondered if he could ever soothe.

A loud pounding on his apartment door startled Jesse from his reflection. He grabbed a towel, wrapped it around his waist, and hurried to the front door as the pounding grew louder and louder.

"Okay, I'm coming!" Jesse yelled toward the door as he approached and finally opened it. When he saw Ben Donovan standing in front of him, he tried to slam the door but Ben put out his arm and stopped it.

"What have you done with her?" Ben demanded as he grabbed Jesse's arms.

Jesse pushed back at Ben. "What the hell are you doing here?"

"Where is she? Where is your mother?"

"How the hell should I know? I haven't seen her since you last saw her. And we both know what a horrific sight that was."

"Never mind that now," Ben said. "I have to find her."

"Well, I haven't seen or spoken to her. In fact, I just got home after finally getting myself free from the bed you tied me to. I couldn't wait to get into the shower and wash the filth from your body off of me."

"I still don't know exactly how your little scheme tonight was supposed to work--"

"--my mother will never speak or even look at you again," Jesse said. "That's all that matters."

Ben grinned oddly. "Don't underestimate me, Jesse. I'll come out on top. Just like I did with you in that hotel bed tonight." Ben turned and left the apartment, the door vibrating as he slammed it behind him.

Jesse pulled the towel from around his waist and hurled it across the room. "Fuck!" Then he headed into his bedroom to put on some clothes.

Meanwhile, Marco Ciancio was on the phone in his hotel room. Standing naked against the dresser with his cell phone in one hand Marco looked down at Rachel Carson as she knelt before him. Her hands wrapped around his muscular thighs Rachel looked up at Marco as he continued his phone conversation.

"Thank you for the update," Marco said. "Keep me posted. And let me know if you hear from my brother. He's been unreachable." Marco ended the call and looked down at Rachel. Running his hands through her long hair, he smiled and said, "Apparently, they are all scrambling to figure out what's what. They received the message loud and clear: don't fuck with me...or my family."

Rachel stopped her activity for a moment to reply, "I like fucking with you."

Marco laughed. "And you do it so well, babe. Don't stop."

On command, Rachel resumed sucking as Marco placed his hand on the back of her head and pushed her further down on him. Then his cell phone rang and he picked it up from the top of the dresser.

"Hello, Father. Happy new year."

"Buon anno," Carlo replied. "How's my son?"

Marco looked down at Rachel. "Couldn't be better."

"Excellent," Carlo replied. "Have you heard from your brother? I haven't been able to reach him."

"Don't worry, Father," Marco said. "I'm sure he's just busy ringing in the new year in his own way." Marco then let out a soft moan.

"Am I interrupting something?"

"No, Father. You're fine."

"How are the Mancinis tonight?"

Marco laughed. "Scrambling."

"What do you mean 'scrambling'?"

"Let's just say their new year came in with a bang."

"A bang?" Carlo paused a moment. "What did you do?"

Marco adjusted his stance and ran his hand along Rachel's face. "Just reminded them whom they are dealing with."

"Without consulting with me first?"

"Trust me, Father. It was necessary and will move our plan along a bit more quickly."

"Don't go rogue on me, my son. There is too much at stake. I haven't come this close to have everything wrecked because you wanted to flex some of your proverbial muscle."

"Relax, Father," Marco said as he spread his legs further apart and Rachel's fingers explored his chest. "I have everything under control."

"You better." Carlo paused again. "When are you returning home? I have another important matter that I need you to attend to here."

"I can be home tomorrow, if you'd like."

"Good. This new project cannot wait."

"I'm on it, Father." Marco smiled down at Rachel.

"Okay. Then I'll see you tomorrow," Carlo said. "And Marco? Dispose of whatever girl you're with right away. You don't need any distractions right now." Marco laughed as Carlo ended the call.

"Everything okay?" Rachel asked.

"Just perfect," Marco said, reaching down and pulling Rachel up from her knees. He wrapped his big arms around Rachel's naked body. Her firm breasts pressed against him as he slapped her butt.

Pushing her backwards on the hotel room bed, Marco grabbed Rachel's ankles and pulled them over his shoulders. Then he knelt forward and pressed his hard cock between her legs as his mouth kissed her neck. Rachel reached over to the night stand and grabbed yet another sabotaged condom, handing it to Marco. Wasting no time pulling it on, Marco forcefully thrust himself into Rachel, who smiled and let out a loud moan.

At the same time, Derek was meeting with Dr. MacMahon outside of Joyelle's hospital room. Bruised from the explosion, Derek's face grew pale and expressionless as he listened as the doctor explained the situation.

"We did all we could to save them," Dr. MacMahon said empathetically.

"My God," Derek mumbled, tears forming in his eyes.

"The good news is that Joyelle is going to be completely fine. That boy Cole shielded her from a great deal of additional harm. Her bruises are minimal -- no worse than your own -- and she will make a full recovery."

Derek sighed. "Cole..."

"That's right. That guy's got a very good reputation around here. I recall him recently taking a bullet for you."

Derek nodded in silence. Then he asked, "Will she be able to have more children?"

Dr. MacMahon smiled. "Of course. The miscarriage was a result of the trauma from the explosion, but there is nothing to indicate she will have any difficulties in the future." Dr. MacMahon added, "You can begin trying again very soon, if that's what you two decide."

"Thank God," Derek said. "Does she know?"

"She does," the doctor replied. "She was conscious when it happened."

"Can I see her now?"

"Of course," Dr. MacMahon replied. "Mr. Mancini, you both have suffered a significant loss today. Be open with each other and help each other through it."

"We will," Derek replied, wiping the tears from his eyes. "Everything will be fine."

"She's been asking for you," the doctor added.

"I'm ready to see her," Derek said.

As Derek entered Joyelle's room, Jesse entered Logan Pryce's condominium. The place was dark and Jesse fumbled for a light switch. As the room illuminated with the flick of the switch, Jesse saw Logan sitting on the couch hovered over a bottle of wine. The light startled Logan for a moment as he turned to see Jesse.

"There you are," Jesse said, walking over to Logan and taking a seat next to him on the sofa. "You're still in your costume."

"Yup," Logan mumbled as he finished the glass of wine on the coffee table in front of him and refilled the glass with what was left in the bottle.

"Logan, I am so sorry," Jesse said. He placed his arm around Logan, who immediately shrugged it off of him.

"Don't touch me," Logan said, his words slurring together.

"Please," Jesse said. "I can explain."

"Explain fucking your mother's husband? I don't think so."

"I can--"

"No!" Logan said, quickly jumping up from his seated position. "And if you can, I don't want you to. Just go."

"Logan, please," Jesse pleaded. "Sit down and let's talk."

"I want you out of here," Logan said. "Now."

"You've been drinking, babe..."

"It's New Year's Eve. Everyone's drinking."

"Let's go to bed and we can talk in the morning."

"Get out!" Logan yelled. "I don't want to be around you anymore."

"Anymore?"

Logan grew angrier. "Ever!" He raised the empty wine bottle above his head as if he were going to hit Jesse with it. "Get out!"

"Okay, okay," Jesse said, standing up. "I'll go...for now."

"Good," Logan said, returning the bottle to the table. Then he picked his ring up off the table and threw it at Jesse. "And take that with you. I don't want it anymore."

Jesse knelt down to pick the ring up off the floor. "No, Logan. It's yours. I love you."

"Get out."

Jesse tucked the ring into his pocket. "I'll hold it for you." Jesse turned toward the door, then turned back toward Logan. "Do you know where my mother is?"

"I dropped her at her hotel a while ago." Logan took another gulp of wine. "She wants nothing to do with you, either. You disgust us."

Jesse started for the door. "We'll talk tomorrow."

"No, we won't..." Logan mumbled.

"Logan?"

"Go!"

Jesse nodded and left the condo. Logan collapsed back onto the sofa and drank what remained in his wine glass. After a moment, he began to cry. Tears poured down his cheeks and his whole body shook. With one quick swipe of his arm, he knocked the wine bottle and glass off the coffee table, sending them across the room. He put his face in his hands and continued to sob.

Jesse made his way back home, while Michael and Keith arrived at Michael's apartment. Once inside,

Michael threw his keys onto the kitchen counter and opened the refrigerator.

"Want a beer?" Michael asked Keith. "Or something stronger?"

"What I want," Keith started as he walked up behind Michael, "is for you to sit down and relax. You could have been killed tonight."

Michael smiled. "But I wasn't. Why are you always so serious? You're like a storm cloud."

"A storm cloud?"

"I think that's what I'm going to call you from now on. 'Stormy.'"

"I'm being serious," Keith said.

"So am I." Michael wrapped his arms around Keith and pulled him close to him. "Stormy, if you're going to continue to be my other half, you have to understand that this is my career. This is my life. Tonight's explosion pales in comparison to some of the situations I've been in. This is Chicago. Anything can happen on any given night."

"I know," Keith said. "But I don't have to like it."

"No, you don't. But you do have to accept it. It's my reality. *Our* reality."

Keith smirked. "*Our* reality, eh?"

"Well, there's a bit of a smile," Michael said. "I'll settle for that, Stormy."

"It took a lot for us to finally be together. I don't want anything to change that."

"Nothing's going to change that," Michael replied. "I promise."

"In your line of work, that's a promise you can't make."

Michael laughed. "It's me, remember? Your knight in shining armor."

"But--"

"Shh," Michael said, putting his index finger across Keith's lips. "Just kiss me."

Keith leaned in to kiss Michael, who pulled Keith even closer to him. Running his hands up and down Keith's back, Michael kissed Keith more deeply. Keith tugged at Michael's costume shirt, eventually pulling it off.

Keith stepped back a moment to stare at Michael -- his handsome face, his hard body. Michael took Keith by the hand and led him out of the kitchen area and into the bedroom. They stood for a moment at the foot of the bed, Michael slowly pulling Keith's scrub shirt off of him.

"I love you, Stormy," Michael whispered.

"I love you, too, Michael," Keith replied.

Michael kissed Keith passionately, his tongue darting in and out of Keith's mouth. Then he began to work his way down Keith's body by kissing his neck, his shoulders, his chest, and his stomach. On his knees in front of his boyfriend, Michael untied Keith's scrub pants and let them fall to the ground.

Running his hands up and down Keith's legs, Michael sucked Keith, who put his hands on Michael's shoulders. Michael opened his own pants and slipped out of them. Then he stood up in front of Keith and wrapped his arms around him, their erect dicks touching.

Michael gently pushed Keith back onto the bed and crawled up on top of him. Keith wrapped his legs around Michael and ran his feet up and down the backs of Michael's calves.

Michael looked down at his boyfriend, running his fingers over Keith's body as if they were exploring it for the first time. As his fingers caressed Keith, Michael worked his hard cock up the inside of Keith's thigh toward his ass. Keith shifted his position beneath Michael and spread his legs apart, inviting Michael in.

As Michael and Keith made love, Tyler returned to the hospital waiting area. He entered the room, and Emmett and Max turned to greet him.

"What did you find out about my brother?" Emmett asked, standing up from his chair.

"And Joyelle?" Max asked.

Tyler raised his hand in effort to slow down the questions. "Just a sec, guys. Just a sec." Tyler looked around the room. "Where are the others?"

"Keith took Michael home," Max replied. "We told them we'd let them know if we found anything out."

"Okay," Tyler said. "Come on, let's sit down." Tyler extended him arm to urge Max and Emmett to take seats as he did the same.

Emmett sighed as he sat. "It's bad, isn't it?"

"I just spoke with Dr. MacMahon and your brother Derek. I have his permission to tell you what's going on."

"Thank you," Max said.

"Derek and Joyelle are going to be fine," Tyler explained. "Just a few scrapes and bruises. So that's the good news."

"And the bad news?" Emmett asked.

"Joyelle lost the babies."

"Oh, no," Max said, putting his arm around Emmett, whose eyes filled with tears.

"The miscarriage was caused by the trauma of the explosion."

"How are they handling this?" Max asked.

"They are together in Joyelle's room now. They are doing as well as can be expected." Tyler paused a moment. "The other good news is that Joyelle will be able to have more children. There shouldn't be any issues with future pregnancies from today's events."

"Well, thank God for that," Max said, relieved.

"I need to tell you that things could have been much worse for Joyelle if it weren't for Cole."

"Cole?" Emmett asked.

"Yes. Apparently, Cole jumped on top of her to protect her from the explosion. He risked his life, but, luckily, he is fine, too."

Max sighed. "Wow."

"Cole saved Joyelle?" Emmett asked. "Incredible."

"He took a bullet for Derek and now this?" Max asked. "That guy's got guts."

"What about that video?" Emmett asked.

"That's another issue," Max said. "Right now, we have to appreciate what he did. Things could have been a lot worse.

"You're right," Emmett replied, turning his attention back to Tyler. "And what about Justin? What did you find out about him?"

Tyler shook his head. "Unfortunately, nothing. He was never brought here."

"Well, then where is he?" Emmett asked.

"I have no idea. I can start checking the other hospitals in the area, if you'd like."

"That would be great," Emmett said. "We need to find him."

"Sure thing," Tyler said, standing up from his chair.

"Thanks, Tyler. For everything," Max said. "We appreciate it."

"It's the least I can do." Tyler smiled at them and then walked out of the room.

Emmett turned to face Max. "I can't believe she lost the twins."

"I know, babe," Max said, hugging Emmett tightly. "But Derek and she are okay and they can have more children."

"How are they going to get past that video?"

47

"They will have to deal with that together, I guess," Max said. "We can help in any way they'll allow us."

Emmett smiled. "You're such a good man."

"I love you," Max said.

Emmett kissed Max. "I love you, too."

"You know, I had a big surprise that I was going to share with you after the party tonight. But things went a bit off track." Max paused a moment, realizing that Emmett was not entirely paying attention to him. "You okay?"

"I feel horrible for Derek and Joyelle." Emmett paused, then added, "And where is Justin? We have to find him."

"You think he's responsible for all of this somehow, don't you?"

"Right now, I just want to find him and make sure he's okay. Where the hell could he be?" Max shook his head and wrapped his arms around Emmett.

Meanwhile, in a medical clinic across town, Gino Ciancio was standing near Justin Mancini, who was lying in a hospital bed. Justin was covered in sheets up to his waist and Gino, still in his bloody costume from the New Year's Eve party and wearing a small bandage on his forehead, was holding his hand.

"Where are we?" Justin asked, his eyes looking toward the ceiling.

"We are at a private clinic," Gino said softly. "I pulled some strings and had you brought here. It's much less public and it's safer for you."

"Thank you," Justin said, his mouth dry.

"You're going to be fine, Justin. I promise."

"Fine? I can't see."

Gino leaned forward and put his hand on Justin's chest. "I know. But everything will be okay."

"I'm blind, Gino. Nothing will ever be fine."

"A specialist friend of mine will see you tomorrow. He's the best in the country. He'll help you."

"Thanks..."

Gino turned and poured Justin a cup of water. "Here. Drink this." Justin fumbled to take the cup from Gino and then put it to his lips to drink. When Justin finished, Gino took the cup and put it on the counter behind him.

"How are the others?"

"I don't know," Gino said. "I've been here with you the entire time."

Justin forced a smile. "You saved my life. You knocked me over and jumped on me."

"I did what needed to be done. That's all."

"Thank you."

"I would never let anything happen to you, Justin. You know that."

"The explosion. How did it happen?"

"You need to rest. We can talk about all that later." Gino ran his fingers through Justin's hair. "Just relax and rest." Justin closed his eyes. "Everything is going to be fine."

As Justin fell asleep, the restaurant building that Max had purchased as a surprise for Emmett stood quietly in the night air. A large bow that Max had placed on the front door remained proudly in place, even though the chaos of the evening had prevented Max from showing Emmett the building as he had intended.

In the alley behind the building, a young, red-headed boy approached the back door of the restaurant. Looking in both directions to make sure no one was around, the boy reached up and unscrewed the light bulb above the door. In the darkness that followed, the boy wrapped his hand in his scarf, quickly punched out a small pane of glass in the door, and reached through to unlock it.

With the door open, the boy quietly entered the building. He pulled the door closed behind him and headed further inside. Arriving in the kitchen area of the old restaurant, the boy looked around. He ran his fingers over the scruff along his jaw line that had resulted from two days of not shaving.

"Perfect," the boy said, as he rubbed his hands together to warm them.

At the same time, David and Cole were leaving the hospital. They passed through the corridor toward the hospital's main exit and David put his arm around Cole.

"You haven't heard from your roommate at all?" David asked.

"Jesse? Nothing. But my phone is dead; it got smashed in all the chaos at the hotel."

"Well, I'm sure he's at home waiting for you. He probably has no idea what happened tonight."

"How could he not? He was at the party. Him not being here to check on me makes no sense."

David shrugged his shoulders. "I don't know what to tell you. I'm sure he'll explain everything once I get you home."

"I want to see Derek."

"What?"

"I want to see Derek."

"I don't think that's a good idea tonight."

"For God's sake, I tried to save his wife. And he loves me. The whole world knows that now."

"Yes...the video." David paused. "I'm not sure this the best time to even bring that up. It's been a long night. Hell, it's been a long year and the year's not even twenty four hours long yet."

"The whole party saw the damn thing. Our relationship is public now."

"Your 'relationship'? Do you really think Derek is going to describe it that way?" David bit his lip and redirected his comments. "Let's just get you home. You can talk to Derek tomorrow. Give him time with Joyelle."

"But--"

"Cole!" David said sternly. "Listen to me. You need to rest. And so do they."

"Okay, okay," Cole said. "You're probably right."

David smiled and put his arm around Cole. "I usually am."

While Cole leaned on David and left the hospital, Derek leaned over Joyelle's hospital bed to kiss his wife on the forehead. Then he wiped the tears from her cheeks as she reached up and took his hand. Dr. MacMahon stood quietly in the doorway.

"I lost them. I lost them," Joyelle repeated several times.

Derek tried to calm his wife. "Shh. It's okay. It's okay, Joy."

"Your twins..."

"It's not your fault, babe. All that matters is that you're okay."

Dr. MacMahon took a few steps forward into the room. "He's right. You're going to be just fine." Dr. MacMahon smiled. "And there will be other babies. There's nothing to indicate you will have any problems in the future. What's important now is that you get some rest."

"Did you hear that, Joy? We can still have a family."

"Well, that's a bit of a Christmas present," Joyelle said softly.

Derek forced a smile. "Christmas present?"

"I was going to give you two little baby outfits for Christmas...as a reminder of our coming twins." Joyelle began to cry again. "Now I can't. But maybe next Christmas?"

Derek tried to reassure his wife. "Yes, Joy. Maybe next Christmas."

"But we have nothing to celebrate this Christmas now."

Derek looked at Dr. MacMahon and then back at Joyelle. "This Christmas? What do you mean, Joy?"

"Christmas. It's in a few days."

At that moment, Tyler passed Joyelle's room in the hallway. Seeing Derek and Dr. MacMahon in the room with Joyelle, he quietly positioned himself just outside the doorway where he could hear what they were saying without being seen.

Dr. MacMahon walked over to the side of Joyelle's bed opposite Derek. "Joyelle, do you remember what happened tonight?"

Joyelle turned her head toward Dr. MacMahon. "You said there was an explosion."

"Yes, there was," Dr. MacMahon said. "Do you remember where?"

"You said it was at the hotel."

"That's right," Derek said.

"Do you remember why you were at the hotel?"

Joyelle closed her eyes, forcing tears down her cheeks, and shook her head. "No."

Derek and Dr. MacMahon exchanged glances as the doctor asked, "That's okay, Joyelle. That's okay. What is the last thing you remember?"

Joyelle shook her head more. "I don't know."

"It's okay, Joy. Just relax and take your time."

"There was a shooting. When you rescued Emmett. And you hurt your arm." Derek nodded to encourage his wife. "That boy was shot. And you both were here in the hospital."

"Yes," Dr. MacMahon said.

"And you had to have physical therapy. You met the therapist here."

"Yes, that's right," Derek said. "We met David here in the hospital. And he helped me with my arm."

Dr. MacMahon nodded and then asked, "And then what do you remember?"

"Waking up here. In this bed."

"You don't remember the explosion?" Derek asked. Joyelle just shook her head. "Or the party before that?" Joyelle shook her head again, more tears flowing. "Putting on our costumes?"

"No," Joyelle cried. "I don't remember any of that."

"What about planning the party?" Dr. MacMahon asked. "For Max and Emmett? You were so excited about it."

"What party?" Joyelle asked, shaking her head and putting her hands over her ears. "I don't remember. I don't remember any of that."

"It's okay," Dr. MacMahon said. "You're going to be just fine."

"What's wrong with me, Doctor? Why can't I remember?"

Dr. MacMahon shifted his focus from his patient to Derek, who was still looking down at Joyelle. She looked toward the doctor for an answer to her question and, when none came, she looked toward her husband. No one spoke, especially not Tyler. The past has a way of working itself into the present.

Episode #23

Time has a way of altering one's perspective. As the unusual mid-January thaw melted Chicago's ice and snow, people took advantage of the above-average temperatures and sunshine in a variety of ways. While some enjoyed a brisk run along the lakefront or ice skating in Millennium Park, others ventured outside to remove holiday decorations and greenery which had begun to turn brown since being wrapped around lampposts and along fences prior to Thanksgiving. With the holidays behind them, Chicagoans were ready for Spring but wise enough to know that this rare streak of warm weather wouldn't last. So they were eager to enjoy the outdoors before the grip of winter returned.

As the sun peered into Derek and Joyelle Mancini's bedroom, Derek rolled over in bed next to his sleeping wife. He kissed her cheek softly. When she didn't wake up, he kissed her again, this time more passionately. His dick beginning to get hard, Derek pressed himself up against Joyelle's naked body. He ran his fingers over her breasts and she finally began to move as she awakened.

"Good morning, Joy," Derek whispered, rubbing his nose along her jaw line. She smiled and wrapped her arm around her husband. "You okay?"

"Yes," Joyelle replied, stretching her legs out from beneath the bed sheets. Derek pulled the sheets completely off of them and ran his right hand down her back to her ass.

"It's been two weeks, babe," Derek said as he kissed her breasts. "Let's try again." Without waiting for a reply, Derek moved into position. Joyelle didn't resist; instead, she kissed her husband's neck and chest, digging her fingers into the small of his back.

Derek used his hairy legs to spread Joyelle's further apart, eventually pulling them up around his hips so he could work himself into her. Joyelle arched her back as he pushed deeper, his thrusts powerful, but not rough. Her fingers caressed his back and shoulders as he gently pushed his tongue into her mouth. They kissed deeply and Derek adjusted his position once again.

Preparing for his release inside of her, Derek stopped kissing his wife and looked down at his cock. His balls slapping against her, Derek's breathing quickened and Joyelle ran her feet along the backs of his legs. She ran her hands along his arms, gripping them for support. Looking deep into his wife's eyes, Derek kissed her and released inside of her. His cock continued to release more seed as he pressed his chest against her hard nipples. Then he rested all his weight on top of her, eventually allowing himself to slip from inside of her.

"I love you," he whispered, kissing her neck. Joyelle hugged him tightly. After a moment, he rolled onto his back next to her. "You okay, babe?"

"That felt so good, Derek," Joyelle said. "It's been so long."

"Too long, Joy. But from now on--"

"Derek," Joyelle said, cutting off her husband. "What if we never have any children?"

"Don't talk like that, Joy. We will. You'll see." Derek wrapped his arm around Joyelle and kissed her forehead. "Maybe we just did."

Joyelle smiled. "Maybe."

"Are you really going into the hospital today?"

"It's been two weeks, Derek. I can't stay in this house forever. It's not helping my memory come back, that's for sure."

"But you have been through a lot, babe. The doctor said you need lots of rest."

"I've been resting non-stop since I got home. I can't sit still anymore. It's driving me nuts." Joyelle ran her hands over her head. "Ugh, if I could just remember more."

"Don't try to force it, Joy. The doctor said your memory will come back in time. You have to be patient."

"In time? How much time? You have no idea what it's like. It's so...frustrating."

Derek squeezed Joyelle tightly in his arm. "I know, I know. But you have to give yourself time, just like you'd tell one of your patients."

"It'll be good for me to get back to work at the hospital, even if it's just part time. I'll get to see my friends at work and take my mind off myself."

"Okay. As long as the doctor said it's okay."

"He did," Joyelle replied. "He encouraged it, in fact. As long as I don't push it and still get rest at home."

Derek rolled over on top of Joyelle again. "Well, there are other ways to distract you besides work..." Derek kissed Joyelle deeply, running his hand along her body and between her legs. "There's no rush to get to the hospital." Derek smiled, preparing to make love to his wife again.

While Derek and Joyelle made love a second time that morning, Keith Colgan was getting dressed in Michael Martinez's bedroom. He dried himself off from his

60

shower, dropping the towel on the floor. As he reached into his duffle bag to pull out some clean underwear, he came across the note that Rachel Carson has anonymously slipped into his hand at the New Year's Eve party.

He opened the crumpled piece of paper and read the handwritten message on it for the umpteenth time: "I know what you did all those years ago." Every time he read the note, he trembled and the fact that he had no idea who put the note in his hand terrified him.

Suddenly, Michael walked up behind Keith and wrapped his arms around his boyfriend. Having also just finished showering, Michael was naked and kissed the back of Keith's neck. Keith quickly dropped the note into his bag.

"Let's start every day off that way from now on, okay, Stormy?" Michael asked as Keith turned to face him.

"Deal," Keith replied, kissing Michael gently. "And who says sex in the shower has to be limited to the morning?"

Michael smiled. "I like the way you think." Michael kissed Keith. "What was that you were just reading?"

"Oh, nothing. Just work stuff."

"You know, today is my day off. Why don't you call in 'sick' to work today and spend the day with me? We don't even have to leave the apartment if you don't want to."

Keith laughed. "That would be great, but I do have to get some things done at the office. And I'm meeting up with Emmett and Derek later, remember?"

"Oh, that's right. The big pow-wow."

"But I could take you to dinner tonight after my meeting. How's that?"

"I've got a better idea. How about if I cook for us? Gives me something to do today besides the gym and errands."

"Sounds perfect. I'd take a night in with you over a night out any time."

Michael smiled. "Okay, handsome. It's a date." Michael kissed Keith and patted him on the ass. "Now you better get dressed and get out of here before I get horny again."

"You're always horny."

"Only when you're around," Michael said, winking. Then he walked over to his closet and began to take out some clothes.

While Keith and Michael got dressed and Keith headed to work, Emmett Mancini and Max Taylor were walking through the restaurant that Max had purchased. As they approached the front corner of the space, they stopped.

"And then the booths would run along this wall all the way to the corner," Max said.

"Perfect," Emmett replied. He turned and looked back toward the opposite wall. "I just can't believe all this."

"What's wrong?"

Emmett smiled. "Nothing is wrong. I just can't believe this is happening. It's so fast."

"Well, when Vince Provenzano contacted me about it and showed me the property, I had to move quickly. Both he and I knew it would be perfect for us."

"It is, Max. I just can't believe you put the deal together so quickly."

"It was supposed to be an engagement surprise for you. But that all got screwed up with the party disaster."

"That wasn't your fault," Emmett said. "And it's the thought that counts. I'm so grateful. For the place, but most of all, for you. I love you so much."

"I love you, too, Emmett."

"I know you told me all about the loan and the finances already. I just want to make sure that we are okay financially. Giving my two weeks notice at work was a scary thing."

"I know. For me, too. But we're going to be fine. With the loan I got, plus our combined savings, plus your inheritance from Todd, and my half of the condo once Logan buys me out, we will be just fine."

"I'm glad we're meeting with Vince again to go over everything. It'll just make me less stressed."

"This is going to be fun," Max assured Emmett. "And stressful, too. But mainly fun. And Shawn's restaurant experience will be helpful, too. He checked everything out with me before the purchase, too."

"Good. Have you heard from him at all?"

"Not since the party. Maybe Jacqueline and he are back in St. Louis? I'm sure he'll be in touch."

"We could always call--"

"Jesse?" Max asked. "Bite your tongue. I haven't seen that little ass since the new year began and that's fine with me."

Emmett changed the subject, pointing to the area beyond where they were standing. "And you're sure about the club part?"

"Well, look at this space, babe. The previous owner had the restaurant on this side and the banquet rooms on that side. We'll convert the banquet side into the club. Staggered openings, of course. Restaurant first."

"We still need a name," Emmett said.

"It'll come to us. There's time."

"Speaking of time, I need to get going."

"I know -- me, too. Should we just meet up at the condo for the meeting then?"

"Sounds good," Emmett said. "It's going to be interesting."

"It's going to be fine. People just want a chance to talk."

"I know. I just don't want it to get awkward. Derek's my brother and I love him."

Max reassured Emmett by hugging him. "It's going to be fine."

"Okay," Emmett said. "Let's be sure to lock this place up when we leave. No more break-ins."

"That was a one-time thing on New Year's Eve. Like the Michael said, it was probably just some drunk kids or something. Nothing was even stolen."

"I suppose. I'm still glad we had the locks changed. Especially since we'll be living upstairs."

"I'll have Michael send extra patrols around the place just to make you feel safe," Max teased.

"Okay, okay. I know when you're making fun of me." Emmett laughed. "Besides, I'm sure Keith has Michael occupied with other tasks."

"I'm sure," Max replied, as they headed toward the door.

Max and Emmett exited the restaurant, locked the door, and headed down the sidewalk. As they crossed the street and continued on their way, they passed right by the red haired boy who had broken into the restaurant. He was leaning against the lamppost in front of the restaurant and watching Max and Emmett as they disappeared down the street. Once they were out of sight, he headed toward the alley that led to the back of the restaurant.

Later that morning, Derek was in his office on the phone with his travel coordinator. Seated behind his desk with his back to the office doorway, Derek provided his friend with his trip details.

"I'd like to head out in the morning. Just an overnight trip," Derek said. "Well, the weather here hasn't been too bad lately, but you're right. California will certainly be warmer." Derek laughed at his friend's response. "Very true, my friend. Okay, great. I'll look forward to hearing from you with my flight information. Thanks."

As Derek hung up his office phone, a voice surprised him. "You could always fly back with me." Derek turned around in his chair to see Gino Ciancio standing in the doorway. "I'll get the jet fired up for us."

"I'd just as soon fly with a kamikaze pilot," Derek replied. "What are you doing here, Gino? Or is it Marco?"

Gino smiled. "It's Gino. Happy new year, Derek."

"What do you want?"

"May I sit down?" Gino asked.

"Of course," Derek said, pointing to one of the chairs across from his desk. "You'll forgive me if I don't stand up."

"I never expect manners from you, Derek, so all is forgiven," Gino said, taking a seat opposite Derek.

"What do you want, Gino?"

"I'm here about your brother."

"Emmett? Or the missing one?"

"Justin."

"Where is the bastard? He's been under the radar even since he tried to blow us all up."

"He had nothing to do with that," Gino said. "He was a casualty of that accident."

"Accident? That's a joke!" Derek pounded his fist on the desk. "That 'accident' cost me my children."

"I was very sorry to hear that, as was your brother. Joyelle and you have my deepest sympathy. Truly."

"Well, Justin will have to live with the fact that he killed his little nieces or nephews for the rest of his life. I will never forgive him for that."

"Derek, I am telling you: Justin had nothing to do with that explosion. In fact, he's blind because of it."

"Blind?" Derek asked. "What the hell are you talking about?"

"He was injured in the explosion, just like the rest of us. He lost his eyesight. He can't see."

"How do you know that?"

"I have been staying with him here in the city since the accident. Looking after him and taking care of him while he adjusts to his condition. He's having a hard time."

"Tell him to try losing his children. Then he'll know what a hard time really is."

"Derek--"

"Look Gino, if you came here looking for sympathy or understanding, I have none to give. My brother is coward. Hiding out for the last two weeks while the rest of us try to move on with our lives that he ruined? That's just pathetic."

"He hasn't been hiding. He's been seeing specialists that I have brought in from all over to try to help him."

"And what have they said?"

"They are at a loss. There is no evidence of physical damage to his optic nerves or his eyes in general. They think it's some sort of psychological response to the explosion. And that hopefully he'll recover."

"Psychological? Where did these 'specialists' of yours go to school?" Derek paused and then said, "Gino, why don't you just get out of here? I don't have time for my brother, you, or your family. I'm too busy trying to save mine."

"Derek, please. He wants to reach out to you. Give him a chance."

"God, you're incredible. Because of Justin, I have to meet tonight with Emmett and all of his friends to try to make sense of everything that has happened lately. Would you please get out of here? Next time, Justin wants to reach out to me, tell him to do so on his own. Not through you. And preferably without a bomb."

Gino stood up from his chair. "You are as stubborn and impossible as he is. What the hell is wrong with you two?" Gino turned toward the door and then turned back to face Derek. "You know, one day the two of you are going to need each other and it's going to be too late for both of you."

"It been 'too late' for us for twenty years, Gino."

"You say you're trying to save your family? Well, like it or not, he's a part of it." Gino turned and left the office. Derek stood up from his desk, walked to the door, and slammed it behind Gino.

At the same time in California, Carlo and Marco Ciancio were having their breakfast and coffee on the terrace overlooking the vineyards on the Ciancio estate. The early morning sun cast a bright yellow hue across the landscape as a soft breeze put a slight chill in the air.

"Have you found out anything at all?" Carlo asked his son.

"I'm looking into it, Father. But finding the fourth Mancini boy isn't something I can do overnight."

"Well, I have my men on it as well. With the old man's declining health, we have to hurry. As soon as he finally passes, his family will know the secret and be looking for that boy, too. We have to find him first."

"Yes, Father," Marco agreed, sipping his coffee.

"And, for now, I don't want your brother Gino to know anything at all about this. He's too closely connected to Justin Mancini and I don't want to put him into a situation that could compromise our success."

"I agree."

"So who's this Rachel Carson who has been occupying your time?"

Marco looked at his father. "How do you know about her?"

Carlo laughed. "I make it my business to know everything about everyone. As should you. Now tell me, who is this girl?"

"She's an ally. She has just as much against the Mancinis as we do. They are responsible for her brother's death. She is a valuable asset."

"Are you sure she's not just an opportunist? From what I understand, she was raised in the gutter and maybe that's where she should stay."

"I know what I'm doing, Father."

"The same way you knew what you were doing with that explosion?"

"It accomplished its purpose. The Mancinis are distracted and Derek's heirs are dead. I thought you'd be proud."

"And there's no way anyone can trace that 'distraction' back to us?"

"None," Marco replied. "Nothing tracks back to us."

"I don't like you making moves like that without consulting with me and considering all the consequences. If the Mancinis become desperate, they become dangerous."

"Don't worry, Father. One by one, they will all fall. And we'll have their company under our control, too."

"Well, think with your head, Marco. Not your libido. I don't want this Rachel getting in the way. Have your fun and then get rid of her."

"The way Antonio Mancini did with mother?"

Carlo grew stern. "Don't you ever speak of your mother in that way."

"I'm sorry, Father. But ever since you told me about the other Mancini son, I have been thinking..."

"About?"

"Mother's affair. And her illness. She was gone all that time in Rome."

"She was in Rome for her cancer treatments," Carlo said. "We had hoped those clinical trials would save her."

"I know, Father. But have you ever considered..." Marco paused. "Have you ever wondered if maybe she and Mancini..."

"That man stole your mother from me. He told her lies about me and took advantage of her kind nature. And when he had his fun, he left her. He used and abused her."

"I understand that, Father. But do you think there's a possibility that during the time they were together--?"

"Don't hesitate, Marco. Say what you mean. Do I think it's possible your mother got pregnant? No, I do not."

"But Father--"

"Your mother never lied to me during our entire marriage. She told me about her affair and what old man Mancini did to her. If she didn't keep that a secret, she wouldn't keep anything a secret. Especially when the cancer came and she knew she was dying. We had many intimate conversations after she returned from Rome and the treatments were unsuccessful."

"Okay, Father. You asked me to investigate and I didn't want to leave any stone unturned."

"That Mancini boy is out there somewhere. And we will find him before they do." Carlo took another sip of his coffee. Marco finished the food on the plate in front of him and gazed out across the property.

As Carlo and Marco wrapped up their morning, Tyler Bennett and David Young were returning from the gym to their apartment. Tyler tossed his gym bag onto the couch and David went into the kitchen. He took his jug of protein powder out of one of the cabinets and scooped the powder into a shake bottle.

"Do you want one, too?" David asked, pointing to the container.

"Sure, thanks," Tyler said, pulling off his sweaty shirt and sitting down on the sofa. David grabbed another cup and filled it with protein powder. "So Joyelle is supposed to come into work today for the first time since the accident."

"Oh, wow," David replied. "I had a session with Derek the other day and he said she's doing okay."

"As good as can be expected, I guess," Tyler said, filling the bottles with water and putting lids on them. He walked over to David and handed him one; they both began shaking them vigorously to mix the powder and water inside. "She still apparently can't remember much."

"That's so weird," David said. "It's gotta be totally frustrating. For her and for Derek."

Tyler sat down on the couch next to David. "I'm not so sure about Derek. This amnesia is pretty convenient for him."

"How do you mean?" David asked, removing the lid from his bottle and taking a drink.

"As long as Joyelle can't remember, he doesn't have to address that video or Cole or anything," Tyler explained. "Hell, he's probably happy she can't remember."

"He lost his children; that's a pretty big tragedy to deal with," David said.

"True. Believe me, I understand that. But he needs to address their marital issues, too," Tyler replied.

"That's their business."

"Aw, come on, David," Tyler said. "I know how much you like Cole, but you can't hope Derek and Joyelle stay together just so you can have Cole to yourself."

"I never said that, Tyler. I would never wish pain on any of them." David took a drink from his cup. "Besides, Cole is obsessed with Derek. He loves him.

He's not available to me, regardless of my feelings for him."

"So you're just going to give up on him? Just like that?"

"Not sure what else I can do. Continue to pursue someone who's in love with someone else?"

"Well, you can't just give up. You deserve to be happy, too."

"And you're hoping Joyelle gets her memory back so that you can be with her? Is that your plan?"

Tyler laughed. "I don't have a plan. But Joyelle deserves to remember the truth and to be with someone who loves and respects her as much as she deserves."

"It's all so complicated."

"True," Tyler said. "It's funny; we'd both be so much better off if Derek were just out of the picture." Tyler took a drink of his protein shake and turned his attention to the painting above the fireplace. "That painting."

"What about it?" David asked.

"It's sort of cool, I think. Of all Todd's artwork that came with this place, I'm glad we kept it."

"I like it, too. It's not really something I would ever purchase, but I like it. The colors are great and it's kind of modern."

"Reminds me of my mother for some reason," Tyler said.

"Looks like a nurse taking care of a patient to me," David said. "Maybe that's why you like it."

"I think it's more of a mother and son. Either way, it's cool."

"We did luck out with this place. And the rent Max and Emmett are charging us is ridiculously cheap."

"Well, we did help them clean out a lot of Todd's stuff. That was part of the deal."

"But we got to keep a lot of it, too."

Tyler smiled. "And we lucked out with roommates, too."

David laughed. "We sure did." He raised his cup to Tyler as if he were toasting him. Each took a gulp of his shake.

While Tyler and David enjoyed their shakes, Cole O'Brien was waiting for Jesse Morgan to join him for lunch in a downtown Chicago restaurant. A waiter refilled Cole's water glass as Cole checked his phone for messages. The waiter walked away; Jesse rushed into the restaurant and over to the table.

"Sorry I'm late, bro," Jesse said, taking a seat at the table. "Had to wrap up a conference call."

"No worries," Cole said. "Any sign of Logan?"

"No," Jesse said. "I've been working at the office nearly two weeks now and he won't see me. His secretary always runs interference for him where I am concerned. And he still won't return my calls or texts."

"Shit," Cole said. "That sucks. You've got to see him. To explain everything."

"Like you said before, the whole fiasco in the hotel room is going to be difficult to explain away, even if he does give me the chance."

"I warned you not to go through with that plan. It alienated both Logan and your mother, just as I feared it would."

Jesse rolled his eyes. "So much for not saying 'I told you so.' I haven't heard back from my mother at all, either. I guess you were right."

"I'm sorry that I was. But there's got to be a way to get through to them both and help them understand what a manipulator Ben is."

"You'd think. I guess we'll just have to wait and see." Jesse glanced at the menu and then back at Cole. "How's your office?"

"Good," Cole replied. "I'm really liking it. And my boss is cool. He's keeping me busy, which is good."

"Takes your mind off of Derek."

"Exactly. Talk about not returning calls or texts. I haven't heard a thing from him."

"Nothing at all? Crap."

"I saw David yesterday and he said that Joyelle is going back to work soon. Maybe that'll give me a chance to get Derek alone."

"She still has no memories of the video or anything?"

Cole shook his head. "I don't think so."

"Damn," Jesse said.

"I know," Cole said. "I do feel horrible for them both. I can't imagine what it's like to lose a child, let alone two of them."

"Cole, you tried to save Joyelle and her babies. That's more than anyone else did, including Derek."

"I know, but I'm sure it's still rough for them. Not sure it's something that they will ever totally get over."

"But without the babies, maybe your chances with Derek are much better? Once Joyelle regains her memories."

"I've thought about that," Cole said. "Seems like a horrible way to 'win' him, though."

"Life works out the way it's supposed to. This whole accident may be an opportunity for you both."

"We'll see," Cole said. "I just want to see him."

"And what about David?"

"We're just friends," Cole said.

"I think he's hoping for more," Jesse added.

"I was drunk when I made out with him. It was a mistake."

"Nothing's ever quite as easy as it should be, is it?"

"As you just said, things will work out the way they are supposed to."

Jesse added, "With a little help from us along the way." Cole smiled as the waiter returned to the table to take their lunch order.

While Cole and Jesse had lunch, Justin Mancini was seated in his hotel room. Dressed casually and facing the hotel room window, Justin picked up the sunglasses resting in his lap and put them on. After a moment, he heard a knock at the door.

"Come in," he said loudly from his chair.

The door opened and Rachel Carson stepped into the room. She scanned the place and, upon seeing Justin in his chair, closed the door behind her and stepped toward him.

"So it's true," Rachel said.

"Where have you been?" Justin asked, recognizing Rachel's voice. "I have been calling you for days."

"I've been busy."

"We have work to continue," Justin said, standing up and turning in Rachel's direction. "And you have some explaining to do."

"Do I?" Rachel asked.

"You had that video shown at the party, didn't you?" Justin received no reply, so he repeated, "Didn't you?"

"What if I did? What difference does it make? You wanted to destroy your brother and that video helped that to happen."

"He thinks I did it. He thinks I'm responsible."

"Good. Then he'll fear you even more."

"But I didn't do it; you did." Justin took a few steps forward.

Rachel stepped forward and put her hands on Justin's chest. "You're just not the man you used to be."

Justin grabbed Rachel's arms. "I'm the same man I always was."

"No," Rachel said. "You've softened. You're weak now. Handicapped."

Justin forced a kiss onto Rachel's lips. "I'm the same man I have always been." Justin kissed Rachel passionately, wrapping his arms around her.

She ran her fingers through his hair as he kissed her mouth and then her neck. As his hands made their way down her back, she tore open his shirt. She ran her fingers over his hard chest, eventually removing his shirt, which fell to the floor.

Suddenly, Rachel broke free from Justin's embrace, pushing him away from her. "You're pathetic. You'll never be who you want to be. I need a real man."

"Damn you."

"You can't handle a woman like me anymore. All you can handle now is a seeing eye dog."

"You bitch."

Rachel walked toward the door. "See you around, Justin." She paused and added, "Oh, that's right. You can't see." With that comment, Rachel left the room, slamming the door behind her.

"Fuck!" Justin said, standing alone in the large room.

Later in the afternoon, Michael was still running his errands on his day off. He dropped some laundry to his dry cleaner and then headed toward the grocery store. The street was quiet and Michael walked with a slow step as he took in the Spring-like air and the streetscape around him.

As he continued north on Halsted, he noticed the red headed boy standing against one of the buildings, one foot against the building and the other on the sidewalk. Michael continued toward the grocery store as the boy whistled toward him.

"Hey, hottie," the boy said, smiling.

"What's up?" Michael replied, without intending to stop his walk.

"This," the boy said, firmly grabbing his crotch. "Want to see it?"

Michael stopped in front of the boy, maintaining eye contact as he pulled his badge from his pocket.

"Officer Michael Martinez, Chicago P.D." At the sight of the badge, the boy put his other foot onto the pavement and lost his smile. "You wouldn't be soliciting me, would you?"

"No, Officer," the boy replied. "Of course, not. Just making small talk."

"Despite what many people in Boystown may think, prostitution is still illegal," Michael explained. "Don't get yourself hauled into the station for something like that." The boy didn't reply; he just looked down at the sidewalk. "Do you understand me?"

"Yes," the boy mumbled.

"Don't let me catch you pulling that crap with me or anyone else again. Consider this a warning."

The boy continued to stare at the pavement, "Thank you."

"Now get out of here." Upon command, the boy took off down the Halsted Street in the opposite direction Michael was headed. Michael watched him run away, then returned his badge to his pocket, and continued on to the grocery store.

As Michael purchased what he needed to prepare his dinner for Keith later that night, Keith arrived at

Derek's condominium for the meeting with his friends. Upon entering Derek's condo, Keith saw that Emmett and Max were already there.

"Come on in," Derek said, welcoming Keith into his home. "I can take your coat."

"Thanks," Keith replied, removing his jacket and handing it to Derek, who left the room with it.

"Hey, Keith," Emmett said, walking toward Keith from the kitchen.

"Hey," Keith responded, giving Emmett a kiss on the cheek.

"What can we get you to drink?" Max asked, giving Keith a hug.

"Whatever you guys are drinking is fine," Keith said.

"Why don't we all sit at the table?" Derek asked, returning to the room.

"We're just waiting on Logan," Max added. "I'm sure he'll be here any minute."

Keith took a seat at the table and looked around the room. "The place looks so empty without all the Christmas decorations."

"I know," Emmett said, smiling. "When I took them all down, the place looked so big. And empty." Emmett sat down next to Keith.

"Same at my place," Keith said as Max handed him a drink. "Thanks, Max."

Max nodded and sat down next to Emmett. "Joyelle is at her mother's. She doesn't know we are all meeting."

"How's she doing?" Keith asked.

"Physically, she's great," Derek said, also taking a seat at the table. "But her memories still haven't returned. The doctors think it may be a while before they do."

"Maybe that's a good thing," Keith said. "There are probably some things we all wish she would never remember."

"Is that why you asked us all to meet, Keith?" Derek asked. "To talk about the video?"

"That was one of the reasons, yes."

Before Derek could ask his next question, the door buzzer rang and Derek popped up from his chair to open the door.

"That must be Logan," Max said.

"Hey, there," Derek said to Logan, who swayed into the condo visibly intoxicated.

"Sorry I'm late," Logan said as he struggled to take off his coat.

"Not a problem," Derek replied. "We were just about to start."

Max got up from the table and approached Logan. "Are you okay?"

"I'm fine," Logan said in much the same fashion he had said it a million times when Max and Logan were together.

"Okay," Max said, hugging his former partner. "Come on in and take a seat." Max escorted Logan to the table as Derek put Logan's coat away and returned to the room.

"Can I get you anything?" Emmett asked Logan.

"A glass of wine would be perfect," Logan replied slowly.

"And a glass of water," Max added, sitting back down. Max gave Emmett a "look," which Emmett immediately understood.

Derek took a seat at the head of the table. "Now that we are all here, Keith was just about to tell us why he wanted to have this group meeting." Emmett returned to the table with Logan's wine and water. He placed the glasses in front of Logan and sat down.

"I think we all know why we are here," Keith said. "It was best to do this all at once, together as a group of friends."

"Friends," Logan mumbled.

"Look, we have all been through a lot together, good times and bad," Keith continued. "Some of our best times together were right in this very room. But what happened on New Year's Eve was horrific and dangerous."

"No one knows that better than I do, Keith," Derek said. "I lost my children."

"I know," Keith continued. "And I am so sorry for that. But in a way, it's your own fault."

"Keith!" Emmett said loudly.

"No, hear me out," Keith said, returning his focus to Derek. "When you decided to fight the Ciancios and Justin for part of your father's company, you put us all at risk. Any one of us could've been seriously hurt or killed. Michael included."

"Is that what this is about? Your boyfriend?" Max asked.

"No. Well, yes. It's about all of us," Keith said.

"I don't see a single scratch on you from that explosion," Derek said. "I don't think you were ever in any danger."

"That's not the point," Keith replied.

"Then what is?" Derek said, growing annoyed. "What is the point of all this? No one sitting around this table lost more than I did that night."

Max tried to calm the situation. "Maybe what would be helpful, Derek, would be an explanation of what happened. The video. The explosion. Everything."

"Yes," Logan said, finishing off his glass of wine. Max pushed the glass of water closer to Logan.

"At least as much as you know," Emmett added.

Derek took a deep breath. "Okay. I will tell you what I can." Derek took a drink from his beer bottle and Max nudged Logan who seemed to be falling asleep at the table. "That video was taken by Justin. He filmed it on his phone at the hospital and then tried to blackmail me with it."

"Justin?" Emmett asked. "Why?"

"He wanted me to sign over my portion of the company to him or he threatened to make the video public."

"Damn," Keith said.

"He made a really bad deal with the Ciancios and needs my part of the company to satisfy his deal with them. I refused, we talked more, and we came up with a plan to make things right with the Ciancios. He promised to destroy the video."

"Cleary, he didn't," Max said.

"Oh, Derek. I am so sorry," Emmett said. "I really thought Justin was trying to change."

"But is it true?" Keith asked. "Are you really in love with Cole?"

"Frankly, that's none of your business, Keith," Derek said. "That entire video was taken out of context. It's not as it appears to be."

"You don't need to explain that to us," Max said. "It's between you and Joyelle."

"And Cole," Keith added.

Derek ignored Keith's comment and continued. "As far as the explosion, I can only assume he is responsible for that, too. He was the one who arranged for the limo that night. And he was probably still angry with me for refusing to sign over my share of the company."

"I told you he hasn't changed," Max said to Emmett. "He's just as awful as he's always been."

"But Michael told me that the limo driver died in that explosion," Keith said. "Wouldn't he have at least spared the driver if he was solely targeting you?"

"God knows what my brother is thinking," Derek said. "We haven't seen or heard from him since that night."

"Something still doesn't make sense," Max said. "If Justin is responsible for the explosion, why would he have been anywhere near it when it went off? He's the one who told Michael to follow him to the car."

"And you said he's blind now," Emmett said. "He would never injure himself in his own plan. If there's one thing we know about him, it's that he's a survivor."

"Well, if Justin didn't set the bomb, who did?" Derek asked.

A voice from the condominium hallway surprised everyone sitting around the table. "I may be able to help answer that question," Justin said, standing just inside the door.

"You!" Derek said, jumping up from the table and rushing toward Justin. "Where the hell have you been?" Derek grabbed Justin and threw him up against the wall as Emmett rushed over to stop him.

"Derek, no," Emmett said, trying to get between Justin and Derek.

"I'm going to kill you!" Derek said, punching Justin in the gut. "You killed my children!"

Max helped Emmett restrain Derek. "Come on, man. This isn't helping." They pulled him away from Justin.

"I'm sorry," Justin said.

"You okay?" Emmett asked Justin, who clutched his gut.

"Yes," Justin said. "I suppose I deserved that. Can you help me to a chair?" Emmett wrapped his arm around Justin and slowly walked him to the table. Feeling the chair, Justin carefully sat down.

"What are you doing here?" Emmett asked.

"And where the hell have you been?" Derek added.

"Gino told me that you were all meeting today," Justin said. "His driver gave me a ride over here."

"So you really are blind," Keith said, receiving a hostile look from Max.

"Yes," Justin said. "I am. I have had appointments with several specialists. Nothing has helped."

"Why did you come here?" Derek asked. "Or did Gino make you?"

"I'm my own man," Justin said. "No one makes me do anything."

"Well, no one made you hide out for the last two weeks like a coward, either. You did that all on your own."

"I understand why you're upset with me, Derek," Justin said. "And I am so sorry for the loss of your children. From the bottom of my heart."

"You don't have a heart," Derek said.

"I have to go," Logan said, abruptly standing up.

"Are you okay?" Max asked.

"I'm fine," Logan replied, walking away from the table.

"Well, don't forget your coat," Max said, following Logan. "I'll get it for you." Max left the room.

Logan walked unsteadily toward the front door. "Bye guys." When he reached the front door, Max appeared with his coat.

Wrapping the coat around Logan, Max asked, "Are you okay?"

"I'm fine."

"You're not 'fine.' You're drunk. What's going on? Did something happen?" Max paused. "Did Jesse do something to you?"

"I'm fine," Logan repeated, putting his arms into his coat.

"I asked you a question. Did Jesse do something to you?" Logan shook his head and left the condo. Max closed the door, mumbling to himself, "I'll kill that kid."

As Max returned to the table, Emmett asked, "Is he okay?"

"Who knows?" Max said, sitting down.

"You promised not to show that video," Derek said to Justin. "I don't know why the hell I ever believed you."

"I didn't," Justin said. "I swear to you. And I know who did."

"You're the only one who had access to the video."

"No," Justin said. "There was one other person. Rachel Carson."

Keith said up in his seat. "Rachel Carson? What does she have to do with this?"

"Who's Rachel Carson?" Max asked.

"She's Nick's sister," Keith explained. Then he looked at Justin. "How do you know Rachel?"

"We met after her brother died in the warehouse."

"So what?" Derek asked. "How would she know about the video?"

"This is difficult to explain," Justin said.

"Do your best, brother," Derek replied sternly.

"Rachel is a loose cannon. She was very close to her brother. She is out for revenge on all of you. She holds you responsible for Nick's death."

"Us?" Emmett asked. "He's the one who kidnapped and raped me." Max put his hand on Emmett's lap. "And he killed Todd."

"She doesn't see it that way. She wants to bring this family down. And she wanted my help doing it."

"And I'm sure you accepted her offer," Derek added.

"No," Justin stated. "She stole the video from me. She was at the party. She is responsible for showing the video."

"Wait," Keith said. "Rachel was at the New Year's Eve party. How do you know?"

"She was my date."

"Oh, no," Keith said. "You're fucking Rachel?"

"How well do you know her, Keith?" Max asked.

"Well enough to know she's bad news," Keith said. "Oh, my God, the note..."

"What note?" Emmett asked.

"She's after all of you," Justin continued. "Keith, she's the one playing those phone tricks on you. With Nick's voice."

"Oh, my God," Keith replied, turning a bit pale.

"Let me get this straight," Derek said. "She stole the video and showed it to hurt me?"

"That's right. I swear to you...I had nothing to do with it."

"Except that you filmed it. Tried to blackmail me with it. And told her about it," Derek clarified. "You are just as responsible."

"No," Justin said.

"And did she plant the bomb, too?"

"I don't know that," Justin said. "I think it may have been Marco."

"Marco Ciancio?" Derek asked. "My God. Was he trying to kill you?"

"I don't know," Justin said, shaking his head. "Honestly, I don't."

"So instead of you being dead, my children are?

"It's not like that," Justin said. "I had nothing to do with it."

"Get out of my house!" Derek said.

"I'm here to help you," Justin said. "I want to help you."

"You've helped quite enough already," Derek said. "Get the hell out of here." Derek turned to Keith. "And you get out of here, too."

"Me?" Keith asked.

"Because this is your fault, too. First, Nick kidnaps Emmett and now his sister tries to destroy me. You think I put everyone here at risk? You did, Keith! You did!"

"I didn't even know Rachel was around. And I certainly have nothing to do with your Ciancio feud. That's all your shit."

"And to think you were almost married into our family at one point. Thank God Emmett came to his senses."

"Come on, guys," Max said. "Enough. You said it yourself, Keith. We are friends. Now we are all turning on each other. We can't do this."

"Friends?" Derek asked. "What a joke!" Derek pointed to Justin and then Keith. "The two of you have placed everyone in this room at risk at one point or another. 'Friends' don't do that."

"Derek, please," Emmett said.

"I want you both out of here," Derek said. "Now!" Derek got up from the table and left the room. A moment later, a door slammed loudly.

"I better go," Keith said. "He's acting crazy."

"Understandably, maybe," Max said. "This is a lot for us all to process."

"I'm sorry," Justin said.

"For what it's worth," Emmett said to his brother, "I believe you."

"Thank you," Justin said. "That means a lot. We'll talk more." Justin stood up from the table. "Can someone help me to the door? Gino's driver is waiting for me downstairs."

"Gino?" Emmett asked, putting his arm under Justin's. "What's going on with you two?"

Justin hesitated and then said, "He's not like Marco."

"I'll walk you out," Keith told Justin. "I want to know more about Rachel." Keith hugged Emmett and then Max. "See you guys soon."

"I'll have the driver drop you home, Keith," Justin said.

"No, thanks. I'd prefer to get home alive," Keith replied.

"Bye," Emmett said, as Justin and Keith left.

Emmett closed the door behind them and turned to Max, who gave him a warm hug.

"Are you okay?" Max asked.

"Yes," Emmett said. "Just overwhelmed. And you're worried about Logan."

"I am. He hasn't been drunk like that in a long time. Something's wrong. And I just know it has something to do with Jesse."

Max and Emmett embraced quietly for a moment and then Derek re-entered the room.

"They're gone," Emmett said.

"Good," Derek said. "I need to talk to you both."

"Are you okay?" Emmett asked.

"I'm fine," Derek said. "I need a favor. I know that you're in the process of moving out of here into your new place above the restaurant. But I'm hoping you can stay here an extra day or two to take care of Joyelle. I don't want her here alone."

"Alone?" Max asked.

Emmett followed up by asking, "Where are you going?"

"I'm going to California for a couple of days. I leave in the morning."

"California? Why?" Emmett asked.

"I'm going to see our father," Derek declared and then turned and left the room. Max and Emmett stood silently staring at one another. Time has a way of altering one's perspective.

All secrets have an expiration date. Just as the snow melting all over Chicago revealed items once buried beneath it, secrets work their way to the surface and eventually emerge for all to know, often altering lives forever.

As Derek Mancini was packing for his trip to California, his brother Emmett walked into the bedroom and sat down on Derek's bed next to his suitcase.

"Got a minute?" Emmett asked as he examined some of the clothes already in the suitcase.

"Of course," Derek said, taking some shirts from his closet. "What's up?"

"It's just you and me now, Derek. No one else is around."

Derek smiled. "I can see that."

"You know how much I love you and that I always have your back," Emmett said. "And you can tell me anything. I will keep it to myself."

"What do you want to know?"

Emmett hesitated. "Do you really love him?"

"Who?"

"Cole."

"He saved my life," Derek said. "I'm very grateful for that."

"You're not answering my question," Emmett persisted. "Do you love him? In the video, you said you did."

"I love Joyelle and we are still going to have a family one day soon."

"Derek, it's me you're talking to. Your gay brother," Emmett said. "You were always so supportive of me when I came out. You never judged me. So you know I'm not going to judge you."

"I know."

"So what's going on with Cole?" Emmett paused. "Are you gay?"

Derek laughed. "Gay? Come on, Emmett. You know me."

"It's okay if you are, you know. A lot of gay men have married women."

"I am not gay, Emmett," Derek insisted. "And I don't appreciate you jumping to that conclusion just from some video clip."

"I'm not jumping to conclusions. I am asking you so I can understand what is going on with you and Cole."

"Nothing is going on with us. We are friends; that's all."

"Derek, you are not just friends. If you were, then Justin's blackmail threat to you would have had no impact. So tell me what's going on."

Derek sat down on the bed next to his brother. "Emmett, I love Joyelle. You know I do."

"That doesn't mean you can't love someone else, too," Emmett replied. "You must be so confused by your feelings."

"I am not confused. I know exactly what -- and who -- I want."

"Then why are you going to see Dad tomorrow?"

"I need to see him before he dies. There are some things I need to say."

"What things? Derek, before the explosion, you said you were interested in the company because you had to provide for your twins. Well, sadly, you aren't going to be a father any more. So you don't need to go back to Dad or his business."

"You're wrong," Derek said. "I am going to be a father, just not as soon as we thought. But certainly one day. And if the Ciancios were behind that explosion that killed my kids, I need muscle and power to go after them and make them pay."

"Make them pay? My God, Derek, do you hear yourself? We both worked really hard to get out of that feud. Why would you voluntarily put yourself back into the middle of it?"

"I have no choice. They killed my children."

"Then why not stay away from all that? Only more bad things can come from interacting with them."

"You'd feel differently if the children who died were yours."

"And what about Cole? What are you going to do about him? Have you even spoken to him since the party?"

"I just told you. Cole is just a friend, who saved my life and tried to save the lives of my children as well. I owe him."

"But do you love him?"

Derek stood up and continued to stuff clothes into his suitcase. "I really have to finish packing, Emmett."

"Okay," Emmett said. "But you know I'm always here for you if you need anything. Even just to talk."

"I appreciate that," Derek said, still packing.

"Have a good trip," Emmett said and then left the room.

Once alone, Derek let out a large sigh and asked himself, "What *am* I going to do about Cole?"

At the same time, not far from the Mancini condominium, people were enjoying the neighborhood's newest restaurant, Boystown Bistro. Only open for a few weeks, Boystown Bistro was attracting diners from all over the city who wanted to check out the new place for themselves.

Cole O'Brien and David Young were seated at one of the restaurant's tables closest to the fireplace. Their waiter, Dustin Alexander, placed drinks on the table in front of them. His blue-green eyes and wide smile sparkled beneath the light hanging above their table.

"Is there anything else I can get you at the moment, gentlemen?" Dustin asked.

"I think we are good for now," David said. "Thanks, Dustin."

"Sure. I'll check back to see how you're doing in a bit," Dustin said and then walked away.

"Cheers," David said. They touched their glasses together and then sipped their cocktails. "I was really surprised to get your call. And excited, too."

"I thought we should probably get together and talk," Cole said.

"I'm glad," David replied. "I like spending time with you. Especially at a great place like this."

"I enjoy spending time with you, too," Cole said. "But I wanted to talk about the New Year's Eve party."

"Okay."

"I was very drunk. Obviously."

David smiled. "You were just having fun like the rest of us."

"I was having a bit too much fun. I should never have kissed you."

"It's okay," David said. "You don't need to apologize for that. Besides, it was a hot kiss and I enjoyed it."

"I appreciate that, David. But I don't want to lead you on. I shouldn't have kissed you, especially knowing how you feel about me."

"Like I said, it's okay. And after seeing that video, I understand why things are so complicated for you. Now that I know who the 'boyfriend' you've referred to is."

"I told you it was complicated. And that we were keeping things quiet."

David laughed. "Well, I think the cat's out of the bag now, don't you?"

"I guess."

"Have you spoken to Derek at all?"

"Not since that night," Cole confessed. "He hasn't taken any of my calls or replied to my texts."

"Well, he has been through a lot. The loss of his children."

"I get it. I do. That was a horrible, horrible thing."

"It's to your credit that you recognize and understand that. He's dealing with a lot, I'm sure."

"I know he is."

"Tell me something, Cole. When Joyelle gets her memory back, what do you imagine will happen?"

"I have no idea," Cole admitted. "I have my hopes, of course. But they aren't necessarily tied to Joyelle getting her memory back."

"You and Derek together, I assume," David said as Cole grinned widely. "Well, I hope you get what you want."

Cole reached across the table and grabbed David's hand. "I'm sorry if that upsets you. That's not my intent."

"Not at all," David said. "I'm fine."

"You'll find the right guy," Cole said. "You're a catch."

"I'm not worried," David replied. "And I'm not necessarily giving up." David winked at Cole. "So consider yourself warned."

"Thanks for the heads up."

"My charm is hard to resist," David said, smiling.

As the bistro hostess was walking Max and Emmett to their table, she led them right past David and Cole's table. She continued on, but Max and Emmett paused a moment.

"Well, hello," Max said, smiling at Cole and David. "Nice to see you both."

"Checking out the competition?" David asked.

Emmett laughed. "Well, I don't know if this place is our competition, but I guess we are."

"When do you think you guys will be opening?" David asked.

"It's going to be a while. Hopefully, summer."

"How are you, Cole?" Emmett asked.

"I'm good, thanks," Cole said. "How's Joyelle?"

"She's doing okay," Emmett explained. "They are both coping with their loss."

"I saw Derek the other day," David added. "He seemed like he was doing as well as could be expected."

Emmett addressed Cole directly. "I understand that you tried to protect Joyelle during the explosion, Cole. That was very brave. Thank you."

"No problem," Cole said.

"It's not the first time you have thrown yourself between danger and a member of my family. I appreciate it." Cole just smiled. "Well, we better get to our table," Emmett continued. "The hostess is showing her fangs."

"Good to see you both," Max said.

"You, too," David said, as Emmett and Max walked away to their table.

"Well," Cole said with a loud sigh, "that was awkward."

David reassured Cole. "You did just fine. Look, Boystown can be a small place and we all know a lot of people in common. You're going to bump into people."

"I know."

"Besides, Emmett seemed pretty grateful to you. And none of what happened on New Year's Eve was your fault anyway."

Cole smiled. "Except kissing you."

"Except that."

As David winked at Cole, Emmett and Max got comfortably seated at their table. The hostess placed menus in front of them and walked away.

"You handled that well," Max told Emmett.

"It was a bit uncomfortable, but I am trying to focus on the good things Cole has done for my family. And he has done a few."

"You're smart to stay out of things for now and let Derek figure it all out. He knows you're available to chat or just listen. And he knows you'll support him. That's what matters most."

"Agreed," Emmett said, taking a sip from his water glass.

"And you're doing okay? I wondered if all the talk of Rachel and Nick brought back any bad memories for you."

"Of the rape? I don't think I'll ever totally get over that," Emmett said. "But I'm okay."

"Good," Max replied. "Your HIV tests have all been negative so far; that should help us both put all that behind us." His phone began to buzz as a text message arrived. He pulled his phone from his coat pocket to check the message. "Oh, wow. It's from Shawn. He'll meet us at the restaurant the day after tomorrow."

"Oh, cool. Guess he'll be back from wherever he was."

"It'll be good to go over the blueprints and renovation plans with him. Get his input before we finalize things with the contractor."

"We still need a name…"

Max laughed. "We'll get there. The main thing was to get the concept. The name will follow."

Dustin arrived at the table. "Good evening, gentlemen. I'm Dustin, welcome to Boystown Bistro."

"Hello, Dustin," Max said. "I'm Max and this is Emmett."

"Nice to meet you both," Dustin said. "Can I get you a cocktail or glass of wine?"

"Definitely," Max replied. They placed their drink order with Dustin who brought it to the bartender.

As the night ended and a new day began, Ben Donovan sat in his car outside of his wife's home. He still hadn't seen her since New Year's Eve and had been frequently visiting her home, but she had not returned, as far as he knew.

Carefully situated beyond some bushes on the far end of Jacqueline's property, Ben watched her property, occasionally checking his phone for a reply from Max. After some time passed, Jacqueline's car pulled into her driveway. Jacqueline got out of her car and Ben hopped out of his, rushing over to her.

"Jacqueline, wait!" Ben yelled.

Jacqueline turned around to see Ben and then rushed toward her front door. "Leave me alone."

"Where have you been? We need to talk."

Jacqueline hurried to open the front door of her house as Ben arrived at her side. "I've been staying with my sister. And I have nothing to say to you."

"I need to explain," Ben said.

"You can't explain this one away, Shawn. Or Ben. Whatever your name really is." Jacqueline walked into her house and Ben extended his arm to prevent the door from closing.

"You're my wife and I love you."

"Not for long," Jacqueline said. "I've filed for divorce."

"No," Ben said angrily as he forced himself into the house. "We are not getting divorced."

"The hell we're not," Jacqueline said. "I don't even know who you are."

"I'm your husband and the father of your child."

"Well, the second part of what you said is unfortunately true. But the first part is about to be remedied. Now get out of my house."

Ben took a few steps toward Jacqueline. "Baby, please. Just hear me out."

"Why? So you can tell me that I didn't really see what you and I both know I saw."

"I'm not denying what you saw. But I am providing an explanation."

"I know what I saw. It doesn't require a commentary."

"No," Ben insisted. "You need to let me explain." Ben reached into his pocket and pulled out a small computer drive. "And I have proof of what I'm saying."

"You filmed it?" Jacqueline asked. "How sick is that?"

"No, your son filmed it. It was all a set up," Ben insisted. "He set me up."

"I don't believe you," Jacqueline said. "And I want you out of here."

"No," Ben said, kicking the front door closed behind him. "I am not leaving and you are going to watch this." Ben grabbed Jacqueline's arm forcefully.

"Let go of me."

"Sit down. You are going to watch this."

Jacqueline struggled to get free of Ben's hold. "You're hurting me."

"Sit down."

"Or what? You're going to beat me?"

"No," Ben paused. "Or I'm going to tell Jesse who his father is."

Jacqueline stopped struggling with Ben and looked into his scowling face. "What are you talking about?"

"Glad to see I finally have your attention." Ben pushed Jacqueline onto the chair situated behind her. "You're going to watch this with me and do as I tell you. Or I am going to tell Jesse that Max is his father."

"How do you know that?" Jacqueline asked quietly.

"And can you imagine what that would do to them? They hate each other. Hell, Max threatened to kill him right in front of us. They'd never forgive you for keeping this secret."

"You bastard."

Ben smiled. "Now get your laptop. It's show time."

As Jacqueline reluctantly watched the video from the hotel room on New Year's Eve, Derek and Joyelle were lying in bed holding each other after making love.

"I love you," Joyelle said, kissing Derek.

"I love you, too, Joy," Derek replied as his phone on the night stand began to vibrate. He reached over and grabbed it. Yet another text from Cole had just arrived. Derek read it to himself -- "Please, Derek, I need to see you" -- deleted it and returned the phone to the table.

"Who was that?" Joyelle asked.

"Just work calling. Nothing urgent."

"Good," Joyelle said, running her hands over her husband's chest. "I'm going to miss you while you're gone."

"It'll only be a day or two, babe," Derek said, kissing his wife. "But I do have to get going to make my flight."

"Okay."

"Emmett and Max will be here to look after you while I'm gone. If you need anything, they will take care of it."

"Honestly, Derek, I'm fine. I can take care of myself."

"I know, but I don't want you to be alone. They love you and are happy to spend the time with you." Derek got out of bed and headed toward the bathroom. Joyelle closed her eyes and eventually fell back to sleep.

While Derek got dressed and made his way to the airport, Justin was straddling Gino's hips. Gino's arms were wrapped around Justin's body as he pushed his way into Justin. Gino kissed Justin's neck, shoulders, and chest as he thrust harder.

Then he flipped Justin over onto his back, pinning him down and raising his hands above his head. He kissed Justin deeply as he forced his hips into him, spreading his legs farther apart. Justin dug his toes into the backs of Gino's calves as Gino kissed his chest. Adjusting his position once again, Gino pressed further into Justin's tight ass. Justin's fingers massaged his back, pulling Gino even deeper into him.

Gino pressed his large chest into Justin's and Justin hugged him tightly. Their tongues wrapped around each other, Gino and Justin kissed and Justin's large dick hardened between their stomachs.

Justin moaned loudly as Gino caressed him. Without trying to prevent it, Justin shot his load all over their stomachs. Not paying much attention to the gooey mess, Gino continued to pound Justin. Pumping more and more rapidly, Gino himself began to moan. In one quick motion, he withdrew himself from Justin, tore off his condom, and shot all over Justin, their cum mixing on his stomach.

"Fuck, you're hot," Justin said, wiping the sweat from his forehead.

"You too," Gino said with a smile. Gino jumped out of bed. "Let me grab a towel."

"Too late," Justin said, using the bed sheet to wipe off his body.

"What's this box?" Gino asked, eyeing a wrapped box sitting on the cabinet next to the television.

"I don't know. The bellman dropped it off earlier. Said it was a special delivery." Justin sat up in bed. "Open it."

"Okay," Gino said, removing the bow from the box. Gino carefully lifted the box top and looked inside. Wrapped in some tissue paper were two movie tickets, a foldable walking stick, and a small note, which Gino read to himself. "Justin, wishing you a quick recovery. Hope to see you back on your feet in no time. The Ciancios."

"What is it?" Justin asked.

"Oh, nothing," Gino said. "Just a tie I had ordered."

"A tie?"

"Yes," Gino lied. "I saw it in the hotel galleria downstairs on my way out earlier and had them send it up. I forgot all about it."

"Sounds nice," Justin said. "I wish I could see it."

Gino returned to the bed. "Speaking of which, I hired a trainer for you."

"A trainer? My body's not hot enough for you anymore?"

"Not a personal trainer," Gino explained. "A trainer to help you get around on your own. And help you use a walking stick."

"You mean to help me be blind better," Justin said, growing upset.

"No," Gino said. "But until you get your sight back you have to learn to become self-sufficient."

"You mean to rely on you less," Justin said.

"Justin, you know how much I care about you. I've been by your side for the past two weeks. But I can't do it forever. You need to get back on your own two feet. You won't be happy until you are."

"Happy? When have I ever been happy?"

"Well, you can be. If you'd let yourself," Gino said. "Don't you realize the life we could have together? If you'd just let go of this need you have to be connected to the family businesses."

"I would just be a burden; you just said so yourself."

"I never said that. You aren't a burden," Gino said. "I just want you to become independent. Stop feeling sorry for yourself. Don't let the blindness defeat you. And don't let your need for revenge wreck what could be a happy future."

"Wreck a happy future? If my future is wrecked, it's your fault."

"My fault?"

"Yes," Justin said. "You and your family. You're responsible for the bomb that did this to me."

Gino stood up from the bed. "I can't believe you'd even say that. God, you're a piece of work. You don't know me at all, do you? I don't know why I even bother." Gino walked away into the bathroom.

"Gino, wait," Justin said.

Gino stuck his head out of the bathroom. "Just so you know, your brother Derek is headed to California to see your father. I thought you'd want to know since that's all you seem to care about anymore. If you're lucky, he'll steal your whole inheritance out right from under you!" Gino returned to the bathroom and slammed the door.

Justin sighed. "Fuck."

In the hospital cafeteria, Tyler Bennett and Joyelle we seated at a table near the window. The beautiful Lincoln Park visible behind them, Tyler and Joyelle each had a cup of tea on the table in front of them.

"It's so good to have you back here," Tyler said.

"Thanks," Joyelle responded. "It's great to be back. I'm always better when I have a routine."

"And the doctor has given you clearance to come back to work?"

"Oh, yes. I'm completely fine. At least physically."

Tyler reached out and put his hand on hers. "I'm so sorry about the babies."

"Thank you," Joyelle said. "It's been difficult, but Derek and I are dealing with our loss together. That makes a big difference. If only I could get my memory back."

"Have the doctors said anything about that?"

Joyelle sighed. "Just that I have to be patient. My memories will come back on their own."

"That must be so frustrating for you," Tyler said. "Is there anything we can do to try to help you get them back sooner?"

"The doctor discouraged trying to force things. He said that would just prolong the process. It has to occur on its own."

Tyler smiled. "You know me. I don't have patience. For anything."

"I usually don't, either. But I don't have much choice."

"Well, I'm glad you're safe and healthy otherwise," Tyler said. "That's what matters."

"And that I can have more children," Joyelle added. "Derek and I have already been trying."

"Ah," Tyler replied.

Joyelle laughed. "Too much information?"

"Maybe," Tyler said. "And you don't remember anything from the New Year's Eve party? Nothing?"

Joyelle shook her head. "I'm sorry; I don't."

"Well, it'll all come back to you. It has to."

Joyelle stood up. "Come on, we better get back upstairs."

"I'm right behind you," Tyler said, standing up and following Joyelle to the elevators. As they passed a recycling bin, Tyler tossed their paper cups inside. Then they hopped into the elevators, which took them back up to their work floor.

As Tyler and Joyelle returned to work, Marco Ciancio was in his office on the phone with his father.

"Yes, Father," Marco said, fidgeting with a pen in his right hand. "I'll head back to Chicago this afternoon to meet with Justin." Marco paused a moment as his father spoke. Then he replied, "Don't worry, Father. I'm on it."

Marco put the phone down, stood up, and turned to look out the window behind him. All of San Francisco was in view and he gazed out over the city he loved. Then he turned back to his desk, picked up the phone, and dialed a number.

"It's Marco," he said. "Change of plans. We're not going to Chicago. Fuel up one of the larger planes; we are headed to Rome."

At the same time, Michael Martinez rolled over on top of Keith in bed. The weight of his body pressing down on Keith, he kissed Keith's ears and neck. Keith ran his fingers through Michael's thick hair and then worked his hands down Michael's powerful back.

"I love you so much," Michael said.

"Mmm, I love you, too," Keith said, as Michael rolled over next to him. "You always make me feel so safe."

"You are safe, Stormy. Always." Michael kissed Keith's forehead. "You didn't say much last night about your meeting with your friends."

"Well, I wanted that fabulous dinner you made to be about us. Not about them."

"So how did it go?"

"Okay, I guess," Keith said. "Justin showed up."

"He did? Where has he been?"

"Apparently hiding out with Gino Ciancio, which is really odd because Mancinis and Ciancios don't usually mix."

"So I've heard," Michael said.

"Have you made any progress at all with the bomb investigation? Justin and Derek seem to think Marco Ciancio was behind it. And me, too."

122

"You? What are you talking about?"

"Well, not the bomb but that video with Derek and Cole."

"What would you have to do with that?"

"Justin took that video with his phone. And he thinks Rachel Carson actually showed the video at the party."

"Rachel Carson?"

"Nick's sister," Keith explained. "Apparently, she blames all of us for her brother's death and is hell-bent on destroying the Mancinis and me."

"Wow."

"In fact, Justin said that she is responsible for the calls with Nick's voice that you and I have received. And the video of Emmett and Nick."

"Do you think that's true?"

"It's certainly possible. I remember Rachel being a total bitch. This would be consistent with how I remember her."

"Besides the calls, has she threatened you? Or any of the Mancinis?"

"Not that I know of. All of this is what Justin said about her. None of us has actually spoken with her directly."

"Well, please let me know if you do." Michael wrapped his arm tightly arm Keith. "And as far as the Ciancios go, we've already questioned both of them. And everyone else at the party or near the explosion. The driver was killed, Justin had been impossible to locate, until now, and there's been little salvageable evidence from the explosion -- so our investigation has been very slow."

"You'll get to the bottom of it," Keith said. "You always do."

Michael smiled and rolled back on top of his boyfriend. "So do you," Michael said, kissing Keith deeply. "And I wouldn't have it any other way." Michael kissed Keith's neck and made love to him again.

As the day progressed, Derek's plane made its way to California as Marco's left California for Italy. Still horrified by what she had viewed in the video that Ben showed her, Jacqueline sat quietly on the sofa in her living room next to Ben.

"I'm sorry that you had to watch all that again," Ben said. "But I wanted you to see that it wasn't my fault. Jesse set the whole thing up."

"You're both at fault," Jacqueline said. "Our entire relationship is based on lies. You and my son were together before you and I ever met. And you never said one word to me."

"Because it was over. It was in the past."

"But it's the only reason you're with me. To get back at him or something."

"No," Ben said. "I mean, yes, that was my plan originally. But as I got to know you, I really and truly fell in love with you. I swear."

"If you loved me, you would have told me the truth. And used your real name all along. And resisted Jesse's advances in that damn video."

"If you loved me," Ben said, "you would have told me that truth about Max."

"That's hardly the same thing. My past with Max didn't motivate my actions regarding you. One has nothing to do with the other."

"Well, now I know that truth. And I will keep it to myself so long as you co-operate."

"So you're going to blackmail me?"

"No, baby," Ben said. "I'm saving our marriage. I love you."

"You don't even know what that word means."

"You can forget all your ideas about divorcing me. As long as you stay with me as my wife and we move forward from this together, your secret is safe with me. Otherwise, I'll go public with my information. They already hate each other. And you will never have any kind of relationship with Jesse or Max again. They'd never forgive you for keeping this secret from them."

"I hate you," Jacqueline said.

"No, baby. You think you hate me at this moment, but that will pass in time." Ben ran his hand along Jacqueline's face. "You will love me like you always have. And we'll raise our family together as we always intended."

Jacqueline pulled her face away from Ben. "Don't touch me."

Ben smiled. "I'm your husband."

"I will remain your wife…for now…but I will never be with you again."

Ben reached into his pocket and pulled out his cell phone to show her. "See this phone? Watch this." He opened an app and a map appeared on the screen. "That dot is your son. I have been tracking his whereabouts for months. Remember that, because even though you want nothing to do with him now, I know you still love him. And you'd hate for anything bad to happen to him." Ben put his phone back into his pocket. "Do what I tell you to do and nothing will."

"You really are a miserable person."

"Not when I'm with you, baby. You make me so happy. And so will our child." Jacqueline rolled her eyes at him. "Do we understand each other?"

"Perfectly," Jacqueline replied.

"Good," Ben said. "Now let's get working on hiring some movers because we are moving to Chicago, as we had planned. I know how much you'd like to be closer to your son…and his father."

As Ben's phone app had indicated, Jesse Morgan was headed toward Logan Pryce's office. In spite of Logan's secretary trying to stop him, Jesse pushed past her and barged into Logan's office with a piece of paper rolled up in his hand. Sitting behind his desk, Logan looked up as Jesse entered followed by the secretary.

"I'm sorry, Logan," she said. "He wouldn't listen to me."

"Not a problem," Logan said, looking up from his computer toward the door. "It's okay."

"Thank you," she replied as she left the office, closing the door quietly behind her.

"What the hell is this?" Jesse said, throwing the paper down onto Logan's desk. "I'm being reassigned to a new division?"

"That's correct," Logan said, turning back toward his computer.

"That's bullshit is what it is," Jesse said, sitting down in the chair across from Logan. "First you won't return any of my calls and texts for the past two weeks and now you want to re-assign me to another division with a different boss? You can't do that. I'm doing very well here and you know it."

"I can do whatever I think is best for the firm."

"Keeping me where I am so that I can do my best work is what's best for the firm," Jesse said. "This isn't about business; it's personal and you know it."

"As you can see, I'm busy," Logan said, keeping his focus on his computer screen. Jesse got up from the chair, walked around to Logan's side of the desk, and sat down on it.

"Look at me," Jesse said, still getting ignored. He grabbed the back of Logan's chair and turned it toward him. "Look at me." Logan reluctantly looked at Jesse. "I love you, Logan. And you love me, too. I know it."

"You slept with your mother's husband. I can never forget or forgive that."

"It wasn't as it seemed."

"Oh? I imagined it?" Logan asked. "I may have too much to drink on occasion, but even I know what I saw. You and him naked in that hotel room."

"Yes," Jesse agreed. "That is what you saw. But it's not what you think. It was my way of exposing him to my mother. His true nature. She wouldn't believe me when I told her about him, so I had to show her. To let her witness it with her own eyes."

"She was traumatized," Logan said. "Heartbroken. And so was I."

"I know," Jesse agreed. "And I'm sorry. That wasn't my intent. I only wanted to--"

"To what? Hurt me? Ruin my life?"

"No, of course not. I would never intentionally hurt you. You weren't supposed to be there."

"Oh, so since I wasn't supposed to see it, I'm supposed to forgive you? And if I hadn't seen it, would you have ever told me about it? Or would you have just kept on lying?" Jesse struggled to articulate a reply. "Never mind," Logan said. "It just doesn't matter."

"But it does. It does matter to me," Jesse said. "I don't want to lose you. I just wanted to protect my mother from that monster."

"Be careful about who you're calling a monster. I could say the same of you."

"How many times do I have to tell you? It was a set-up. I just wanted to protect my mother."

"And in the process, you lost her. And me."

"No," Jesse said. "I refuse to believe that we are done."

"Well, we are," Logan said, turning away from Jesse.

Jesse put his hands on Logan's shoulders. "No. We just need time. I just need time to make things right and show you how much I love you."

Logan pulled his shoulders from Jesse's grip. "You couldn't do that in ten lifetimes."

Jesse paused and looked around the office for a moment. Then he spoke again. "The fundraiser. For Cole's mother. You promised you'd help me."

"That was a long time ago."

"Yes, one of the first times we ever met, in fact. But you promised and it's for a good cause and a special person. You can't go back on your word." Logan didn't respond. "You have to help me plan it. I can't do it alone. I'm counting on you."

"Yes," Logan mumbled. "I promised I'd help you."

"Yes!" Jesse repeated, excited. "We will work on it together."

"I'll do what I can to help," Logan said. "But that's all."

Jesse smiled. "I'll take that. It's a start." Jesse walked toward the door. "And you won't transfer me?"

"You can stay," Logan said. "Like you said, it's best for the firm. This is your division."

"Thank you," Jesse said. "I promise you won't regret this."

"I already do," Logan said, returning to his work on the computer.

"I love you," Jesse said before opening the door and leaving the office.

Logan remained seated and looked toward the door where Jesse had stood moments before. He mumbled to himself, "I still love you, too…"

While Logan tried to refocus on his work, Keith was engaged in his own work in his office. When his phone rang, he quickly answered it.

"Hello?"

"Hello, Keith. It's Nick. I'm not finished with you yet."

As Keith listened to what he knew to be a fake call, the voice grew louder. Keith turned around only to find Rachel Carson standing in his office with her cell phone in "speaker" mode. She laughed and soon the message with the voice of her dead brother stopped playing.

"Rachel! What are you doing here?"

"It's been a long time, Keith. Far too long," Rachel said, closing Keith's office door behind her. "You're looking as fit and handsome as ever."

"Why have you been calling me with that recording of Nick?"

"Maybe it was just to amuse myself. Or maybe I was just bored," Rachel said, sitting down in a chair across from Keith's desk. "Or maybe I hold you and your friends responsible for my brother's death."

"That's insane; none of us had anything to do with that. He brought it upon himself. He was a reckless drug user."

"Only because he dated you," Rachel replied. "He never touched drugs until you came into his life. And then you left him in prison. Alone."

"Rachel, he was selling and distributing drugs. I told him not to. There was nothing else I could do to stop what happened to him from happening." Keith sat down in his chair. "And then he kidnapped Emmett, too."

"He loved you," Rachel said. "Love makes you do crazy things sometimes."

"When we were together, I loved him, too. But his behavior got out of control. What happened at the warehouse is his fault and nobody else's."

"Well, that's where we disagree," Rachel said. "I blame you and your friends. And so you have to pay."

"By listening to that recording over and over?"

"Oh, honey, that's just the start. I have big plans for you. For all of you." Rachel smiled. "Did you get my note?"

"Your note? The one you shoved in my hand at the party?"

"That's the one."

"Yes, I got it. Although it makes no sense to me."

"Oh, come on, Keith. We both know exactly what I'm referring to. Nick told me everything. In fact, he unknowingly gave me all the tools I need to bring you all down."

"I have no idea what you're talking about."

"Let me refresh your memory. The accident. All those years ago. The one you never did time for." Rachel grinned. "Sound familiar?"

Keith slumped in his chair. "What do you want from me?"

"Today? Nothing, really. Just for you to understand that I hold all the cards." Rachel stood up. "I'll be in touch." Rachel blew Keith a kiss and left the office. Staring blankly at the door, Keith remained silently in his seat.

At the same time in Rome, Marco sat quietly in a cavernous room of the convent. Sun streaming through the beautiful stained glass windows created colorful patterns on the walls and floor. Magnificent tapestries featuring Biblical scenes on the walls fascinated Marco and he carefully examined them as he waited for someone to enter the room.

Eventually, the door to the room opened and two nuns -- one young and one old -- entered the room, the younger one carefully guiding the elderly one. Marco stood from his seat and approached the women. Both he and the younger nun helped the older woman onto a nearby sofa.

"Grazie," the younger nun said. Once the elder nun was seated comfortably, the younger one nodded in Marco's direction and quietly left the room.

The older nun turned to Marco and, with a sparkle in her eyes, reached out and put her hand on Marco's cheek. "Marco," she said with a wide smile that wrinkled her face. "It's good to see you."

Marco sat down next to the woman on the couch. "Aunt Connie, it's good to see you, too."

"My eyes are so bad and it's been so long, I can barely tell it's you."

"It's me," Marco said. "Marco."

"I never could tell Gino or you apart, even when I was younger." Concetta paused a moment and took a labored breath. "Last time I saw you both, you were young children."

"It's been a long time."

"I was so surprised when they came to get me. I don't often have visitors, from America or anywhere. How's your father?"

"He's good. He sends his love, of course. And Gino, too."

"Ah, Gino," Concetta said quietly. "You were both such good boys. How your mother loved you both."

"Actually, Aunt Connie," Marco said, "I am here because of mother. I need to ask you some questions about her."

"What questions?"

"About the time she spent here with you. All those months."

Concetta paused before responding. "Very sad times those were. Cancer is a terrible thing."

"I know," Marco said. "But you offered her great comfort."

"We were sisters. I did what I could."

"Aunt Connie, I'm sure she told you about her affair. She trusted you with the most delicate information."

Concetta nodded. "We trusted each other. Very much."

"So when she was here did she tell you anything about the affair?"

"It was something she greatly regretted. We prayed together many times in this very room. She wanted forgiveness from your father and from our Heavenly Father as well."

"Father forgave her," Marco explained. "And he's not a forgiving man. But he loved her very, very much."

"And she loved him, too, Marco," she said. "I'm sure he knew that."

"Was there…was there any possibility that she may have been pregnant during her time here with you?"

Concetta's eyes grew large behind her thick glasses. "Pregnant? Your mother was here in Rome for special cancer treatments. There was no pregnancy."

"You're sure?"

"Marco," Concetta said, putting her frail hand on top of Marco's, "my sight and my hearing may be all but gone, but my memory is not. The only pregnancy I know of is when she delivered you and Gino. That's all." Concetta paused. "I'm getting tired."

"Of course," Marco said. "We can get you back to your room."

"How long are you here in Rome?"

"I came to see you," Marco said. "But I'll check in at our Rome office while I'm here. Then I'm heading back home."

"It's good to see you," she replied. "If you have time, come back and eat with me. I want to know how the rest of the family is doing."

Marco smiled. "Sure. I'll see you tomorrow before I leave for California. Come on, I'll help you back to your room."

Marco carefully helped Concetta from her chair and aided her as they slowly made their way out of the room.

While it was quite warm in Rome, the temperature in Chicago was dropping as winter engulfed the city once again. Despite the cold outside, the inside of Rebound was hot and lively, packed with mostly men dancing, socializing, and partying. The male strippers dancing on blocks throughout the club entertained the patrons as did the bartenders who were rushing around trying to keep up with the crowd's drink orders.

Already a bit tipsy, Jesse, Cole, and David were at the main bar ordering shots from their bartender. As he placed four shots on the counter, David handed him some money. The bartender put the money to the side momentarily and picked up one of the four shots. Jesse, Cole, and David each picked up a shot as well.

"To us," David said and the four men touched their glasses together before chugging their shots. Then they put their empty glasses on the bar and the bartender took them away.

"This was a great idea," Jesse said to David. "We all needed a carefree night out."

"Damn right," Cole said.

"I thought it would be fun," David said, picking up his martini.

As they continued to drink and chat, one of the strippers dancing on the bar made his way over to them. He was the red haired boy who had broken into Emmett's restaurant and had propositioned Michael on the street. Once in front of the guys, he began dancing, occasionally thrusting his crotch toward their faces.

"I think he likes you," David said to Cole, laughing.

"Right," Cole said. "Just what I need in my life now." Cole pulled out his cell phone.

"Oh, no," David said. "Drunk texting."

Jesse added, "Cole, don't." But Cole sent a text to Derek anyway.

"He hasn't replied in two weeks," Jesse said. "What makes you think he's going to reply tonight?"

"You just said it yourself," Cole replied. "We're drunk so I'm not thinking at all."

The stripper knelt down on the bar. "Hey, boys."

"Hey," David said, smiling back at the boy.

"Having fun tonight?"

"We are," David replied. Jesse put a dollar into David's hand and David worked it into the stripper's underwear. "There you go."

"Thanks," the stripper said, turning his face toward Cole. "You look familiar."

"I do?" Cole asked.

"That's funny," Jesse said. "Most people usually recognize him from the back."

"Are you all single?" the red head asked.

"We are tonight," Jesse replied.

"You're all hot," the stripper added

Cole laughed. "Thanks. That deserves a tip." Cole put a few bucks into the stripper's underwear as he put his arms over Cole's shoulders.

The stripper smiled. "Thanks, baby. What's your name?"

"I'm Cole."

"I'm Jensen," the stripper said.

"And this is David and Jesse," Cole continued.

"Nice to meet all of you boys."

David put his arm around Cole's shoulders, displacing Jensen's arms. "Same."

"Well, I'll check back with you boys in a bit. Have fun." Jensen walked back to the other end of the bar and continued to flirt with other patrons.

"What a piece of work," Jesse said. "Too funny."

"He's just trying to make a living," David said, his arm still wrapped around Cole.

"I guess," Jesse said as he noticed Logan across the room at the other end of the bar. "Logan."

"What?" Cole asked.

"Logan. He's over there sitting alone at the end of the bar. He looks pretty hammered."

"Ugh," David said.

"Maybe I should check on him?" Jesse leaned over the counter and asked the bartender to come over. "How long has Logan been there?"

The bartender looked down the bar toward Logan. "He's not in my service area. But he's been here a while. Looks sort of out of it to me."

"Me, too," Jesse said. "I'm going to check on him." Jesse walked away in Logan's direction.

"You two doing okay?" the bartender asked Cole and David.

"Let's have another round," David said.

"Sounds good," he replied, turning around to grab a vodka bottle.

"You okay?" David asked Cole.

"I'm great," Cole said, holding up his drink and chugging it.

"Good," David said, smiling. Then he leaned in and kissed Cole. Cole pulled away momentarily. Then he stepped closer to David and kissed him back. The kiss grew in intensity and they wrapped their arms around each other.

When the long kiss was over, David put his forehead against Cole's. "I told you I'm not giving up on us."

"I'm not sure I want you to," Cole said, leaning forward and kissing David again.

While David and Cole kissed, Jesse approached Logan, who was sitting on a stool at the bar and was clearly intoxicated.

"Hey, handsome," Jesse said, putting his hand on Logan's back. "You okay?

Logan turned his head toward Jesse and squinted his drunk eyes to see who was touching him. "I'm fine," Logan said, slurring his words.

"Maybe I should help you get home?"

"You? Help me?" Logan sat up more erectly. "I'm fine."

"Naw," Jesse said. "You've been over-served."

"I'm fine."

Jesse waved at the bartender. "What does he owe you?"

"He's all set," the bartender replied. "Just get him home safely."

"Thanks," Jesse said. "I will." Jesse wrapped his arm around Logan to help him up from the bar stool. "Come on, let's go."

Logan reluctantly and unsteadily began to stand up. Jesse held him tightly and started walking him toward the door.

Upon arriving at Logan's home, Jesse carefully helped him into the bedroom. Sitting him on the edge of the bed, Jesse pulled Logan's shirt off of him and then removed his shoes. As Jesse helped Logan onto his side and pulled the bed covers up over him, Logan mumbled a bit, shifted his position in the bed, and fell asleep.

Jesse took a few steps back and leaned against the wall opposite the bed. Watching Logan sleep, Jesse reflected back on New Year's Eve and all that had happened since. His eyes flooded with tears as he watched Logan's chest rise and fall beneath the sheets.

"I love you, Logan," Jesse whispered softly. "And I'm going to make things right again for us. Please just give me the chance."

Jesse eventually turned off the light and left Logan's bedroom as Keith rushed into his. His conversation with Rachel roaring through his mind, Keith tore open his wardrobe and reached deep inside. His fingers grasped a large box and pulled it out into the room.

Turning around and placing the box on his bed, Keith recalled Rachel's words: "Let me refresh your memory. The accident. All those years ago. The one you never did time for." He lifted the lid from the box and carefully removed the note that she had pressed into his hand at the New Year's Eve party: "I know what you did all those years ago."

Then Keith took newspaper clippings from the box and placed them all over the bed. When finished, he scanned the articles' headlines. "Hit and run victim D. O. A." "Hit and run driver still at large." "Beloved father killed in hit and run." "P. D. mourns loss of one of their own."

At the same time in Rome, Concetta slowly opened the wardrobe in her bedroom. Her frail hand inserted a key into the keyhole of one of the drawers inside the wardrobe. Unlocking the drawer, Concetta pulled it open and gazed inside at its contents.

She moved some items to one side to uncover a leather-bound diary. Struggling to wrap her arthritic hands around it, Concetta eventually lifted the book from the drawer and carried it over to her rocking chair. She sat down, holding the diary in her lap. Running her fingers over the brass lock on the diary, she looked up at the crucifix on the wall of her room.

"Maybe it's time," Concetta quietly said to herself, her eyes focused on the wall. "Maybe it's time to reveal the truth." She looked down at the book in her lap and then back at the cross on the wall. All secrets have an expiration date.

Episode #25

Chicago snowstorms bring out the best and worst in people. An early-February snowstorm replaced the unusual January thaw, putting Chicago back into winter's tight grip. Chicagoans were used to these kinds of changes in the weather and tried to go about their business un-phased by the quickly-accumulating snow. But this storm showed no signs of letting up, perhaps heading for the record books.

Some neighbors helped to shovel each other's driveways or dig out each other's cars from beneath the heavy snow. Others were more territorial, "reserving" their shoveled street parking spaces with folding chairs and other items. Some checked in on neighbors and friends who needed a helping hand while others "bunkered down" in their homes tending to themselves and waiting for the storm to pass.

As the snow and wind fell outside of their new restaurant location, Max Taylor and Emmett Mancini were reviewing plans and renovations with Ben Donovan. Standing over the blueprints that were draped over a table, the men were discussing several of the renovations. Ben snapped photos of all the plans with his cell phone.

"They did a great job with the booths," Max said. "I just think the light fixtures need to be centered over the tables."

"I agree," Emmett added. "They seem a bit chaotic. If we're going for a classic Golden Age of Hollywood look, lines need to be cleaner."

"I'll talk to the electrician in the morning," Ben said.

"The city inspector is supposed to come by Friday," Emmett said. "It would be nice to have the electric work done by then."

"And I'm supposed to meet with Logan," Max said. "He wants to talk about doing a charity event here."

"Are we going to be ready for that?" Ben asked. "When is he thinking?"

"I don't know yet," Max replied. "If it's soon, I was thinking we could hire a caterer to use our kitchen here. It might be a nice way to 'preview' our space and cause some neighborhood buzz."

"Well, let's see what he has in mind and then we can decide what we can pull together, if anything," Emmett said.

"Can we take a look at the club lighting again?" Ben asked. "The more the electrician can work on at once, the better."

"Sure," Max said. The three men walked over to the large plastic tarp that divided the restaurant area from the club area. Max pulled the tarp back, allowing the other two to pass under it. Then he followed them into the club space.

As the three men disappeared behind the tarp, Jensen Stone, the red-headed stripper from Rebound, quietly emerged from the kitchen area. He walked over to the table where the men were previously situated and found Emmett's keys resting on the table. He grabbed them, shoved them into the pocket of his hooded sweatshirt, and then headed out of the restaurant through the alley exit.

Max, Ben, and Emmett eventually returned to the restaurant space and once again hovered over the renovation drawings on the table. Max pointed to one part of the drawing.

"See? This is what I was talking about," he explained. "I think the stage needs to come out further in this direction. It'll improve the interaction between patrons and performers."

"It's not a problem," Ben said. "We can make that happen. Better to get your ideas out now while they are less costly to implement. Once things are built, changing them will blow your budget."

Emmett began patting down his pockets and then lifting the corners of the plans. "Have either of you seen my keys?"

"Your keys?"

"I thought I left them here on the table."

"Are you sure you had them with you at all?" Max asked.

"Duh," Emmett replied. "Remember who unlocked the place when we all got here?"

"Oh, that's right," Max said. "Well, don't stress out. They have to be around here somewhere." Just then, Max's phone began to vibrate deep within his pocket. He pulled it out to see who was calling and said to Ben, "Hey, it's your wife."

Ben looked up from the drawings. "Oh?"

"You want to take it?" Max asked, holding his phone out to Ben.

"Sure," Ben replied, taking the phone and slowly walking away from the other two. "Hey, baby. It's me."

"Ben?" Jacqueline asked.

149

"That's right," her husband replied. "Max just handed the call to me. Disappointed?"

"I don't know what you're talking about," Jacqueline said. "I just need to tell Max something."

"What, exactly?" Ben asked, looking over his shoulder to make sure that Max and Emmett were otherwise occupied.

"It's none of your business," she replied.

"Everything you do is my business, baby," Ben said. "I'm your husband." There was a moment of silence and then Ben continued, "Just don't do anything stupid. Remember what we talked about."

"You don't need to worry about my memory," Jacqueline said before quickly ending the call. Ben returned to the others and handed Max his phone.

"Everything okay?" Max asked.

"Perfect," Ben said with a smile. "Maybe we should wrap up for now. It's getting pretty ugly outside."

"Agreed," Max said. "Why don't you go on? We'll close up here."

"Thanks," Ben said, pulling on his heavy overcoat. "I'll see you guys soon."

"Thanks," Emmett said, still looking around the area for his keys.

Max escorted Ben out of the front door and then locked it behind him. "It's pretty bad out there."

"Luckily, we just have to walk upstairs to get home," Emmett said. "Pretty nice, don't you think?"

Max smiled. "A home that I share with you is better than 'pretty nice.' It's perfect." Max kissed Emmett and then noticed his keys lying on the floor near the entrance to the kitchen area. "Hey, look." Max walked over and picked the keys up off the floor.

"How did they get all the way over there?"

"Not sure," Max said. "You must have dropped them or maybe one of us kicked them across the floor without knowing it. Who knows? In any event, they aren't lost, so all is good."

"I guess so," Emmett said, still pondering the location of the keys.

"Come on," Max said. "Let's lock up, get into our PJs, watch a movie, and eat bad food."

Emmett laughed. "Sounds like a date to me."

Emmett and Max proceeded to lock up the restaurant and club and head upstairs to their new condo. Once they were upstairs, Jensen emerged from the basement storeroom. With only the street lights from the sidewalk lighting the interior of the restaurant, Jensen made his way to the window. From inside the restaurant, he watched the blustery snowstorm outside.

If Jensen had been able to see further down the street, he would have seen Derek Mancini's car slowly making its way down Roscoe Street. Inside the car, Derek was on his phone talking to wife.

"I'm driving as carefully as possible, Joy," Derek reassured her. "There's no other cars driving on the street anyway."

"That's because they're smart enough to be inside," Joyelle said. "Not driving out in a blizzard like my crazy husband."

"I told you -- I had to meet a client."

"Clients can be rescheduled."

"Okay, Joy," Derek said. "At this point it doesn't make much difference, right? How are things there?"

"That's why I'm calling," Joyelle explained. "A lot of my coworkers couldn't make it in, so I'm going to have to stay."

"Aww, Joy," Derek sighed. "How long?"

"Probably over night," Joyelle said.

"You still need your rest, babe," Derek replied. "That's too long a shift for you."

"I'm fine. I promise. Besides, it's safer for me to be here than trying to get home in this storm. Tyler is here with me -- and I'm surrounded by doctors. I'll be fine."

"Okay, okay. Just please take it easy," Derek said.

"I will. Don't miss me too much tonight."

"I'm beat," Derek replied. "I'm just gonna crash once I get inside."

"Great. Okay, I need to get back to work."

"I love you."

"I love you, too," Joyelle responded and then disconnected the call.

As the call concluded, Derek made the turn into his driveway. A snowplow had recently been down the street, causing high mounds of snow along both sides of it. While Derek's car made the turn, his tires cut into the snow mound and lost traction. He quickly realized that he was stuck.

"Fuck!" Derek yelled out as he pounded his fists on the steering wheel. He opened the car door to assess the situation and then began shifting the car from "drive" to "reverse" and back again in an attempt to "rock" the car through the mound. With the snow continuing to fall heavily, the situation only grew worse and Derek made no progress.

Across the street, Cole O'Brien was making his way home from the bus stop. Wrapped warmly inside his thick winter coat, Cole trudged through the storm, his scarf waving in the wind behind him. As he approached his apartment, he saw Derek's car stuck in the snow.

Without wasting a second, Cole made his way across the street to assist Derek, who was getting out of his car. Derek turned and looked at Cole through the falling snow.

"I'm okay," Derek said. "You should get out of the storm."

"Hardly," Cole replied. "You're stuck. I'll help you get out."

"I don't need your help."

"Stop being stubborn, Derek. Get back inside the car and I'll push."

Without arguing, Derek got back into the car and pulled the door closed loudly. Cole made his way around to the back of the car and placed his gloved hands on the trunk. Pushing forward, Cole's feet slid in the slick snow. As Derek accelerated, Cole continued to push, his feet finally gaining some traction in the snow. The car's back tires kicked snow up at Cole, who persisted in his pushing until the car was finally free.

Derek pulled the car a bit further up the driveway and then stopped and rolled down the window. Sticking his head out, he looked toward the back of the car to thank Cole; however, Cole quickly opened the passenger side door and hopped into the seat next to Derek.

"What are you doing?"

"We need to talk," Cole said.

"Look, I appreciate your help but--"

"I think you owe me at least that," Cole added. "Please."

Derek sighed. "Okay. Joyelle's at the hospital. Let's park the car and go inside."

"Great," Cole said with a smile as Derek pulled his car into the garage.

As Cole and Derek headed inside, Jesse Morgan sat inside Logan Pryce's condo. They were meeting to discuss the charity event they were co-planning. Seated on the sofa across the room from Jesse, Logan had a bottle of wine and a half-full glass of wine on the coffee table in front of him.

"I have a few ideas for entertainment," Jesse said, a notepad on his lap and a beer in his hand.

"Oh?" Logan said, drinking his wine and then refilling his glass.

"I was thinking about Whiskey and Cherries, the group from Emmett and Max's engagement party. Plus Amy Armstrong and maybe even Steve Grand. They all have ties to Chicago so I thought maybe they'd be willing to help out."

"If you can book them, that'd be great," Logan said. "Did we ever decide on a theme?"

"Golden Age of Hollywood, remember? It's the style of Emmett's new restaurant so it'll be easy."

"Right."

"I haven't told Cole about this yet, because I wasn't sure that it was really going to happen. But I will now. I think he'll be really excited."

"Are you going to invite his mother?"

"I'm going to leave that up to him," Jesse said. "While she's the inspiration for the event, it's really much broader." Jesse stood up and walked to the window. "Man, it's really coming down out there."

"Maybe you should get going?"

Jesse walked over to the couch and sat down next to Logan. "Is that what you really want? For me to go?" Jesse put his hand on Logan's lap. "Babe?"

Logan looked away. "Don't call me that."

"We need to talk about us," Jesse said.

"There is no 'us' anymore," Logan said, reaching for the wine bottle. Jesse took it from his hand before Logan could pour another drink.

"You've been drinking a lot lately," Jesse said. "Too much. Like when you and I first met. Is it because of me?"

"It's because I want to," Logan said, tearing the wine bottle from Jesse's hand and refilling his glass again.

"I wish you'd slow down," Jesse said. "I'm worried about you."

"Worried about me? You sure weren't worried about me on New Year's Eve, were you?"

"That's not fair," Jesse said. "I thought I explained all that to you."

"You tried. But I didn't buy it. Still don't."

"Logan, please."

"Is there anything else we need to discuss about the party? Otherwise, you should go."

"You're really going to send me home in the middle of this storm?"

Logan hesitated. "No. But sit back over there," Logan said pointing to the chair across the room.

"You don't want me next to you?"

"No," Logan said.

"Come on, Logan. You can't keep me away forever."

"How many times do I have to say it? I'm happy to help you with the fundraiser because I promised you that I would, but that's all."

"I don't believe that," Jesse replied. "I love you and I know you love me. And I know I hurt you."

"What you did is unforgiveable."

"I told you I will make it up to you. Prove myself again."

"That's not possible," Logan said. "Now, please, either sit back over there or go."

Jesse walked back over to the chair. "Fine. For now. So let's get back to business -- and get this event planned."

While Logan and Jesse continued planning their cancer charity event and the snow piled up outside, Cole and Derek were talking in Derek's kitchen. Cole was seated at the counter on which stood his beer bottle and Derek was standing, leaning against the stove, with a beer in his hand.

"I'm sorry that we haven't been able to talk," Derek said. "There's been a lot going on, as you know."

"I understand," Cole replied. "And I really am sorry about the children."

Derek smiled. "Thank you. It's been rough. For both of us."

"I feel like you blame me for that video. And that's why you have been avoiding me."

"No," Derek said. "I know who is responsible. You had nothing to do with it."

"It shocked me as much as it did you."

"Maybe more," Derek said.

"What do you mean?"

"I knew for a while that the video existed. My brother Justin took it on his phone."

"He did? Why?"

"To try to blackmail me. He wanted something from me."

"Wow," Cole said, taking a sip of his beer. "I'm sorry to hear that."

"It doesn't matter much now," Derek said.

"Except for the fact that Joyelle doesn't remember seeing it. From what I understand anyway."

"That's true," Derek replied. "But the doctors expect her memory to return."

"And then?"

"And then we'll have to talk about it."

Cole stood up from the counter and took a few steps toward Derek. "Where does all of this leave us?"

Derek looked down at the floor. "Cole…there can't be anything between us anymore."

"But you said you love me. And the whole party heard you say so."

"I do," Derek said, raising his eyes from the floor to look directly at Cole. "But that doesn't matter. It can't."

"How can you say that? Look how long we've waited to be together."

"I've been married to Joyelle longer."

"But you don't love her like you love me."

"I love her very much and we have known each other for a long time."

Cole stepped even closer to Derek. "Look, when you were going to have kids together, I tried to understand the difficult situation you were in and see things from your point of view. But you aren't having kids with her anymore. There's nothing stopping us from finally being together like we both want."

Derek walked across the kitchen and leaned against the counter opposite Cole. "Just because we lost the children doesn't mean we aren't going to have more. In fact, we are trying often."

"Why would you tell me that? Just to hurt me?"

"Of course not, Cole. I am trying to make you understand. Family is important to me." Derek paused to drink his beer. "I just got back from visiting my father. He's dying. And although he and I rarely saw eye to eye through most of my life, it was important to me to try to make amends. Blood matters to me."

"And since I can't give you children, I'm not worth being with?"

"You just don't understand," Derek said.

"I'm trying to. But none of this is making sense to me. We love each other and we should be together. It's pretty simple."

"I do love you," Derek said. "I honestly do. But I'm choosing a different lifestyle for myself. Almost having children and then losing them has changed my perspective. And my priorities."

"And I'm no longer a priority?"

"I'm sorry," Derek said. "I really am. I don't want to hurt or upset you."

Cole shook his head. "I refuse to believe this. We have been through too much--"

"So has Joyelle."

"This isn't about her. I have nothing against her; you know that. Hell, I tried to protect her and your children in that explosion."

"And we will always be grateful for that. More so than you probably know."

"Do you really think she's going to want to stay with you once she remembers everything? She may want nothing to do with you."

"Hopefully, she'll be pregnant again by then."

"So that's your plan? To trap her?"

"I'm not trapping her. I'm trying to give her what we both want -- a family. And I will explain away the video as best I can."

"You can't explain away the truth," Cole said. "And that video was true." Cole walked toward Cole. "And the truth is that you love me."

"But I am not..."

Cole reached out and put his hands on the counter on each side of Derek, blocking him from moving anywhere. "And nothing you can say is going to make me believe otherwise." Cole leaned in and kissed Derek. Their lips touched for a moment and then Derek pushed Cole away from him.

Cole stepped forward to kiss Derek again, but Derek stepped to the side. Determined, Cole grabbed Derek's arm and pulled them toward him, once again attempting a kiss. Derek twisted his arm out of Cole's grip and punched Cole in the stomach, causing Cole to buckle over. As Derek walked away into the dining room, Cole lunged at him, pushing into his back and knocking him to the floor. Derek quickly turned himself over to face Cole and then jumped up at him, grabbing him around the waist.

Falling backward, Cole knocked over a large plant in the corner of the room. Some dirt flew out of the pot as the plant crashed to the ground. Paying little attention, Derek and Cole continued to wrestle, each trying to overpower the other. Cole managed to put his feet against Derek's chest and kicked him back into the middle of the room. As Cole rushed to get on top of Derek, Derek raised his legs, tripping Cole, who fell forward into the archway dividing the living and dining rooms.

Derek got back onto his feet and rushed forward, tackling Cole and pinning him to the ground. Wrapping his legs around Derek, Cole flipped over on top of him, sending a chair flying across the room in the process. With his hands gripping Derek's wrists, Cole tried to overpower Derek and end their battle, but Derek continued to struggle.

Using all his strength, Derek pushed Cole off of him and climbed on top, once again pinning Cole down. Cole struggled to get free, but Derek had his hands pressed against the floor. After a few futile attempts to free himself, Cole rested below Derek, trying to catch his breath.

Both breathing heavily, the two men looked into each other's eyes. Looking up at Derek, Cole made a hint of a smile. Maintaining control, Derek slowly lowered his head and kissed Cole. Growing more aggressive and passionate, Derek kissed Cole's neck and used his feet to force Cole's legs apart.

Thrusting his hips into Cole's crotch, Derek released Cole's arms and tore open his shirt. His tongue wasted little time exploring Cole's chest and nipples as Cole struggled to open Derek's shirt. Once it was open, Cole pulled it of Derek, revealing his muscled torso.

Suddenly, Derek jumped to his feet, pulling Cole up with him. He lifted Cole off the ground and Cole wrapped his legs around him. Digging his fingers into Derek's back and kissing him deeply, Cole held onto Derek as he carried Cole into the guest bedroom.

Once inside, Derek threw Cole onto the bed, shedding his pants before climbing on top of his boy. Cole reached back and grabbed the headboard as Derek tore Cole's pants and underwear off him. Derek looked down at Cole, running his hands over his arms, armpits, chest, stomach, cock, and legs. Then he leaned forward to kiss Cole's chest as their hard dicks rubbed against one another.

Grabbing Cole's hips, Derek pulled Cole toward him, forcing himself into Cole's tight ass. He kissed Cole's thighs and ankles as he pulled them over his shoulders, allowing him to penetrate deeper.

Curling his toes each time Derek hit deep inside of him, Cole moaned loudly and clawed at Derek's back. Pulling Derek's torso down toward him, Cole bit Derek's nipples, causing him to moan loudly.

"Oh, fuck," Derek said as he released deep inside of Cole. When Derek finally collapsed onto Cole, Cole kissed him and held him tight. Then Derek rolled over onto his back next to Cole.

"Why can't I get you out of my system?" Derek asked, running his hand over his forehead.

"Because you love me," Cole said, adjusting his head on Derek's chest. "And because we are meant to be together."

"You may be right," Derek said. "I apologize for ignoring you this past month or so."

Cole smiled. "I think I can forgive you."

"Thanks," Derek replied, kissing Cole's forehead.

"You've been under a lot of stress. I get it." Cole ran his hand down Derek's side. "But we need to be together now. I will make you so happy."

"You already do." Derek paused a moment. "Fuck, why does this have to be so complicated?"

"It doesn't have to be," Cole said. "Divorce Joyelle and marry me."

"Wow. Was that a proposal?"

Cole looked into Derek's eyes. "Only if the answer is 'yes.'"

"We'll work it out. I promise."

"I've heard that promise before."

"I know; I'm sorry. I'm trying my best to figure this all out."

"You know, David has been dying to date me. Better be careful or he might steal me away from you," Cole said with a smile.

Derek laughed. "We both know that's not possible. You're mine."

"Then we need to make it official and public soon. I can't live life in the dark forever."

"I understand. I just need some time, that's all."

"Time to get Joyelle pregnant?"

"Stop that," Derek said. "No. Time to make sure she'll be okay."

"I know. I didn't mean to be snarky."

"It's okay. This is difficult for both of us." Derek rolled over on top of Cole. "I promise it's going to get better. Soon."

"I love you," Cole said, kissing Derek.

"I love you, too." Derek pushed his feet between Cole's legs to spread them again and began kissing him passionately. Cole grabbed Derek's ass and pulled him closer to him as Derek worked his way back inside Cole.

While Derek fucked Cole again, Michael Martinez and Keith Colgan were cooking in Michael's kitchen. Michael sautéed some onions and peppers on the stove while Keith prepared a salad.

"Can't you question them all again?"

Michael smiled. "You're cute. No, I can't keep hauling people back into the department to question them over and over about the explosion because my boyfriend wants me to. There are procedures in place. Besides, I have already questioned everyone who was there, including

Gino and Marco. And now Justin, too. There's no new information."

"But I know Marco is behind it. Justin said so," Keith replied, tossing some tomatoes into the salad bowl.

"I know that's what Justin said, but he has nothing to back that up. And Justin has a bone to pick with that family anyway, so he's hardly an unbiased source."

"Can't you just question Marco again? For me?"

Michael turned from the stove and kissed Keith. "It's sweet that you care so much about your friends, but I'm doing all I can."

"I care more about you. You could have been killed in that explosion."

"But I wasn't," Michael said, adding some tomato sauce to the pan. "I would like to question that Rachel, though. Now that we know she was at the party. Any idea where she might be?"

"Rachel? She could be anywhere."

"And you haven't heard from her at all?'

Keith hesitated a moment. "No. Not since December."

"You okay? You get jittery every time I mention her."

"I'm fine," Keith said, refocusing on the salad. "Her name just brings up a lot of bad memories; that's all."

"I'm sorry," Michael said. "I won't bring her up again. But if you do hear from her, you'll tell me, right?

"Of course."

"I have a question for you. My father's birthday is tomorrow and I always visit his grave on his birthday. Would you like to come with me, Stormy?"

"Sure," Keith said, planting a kiss on Michael's cheek. "Thank you for asking me."

"Well, you're my other half now. It's time you meet him. If we can find his grave marker under all this snow."

"It'll be my pleasure." Keith finished tossing the salad. "Okay, this is ready to go. What else can I help you with?"

Michael wrapped his arms around Keith and pulled him tightly toward him. "Just this." Michael kissed Keith.

Michael and Keith finished preparing their dinner while Emmett and Max were wrapped up with each other under a blanket on the sofa in their new living room. Boxes from their recent move stood in the corner of the room and the walls were still bare. The glow from their television lit the room as the movie *Mommie Dearest* played.

"I never get tired of this," Max said as he kissed Emmett on the forehead.

"The movie? Or me?"

Max laughed. "Both."

Emmett looked around the room. "We still have a lot of unpacking to do."

"Not tonight," Max said. "Tonight is about cuddling with my fiancé in a snowstorm."

"With Joan Crawford," Emmett added.

"Between the two of us, we know this movie line for line."

"Of course," Emmett said. "Can't be gay if you don't."

Max laughed. "Can I ask you something?"

"Anything."

"Did hearing about Derek's visit with your father make you regret not going with him?"

"Not at all," Emmett replied. "Seeing my father would only bring back all the pain of Justin outing me to him and him throwing me out. I don't need to relive that."

"You sure don't."

"If Derek has a need to make up with our dad, that's his business. It's only motivated by his interest in the company anyway. My father and I have said all we ever need to say to one another."

"Okay," Max said. "I guess I just wanted you to know that I'd support you if you wanted to go see him. I support whatever you decide."

Emmett kissed Max. "I know. And I love you for that. But I'm good."

"Good."

The two shifted their focus back to their television. They watched as Joan Crawford drove her daughter home from boarding school.

Emmett said Christina's line, "There's a liquor store to the right."

Then Max recited Joan's line, "I should have known you'd know where to find the boys and the booze."

They both laughed and then looked at each other.

"Oh, my God," Emmett said.

Max smiled. "That's it!"

"The boys and the booze," they said simultaneously.

"I think we have our name," Emmett said, kissing and hugging Max.

While Emmett and Max celebrated their new club's name and finished watching their movie, Jacqueline stood in front of the hotel room mirror, examining her naked body. Her pregnancy was finally beginning to show a bit and she ran her hands over the small baby bump in her abdomen. While most people wouldn't be able to notice it, especially when she was fully dressed, Jacqueline was well aware of her changing physique.

Startling her as he entered, Ben came into the hotel room abruptly but stopped when he saw her standing in front of him. He pulled off his winter coat, hat, and scarf, tossing them onto the nearby table.

"Babe, you look beautiful." Jacqueline didn't reply; she maintained her focus on the mirror. Ben pulled off his shirt and walked over behind her so they both were visible in the mirror. He wrapped his arm around her, placing his hand on her abdomen. "How's my little one doing?"

"Just fine," Jacqueline said frankly. "How long are we going to be staying at this hotel?"

"Not much longer," Ben replied. "I think I have finally found an apartment for us. It's close to Jesse's place and the restaurant. And even Max."

"How convenient."

Ben began to kiss the back of Jacqueline's neck. "Do you know how much I love you?"

Jacqueline stepped away from Ben and picked up her night gown from the bed. "You have an odd way of showing it."

"Come on, Jacqueline. I'm trying to help us move forward together and get past what happened on New Year's Eve. You have to try to as well." Ben kicked off his boots.

"That's like asking me to move a mountain. You were sleeping with my son."

Ben pulled off his pants. "It wasn't my fault. You know that."

Jacqueline turned away from Ben, who walked up behind her and hugged her. "Let go of me." Ben ignored his wife's request and ran his hand down her stomach, his mouth kissing her shoulders. "What do you think you're doing?"

Ben ran his leg along Jacqueline's as his dick grew hard inside his underwear. As it pressed up against Jacqueline's ass, she spun around to face him. He leaned in to kiss her, but she turned her face away from him and stepped to the side.

"We are not doing this," Jacqueline said. "Not tonight. Not ever again."

"I love you," Ben declared, walking toward his wife. He pulled his underwear off, revealing himself to her. Jacqueline kept stepping backwards until she was up against the wall. Ben put his hands against the wall on each side of her and kissed her neck again.

"We are not doing this," Jacqueline repeated. Ben's right hand worked its way down the side of her body, eventually fingering between her legs, and his lips kissed her ears and her jaw line. As his mouth approached hers, she turned it away from him. His left hand grabbed her face and turned it back to him so that he could finally kiss her. Their kiss lasted a moment and then Jacqueline quickly stepped out from against the wall.

"We are not doing this," she said once more as Ben turned and walked to her. She stepped backwards against the bed, losing her balance and falling onto it in a seated position. Ben quickly dropped to his knees between her legs and kissed the inside of her thighs.

Jacqueline looked down at her husband. "We are...not..." Her hands gripped the bed sheets as Ben kissed his way up to her stomach and then her breasts. Ben's dick

174

pressed between her legs and his mouth on her right nipple, Jacqueline finished her thought, "...doing...this."

Ben looked into Jacqueline's eyes, his muscled body weighing her down. She ran her hands over his tattooed arms as he kissed her deeply. Their tongues embraced for a moment until she turned her head to the side.

"I hate you," she said.

"No, baby," he replied with a smile as he worked himself into her. "You love me. And you want me more than you ever have."

"I..." she said, digging her fingers into his back and wrapping her hips around him. "Hate..." He plunged deeper inside her as her hands ran down his back to his firm butt. "Oh, Shawn."

Giving in to her husband, Jacqueline kissed his neck and his chest. He pushed himself up on the bed, adjusting his position to get deeper inside her. His new angle allowed his cock to penetrate more effectively and Jacqueline squirmed beneath him.

Ben smiled at her as he prepared to fill her. He thrust deeper and harder as she ran her feet up and down the back of his legs. She kissed him deeply, running her hands over his head and neck. Finally, he released inside of her. "I love you, baby."

Jacqueline didn't reply; she just lay quietly on the bed. Soon, Ben got up and slapped her gently on the butt. Then he walked into the bathroom and closed the door. Staring at the bathroom door, Jacqueline remained on the bed for a moment. After a moment, she jumped up and grabbed her phone from the night table. She quickly texted her son: "Be careful. Ben is monitoring your phone."

As the snow continued to coat Chicago in white, Tyler Bennett and Joyelle were walking from the nurse's station on the fifth floor of St. Joseph Hospital to the elevators.

"This is crazy," Tyler said, pushing the button to call the elevator. "If we get one more broken wrist tonight..."

Joyelle smiled. "Everyone is slipping on the ice."

"Everyone should be staying inside," Tyler said as the elevator doors opened in front of them.

"If I weren't here, that's where I'd be -- inside at home," Joyelle replied as she stepped into the elevator. "I don't do well outside in blizzards."

Tyler laughed and followed her into the elevator. "Apparently, neither do these people we're treating tonight."

Joyelle pressed the button for the first floor and the elevator doors closed. "Well, at least we're on duty together. We have each other to 'vent' to."

"Exactly," Tyler agreed as the lights in the elevator began to flicker. "Oh, shit."

"This isn't good," Joyelle said as the elevator halted abruptly, causing both of them to lose their balance momentarily.

"You okay?" Tyler asked as the light in the elevator went out.

"Fine," Joyelle said. "Storm must have knocked out the power."

"The hospital has generators," Tyler said. "We'll be okay." The light in the elevator turned back on, more dimly than before. "See? That's better."

Joyelle hit the emergency button on the elevator panel but nothing happened. "Well, that's helpful," she said sarcastically.

"We just have to sit tight for a bit. They are probably resetting the system."

Joyelle sat down on the floor. "Might as well get comfortable, right?"

"Sure," Tyler said, sitting on the floor as well. "So enough about our patients. How are you doing?"

"I'm okay," Joyelle said, folding her arms to try to keep herself warm. "Chilly in here."

"Have the doctors said anything else?"

"Anything else? About my memory, you mean?" Tyler nodded. "Nothing. Physically, I'm fine. Just have to be patient, as you and I have discussed."

"Joyelle, do you remember our talks about your wedding ring?"

Joyelle looked down at her hand. "My wedding ring? No. Why were we discussing that?"

"It's hard to explain," Tyler said. "What about Cole? Do you remember anything we discussed about Cole?"

"My neighbor? No. What were we saying about him?"

"You remember that he took that bullet for your husband, right?"

"Yes. That I do remember. He saved Derek's life."

"Do you know that he saved yours as well?"

"Mine? What are you talking about?" Joyelle rubbed her arms more to keep warm.

Tyler moved himself next to Joyelle and put his arm around her. "Here, let me see if I can help with that."

"What do you mean that Cole saved me?"

"At the explosion. He jumped onto you to protect you and your children."

"My God," Joyelle said. "Why didn't anyone tell me that?"

"I was sure they had," Tyler said. "I guess it was like karma, since I am told that you saved him a while ago when he got mugged."

"It's hardly the same thing," Joyelle declared. "I happened upon him after he was attacked. It sounds like he put himself directly in harm's way to try to protect me."

Tyler nodded. "He did."

After a moment of silence in the elevator, Joyelle spoke again. "Wow, what else aren't people telling me that I should know?"

"Everyone is respecting what the doctors said. You can't force the memories; they have to return on their own."

"Just makes me wonder," Joyelle said, putting her head on Tyler's shoulder. "About all the things I'm missing."

"It'll get better, Joyelle," Tyler said, tightening his arm around her. Suddenly, there was a violent jolt as the elevator began operating again. The light came back on fully and the elevator was in motion. Tyler smiled. "See? They are getting better already."

As Joyelle and Tyler took care of more patients who fell victim to the Chicago snowstorm, Justin was standing on his balcony in sunny California. Wearing his sunglasses and enjoying the warm breeze, he spoke into his cell phone.

"Call Rachel Carson." Justin waited while the call connected. After a few rings, Rachel's voicemail answered the call and Justin left a message. "It's Justin. We need to talk. Call me."

He ended the call and paced back and forth on the balcony. Then he spoke into his phone again. "Call Gino Ciancio." Justin waited for the call to connect, but it, too, eventually went to voicemail. Justin ended the call without leaving a message.

Before he could put the phone down, it rang. He immediately answered it, assuming it was either Rachel or

Gino calling him back. "Hello?" Justin paused as he listened to the voice on the other side of the call. "My father? I'll be right there." Justin shoved his phone into his pocket and slowly made his way to the door of his home.

When Justin called Gino, his cell phone lit up brightly. It was lying on the table next to Gino's bed, unnoticed by Gino whose attention was focused on his house staff member, Bella. Naked, Gino stood on one end of the bed as Bella wrapped her mouth around him. Gino maintained his balance by leaning forward and placing his hands on his brother Marco's shoulders.

Marco was situated behind Bella, fucking her deep and hard. He looked up at his brother and then back down at Bella who pushed against him as she sucked Gino. Marco adjusted his position, raising his left leg alongside Belle's curvy body. Each time Marco pushed into her, her breasts bounced and her throat took Gino deeper.

Gino grabbed Bella's arms, lifting her up against him. Her fingers explored his hard chest as he kissed her deeply. Running his hands through her wavy, black hair, Gino kissed her mouth and then her large breasts.

Marco pulled himself out of Bella and stood up on the bed beside his brother. Bella turned slightly so she could suck both brothers simultaneously. The brothers put their arms around each other's shoulders as they watched themselves bounce in and out of Bella's mouth.

Digging his hand into Gino's shoulder, Marco erupted, spewing into Bella's mouth. Smiling as she looked up at the twins, Bella anticipated Gino. Looking up at the ceiling, Gino released, filling Bella's mouth.

Marco hopped down off the bed, tapping Bella's ass as he did. Bella smiled and stood up from the bed. She picked her clothes up from the floor and started to pull them on.

"Hot as always," Gino told her as he got off the bed and searched the floor for his pants.

"Just like when we were kids," Marco added.

"I love you boys," Bella said. "But I better get out of here before your father starts looking for me. It's almost dinner time." Bella blew each twin a kiss and then left the room.

"Thanks, Bella," Gino said. "I'm going to hop in the shower." He turned to his brother. "And then you and I are going to have a talk."

"Sounds ominous," Marco joked.

Gino went into the bathroom to clean up while Marco pulled on his shirt. Bella knocked on the bedroom door and stuck her head back into the room.

"Can you tell Gino that he has a call from Rome waiting on his room line?"

"Sure," Marco replied as Bella winked at him and closed the door when she left.

Marco checked to make sure that Gino's bathroom door was still closed. He could hear the shower running within. He walked over to the house phone on the table, pressed a button, and answered the call.

"This is Gino," Marco lied.

"Gino," a woman's voice said. "It's your Aunt Concetta. How are you, my dear?"

"Aunt Connie, it's good to hear from you. I'm great. How are you? It's been way too long."

"It has," she said. "But I need to see you. It's important."

"Is something wrong?" Marco asked. "Are you okay?"

"I'm fine, dear. Thank you. I just need to deliver something to you in person. In about a week."

"What is it?"

"Gino, it's very important that no one know I'm coming to see you. Especially not your father or brother. Is that understood?"

"Of course," Marco said. "Whatever you want."

"I just need to meet with you in confidence. Let me give you my flight information."

"Sure," Marco said. "I'll meet you at the airport. And Aunt Connie, let me give you my private cell phone number. It's safer."

Marco shared his cell phone number with his aunt and took down her flight information. When the call was over, he grabbed the rest of his clothes and left Gino's room, while Gino concluded his shower.

The next day in Chicago brought with it the sounds of snow plows and shovels as the city began to dig out from under the snow that the storm left behind. City crews worked around the clock to clear streets and residents did their best to return to normal routines under a blanket of white.

Inside his apartment, Jesse made himself a protein shake for breakfast. He gulped it down and peeled a banana, which he also ate quickly. Then he picked up his phone and re-read the text message from his mother.

Wearing only his sweatpants, Cole emerged from his bedroom, running his fingers through his messed hair.

"What time did you get home?" Jesse asked. "There was no sign of you when I finally went to bed. I thought maybe you were trapped in a snowdrift or something."

"Even better." Cole smiled. "I was with Derek."

"No shit. How'd that happen?"

Cole opened the refrigerator and pulled out a water bottle. "Long story. But it was good. We finally got a chance to talk and to--"

Jesse covered his ears. "Uh, I don't want to hear the rest of that sentence."

Cole laughed. "I was going to say 'sort things out.' But we did get to do what you were thinking, too."

"So...what did you sort out?"

"I think we're going to be together after all. It's just going to take some time."

"That sounds like what he always says."

"No, I think he's serious this time. He just wants to make sure Joyelle is okay first. Which I totally get."

"As long as you're okay with it. I'm kind of tired of telling you to be careful. You're a big boy."

"Yes, I am," Cole said, sitting down on the sofa.

"Well, if he ever fucks you over, he'll answer to me.

"Down, boy," Cole said. "I can handle myself."

"Guess what," Jesse said, changing the subject. "I heard from my mother last night. She sent me a text."

"Hey, that's great. Are you two okay now?"

"Hardly," Jesse said. "It was just a sentence. But at least it shows she's thinking about me and still cares."

"Well, of course, she does," Cole stated. "She's your mother. She loves you."

"I have other good news I'd like to talk to you about, too," Jesse said, sitting down on the chair across from him.

"What's that?"

"For some time now, I have been thinking about throwing a small fundraiser for your mother. Well, not exactly for her, but inspired by her. A cancer research fundraiser."

"Wow."

"Logan and I are working on it together and we have a lot of the plans done already."

"You and Logan? How's that going to work?"

Jesse smiled. "Well, we first discussed it a long time ago. And now we're using it as a way to re-build our friendship, I guess. It's something we can work on together and spend time together in the process."

"And he's cool with that?"

"He's cool with the fundraiser part. Us becoming close again is a side perk that I need to make happen."

"Ah," Cole said. "An ulterior motive, eh?"

"Sort of. But the event will be amazing. It's going to be at Emmett's new place, before it's open to the public. Not a huge crowd but food, entertainment. Just a way for me to celebrate my friendship with you and my love for your mom."

"That's really sweet. Thank you so much, bro."

"I know your mom isn't always able to travel, so she's certainly welcome to attend. But we'll leave that to you and her to decide."

"She'll be very touched when I tell her. Or do you want to tell her? This is your idea."

"No," Jesse said. "I want you to tell her. And then you two can decide if she wants to attend."

"Thank you so much. This really means a lot."

"You're my family, Cole," Jesse said. "And I love you."

"Love you, too," Cole replied, hugging his friend. "Thank you."

"Gym time?"

"Let's do it," Cole said, getting up from the couch. Jesse and Cole headed into their rooms to grab their gym gear.

Across the street, Joyelle was arriving home from her overnight shift at the hospital. She pulled off her coat and scarf as Derek greeted her with a kiss and a hug.

"You must be exhausted," Derek said.

"I am," Joyelle said. "But it wasn't too bad. Other than the few minutes when the power went out."

"Oh, boy," Derek said.

Joyelle kicked off her boots. "Why didn't you tell me that Cole saved my life?"

"What?" Derek asked, surprised by the question.

"Tyler said that Cole tried to save me and the babies from the explosion. Why didn't you tell me?"

"I didn't think it was important. I was more focused on you."

"You didn't think it was important that I know someone risked his life for me and our babies?"

"The doctors told us not to pressure you into remembering."

"But that's something pretty important. I need to thank Cole for that. Take him cookies or something."

"No!" Derek said. "You don't need to say anything. I'm sure he knows you're grateful. He knows you're still recovering."

"Derek, if I want to thank someone for trying to save our babies, I'm going to."

"I don't know why Tyler is telling you stuff like that anyway."

"Because he thought I should know. And I think so, too."

Before Derek could reply, his cell phone started to ring. The phone screen said the call was from "Justin," so Derek answered it. "Hello?"

As Derek took the call, Joyelle went into her bedroom to pull off her scrubs and pull on some sweatpants and a sweatshirt. Once changed, she returned to the hallway where Derek was standing.

"That was Justin," Derek said.

"What did he want?"

"My father died last night."

As Derek shared with Joyelle the news of his father's passing, Michael drove Keith through the gates of

Chicago's Graceland Cemetery. They slowly made their way through the cemetery until Michael stopped and parked the car so they could walk across the snow-covered cemetery to his father's grave.

"I'm sorry to drag you out in this snow, but it's my tradition on my dad's birthday," Michael explained.

"I understand," Keith said. "Besides, they already have the paths pretty cleared of the snow."

"Just a bit further," Michael said as he saw the top of his father's gravestone protruding from the snow. The two made their way to the grave unaware of a person watching them from a safe distance.

When they reached the spot, Michael pushed the snow off the gravestone with his hand. The snow tumbled to the ground, slowly revealing the shape of the marker and the writing on it. Michael knelt down to brush the remaining snow from the face of the stone so that Keith could see the details.

"This is my father," Michael said. "Feliz cumpleaños, Papa."

Keith stared at the name on the grave. "Sergeant Ricardo Gomez. But that's a different last name."

"Yes," Michael explained. "I have my mother's last name, Martinez. They weren't married. Michael was my mother's dad's name and my middle name is Ricardo for my father."

"My God," Keith said as his knees buckled slightly.

"Are you okay?" Michael asked. "You don't look so good."

"Just the wind, I think. Hard to catch my breath."

"It is cold out here. Maybe we should get back to the car."

"Why don't I head back and you can have a moment with your father?" Keith said. "I'll wait in the car."

"Okay," Michael said. "You sure you're okay?"

"Yes," Keith replied, already walking back toward the car.

As he made his way through the snow, he passed a tree, behind which Rachel shifted her stance so she wouldn't be seen by either man. She watched Keith get back into Michael's car and then turned her attention back to Michael and his father's grave. A gust of wind kicked up some snow from the ground. Chicago snowstorms bring out the best and worst in people.

Episode #26

One's identity may change in a moment. As Marco Ciancio prepared to see his Aunt Concetta again, he transformed himself into his brother Gino. Dressed in one of Gino's suits and wearing his hair more in Gino's style, Marco waited patiently in the back of his limousine for his aunt to arrive.

When he saw his chauffeur escorting his elderly aunt to the car, Marco stepped out of the back seat and greeted her. Embracing her with a warm hug, Marco made sure not to make direct eye contact with the old lady, whose eyes were shielded by thick sunglasses.

"Gino!"

"Aunt Connie," Marco said with a smile. "So good to see you."

"You look just like your brother," Concetta said. "I still can't tell you two apart. Did I tell you that he came to visit me recently?"

Marco acted surprised. "Marco visited you? In Rome?"

"He's a good boy, too." Concetta patted Marco on the cheek. "I have much to share with you."

"Let's get you into the car and out of this hot sun," Marco said, carefully helping his aunt into the back seat. "I made all the arrangements for your hotel just as you asked. No one else knows you're in town."

"Thank you," she replied, getting comfortable in the car. Marco got inside next to her and the chauffeur returned to the driver's seat.

As the limousine left the airport and headed into the city, a taxicab pulled in behind it. The driver got out and walked around to the trunk while Derek Mancini got out of the back seat and met the driver behind the car. The driver removed Derek's luggage from the trunk and placed it on the curb.

"Thank you," Derek said, putting some cash into the driver's hand.

"My pleasure," the driver replied. "Have a good flight back to Chicago."

Derek smiled, picked up his luggage, and headed into the airport terminal.

As Derek headed home to Chicago and Marco drove his aunt to her hotel, Gino Ciancio was visiting Justin Mancini in his home. After placing a gigantic floral arrangement on the counter in Justin's study, Gino hugged Justin tightly.

"How are you doing?"

"I'm okay," Justin replied. "Just tired. Been running around nonstop."

"I know you can't see them," Gino said, "but I knew you'd love these flowers because you love the scent. I remember that."

"I knew what they were as soon as you brought them in," Justin replied. "Thank you."

"My pleasure," Gino said. "I'm so sorry for your loss."

"I appreciate your support over the last week very much." Justin paused a moment. "I'm glad you're here because I want to apologize to you."

Gino smiled. "Oh?"

"Yes. The last time we were together, before my father passed, I said some horrible things to you. I was feeling sorry for myself about the loss of my vision and I accused you of being the cause. I'm sorry."

"I understand how frustrated you are."

"That doesn't justify me lashing out at you. You have been the one person in my life lately who I can trust and count on. You have my back, even when my own family doesn't. So I'm sorry.

"I love you, Justin," Gino said.

"Thank you," Justin said. "I guess I love you, too, in my own way."

"And because I love you, I'm worried about you. Now more than ever."

"Why?" Justin asked. "I've been working with a trainer like you suggested. Getting around with a walking stick and learning to rely more on my other senses. I'm doing well."

"Your vision isn't why I'm worried about you."

"Then what?"

"Now that your father is dead and you officially own one fourth of Mancini Global, my family is going to come after you like never before. You owe them a large debt and they intend to collect." Gino paused and then continued. "I will do whatever I can to protect you, but sometimes they don't keep me in the loop about their plans. You need to be careful. All of you."

"One fourth? Can you believe it? Who knew my father had another son?"

"I'm sure you were all surprised by that fact during the reading of the will. It's unbelievable."

"Not really," Justin said. "Knowing how often my father cheated on my mother, I'm surprised I don't have more half-siblings out there."

"Well, as executor of your father's estate, you need to locate this person. Quickly."

"I'm not even sure about how to begin. Even in death, my father is manipulating us."

"I'm here to help, no matter what you need."

Justin smiled. "You always are. Not sure what I ever did to deserve that."

"I'm not, either," Gino said jokingly. "But it's true nonetheless. And maybe one day when you're not so focused on business, you'll realize that we should be together." Suddenly, Justin began to stagger as if he were about to faint. Gino reached out and grabbed him. "Whoa, are you okay?"

Justin put his hand up this head. "I think so."

"Do you need to sit down?"

"No, no. I'm good. Thanks, though."

"I have an idea. Why don't I come by later on and take you to dinner? Just the two of us."

"That would be great," Justin replied.

"Perfect. I have a meeting to get to now, but I'll catch you later then."

"Looking forward to it," Justin said as Gino left the room. Still rubbing his temple, Justin sat down on a nearby bar stool.

As Justin relaxed in the silence of his home, the Chicago restaurant was loud with the sounds of carpenters and designers, who were busy bringing the design plans for The Boys and The Booze to life. Workers on ladders with hammers and saws, with electrical wire and light fixtures, with fabric and paint filled the space, making it difficult for Max Taylor and Emmett Mancini to walk through the area.

"It's like war zone in here," Emmett said. "I can't believe it."

"Well, Shawn really had the team step it up when I told him the date for Logan's fundraiser. It's gonna be close, but I think we'll be okay."

"Amazing," Emmett replied.

Max stopped and put his hands on Emmett's shoulders. "Are you sure you're okay? You look really tired."

"I'm okay. It's just everything with my father and all of this, too."

"If this is too much, we can put it all on 'hold'. There are lots of places they can hold the fundraiser. It's not worth stressing out about."

"No," Emmett said. "I'm fine. Just tired. Besides, this is all a good distraction from my family stuff. Speaking of which, I need to get going to pick up Derek at the airport."

"Are you sure you don't want me to go with you? I can cancel my meeting with Logan."

"Don't be ridiculous. I'm fine. You need to meet with Logan so we can get more details about the party."

Ben Donovan approached the two men. "I'm sorry to interrupt, but I need your approval on something."

"You two handle it," Emmett said, giving Max a quick kiss. "I have to go."

"Drive carefully," Max said as he watched Emmett rush out the front door. Then he followed Ben over to the far area of the club. In the midst of all the chaos of the renovations, Jensen Stone emerged unnoticed from the basement area.

He watched Ben and Max walk away toward the far area of the club and then quickly scanned the room, checking out all the workers and their activities. A few steps away, he spotted a clipboard, work helmet, and wallet sitting on an electric saw table. He walked near the table, reaching out and grabbing the wallet as he passed it, and returned to the kitchen area. Standing behind the wall, he pulled the cash from the wallet, dropped the wallet onto the floor, and headed out the back alley door of the restaurant.

As Jensen rushed from the restaurant, Keith rushed into his bedroom. He tore open his wardrobe and removed the box containing the newspaper articles from his past. Sitting down on his bed with the box in his lap, Keith opened it and began pulling out clippings until he located the one with the headline, "Beloved father killed in hit and run."

His eyes quickly scanned the article. "Sergeant Ricardo Gomez was killed early Thursday in an apparent hit and run accident." He continued to read until he reached the end of the article. "Sergeant Gomez is survived by his children Michael, Rosa, and Mateo."

Keith's eyes welled up with tears as he crumbled the article in his hands. "It can't be true. It's can't be."

While Keith tried to face the reality of his situation, Marco slowly helped his aunt into the chair in her San Francisco hotel. Deliberately leaving the room dark, Marco sat himself in a chair to Concetta's side. Holding a cloth bag in her lap, she turned slightly to her side to try to face her nephew from behind her thick glasses.

"Thank you for arranging this hotel room for me, Gino," she said softly. "It's lovely."

"No problem at all, Aunt Connie. As I'm sure you can understand, I am eager to hear what you have to tell me."

"Of course," she replied. "Your mother and I were sisters. Few sisters are as close as we were. We told each other everything."

"She always spoke very highly of you."

"So whenever our lives got crazy or stressful, we turned to each other for support and help, as I hope you and Marco do as well."

Marco smiled. "We do."

"You know that her affair with Antonio Mancini was something that she struggled with for a long time after it was over. She loved him. But she loved your father, too."

"I know she did."

"So when it ended and something happened, she turned to me for help."

"Something happened?" Marco asked. "You mean her cancer?"

"No," Concetta replied. "Your mother didn't actually have cancer at the time she came to stay with me."

Marco's eye widened. "What? But that's why she went to Rome. To participate in those experimental studies. Why else would she have left us for so long?"

"The cancer and those treatments was a story that she and I made up so that she could get away and stay with me for an extended period of time."

"You lied to all of us?"

"I protected my sister."

"From what?"

"From the truth," Concetta stated, clearing her throat. "Your mother came to Rome with a medical condition, but it wasn't cancer. She was pregnant."

"Oh, God," Marco said.

"She came here to live until she had the baby so that no one at home would know."

"But she died of cancer."

"She did," Concetta said with a nod. "Which they ironically discovered while she was here. So her lie became the truth." Concetta paused for moment to catch her breath. "She always said that cancer was punishment

201

for the sin of her affair. God's punishment. I tried to explain to her that God doesn't work that way."

"And what happened to the baby? Did she have it?"

Concetta nodded again. "She did. A baby boy."

"So I have a half brother?"

"You do. But, Gino, remember what I told you. This information is for you and you alone right now."

"But why?"

"Your mother loved and trusted you more than anyone else in your family. Even me."

"How is that possible? She told you everything."

"No," Concetta said, reaching into the cloth bag on her lap and removing a large, leather covered book. "She told *you* everything." She handed the diary to Marco.

"What is this?"

"Your mother kept a diary during her time in Rome. She said it helped her process and work through all that had happened and how she felt about her pregnancy. Even after she gave birth, she kept writing. She wrote in it all the time, until she decided it was time to return home to America and her family."

"And she gave it to you."

"When she left, she gave me very clear, strict instructions. After her death, at a time determined by me, I was to give the diary to you. She specifically said it was to go to Gino and no one else."

"I see..."

"No one has ever opened that book since she locked it closed. Even I have no idea what's inside of it. But when your brother Marco visited me recently and began asking questions about your mother, I knew it was time to deliver this to you as I had promised."

"And what about her other son?"

"I have no idea what happened to the boy after she gave birth to him. I never saw him again and she never spoke of him again. She said everything that you would need to know about him -- and other things -- would be found in there."

"What kinds of things was Marco asking?"

"Questions about your mother and the affair. I provided as little information as possible. As I promised your mother."

"Is there a key to this?"

"She destroyed it," Concetta said. "She said you'd have to break it open; that way you'd know no one else had ever been in it."

Marco ran his fingers over the book's lock. "Mom was certainly clever, wasn't she?"

"Gino, please remember this. That book is like Pandora's Box. Once you open it, you may learn things about your mother that you never knew. And your family as well. Whether or not you choose to open it is entirely up to you. I promised my sister that I'd deliver it to you and I have. Be careful and think long and hard before you break that lock."

"Of course, Aunt Connie. I understand."

"Good, my boy. Now, I have done what I came to do. And I need to rest before my trip back to Rome tomorrow."

"Yes," Marco said. "And you're sure you don't want to see anyone else while you're here? Even just to say hello to Marco or my father?"

"No one must ever know I was here."

"I understand," Marco said, standing up. "Your secret is safe with me. Is there anything else I can get you before I go?"

"No, dear. I just want to rest now."

"I'll go then. Thank you so much for this conversation. And the diary." Marco kissed his aunt. "I'll be back to drive you to the airport in the morning."

"Thank you, Gino," Concetta said. "And remember what I told you about opening that book."

Marco nodded and then left the room. Once in the hotel hallway, he looked at the diary and smiled wildly. Then he headed to the elevator.

While Marco got into his limousine to head back to the Ciancio estate, Gino and his father Carlo were speaking in the mansion's library. Carlo was seated in the large leather chair to the left of the fireplace and Gino was pouring himself a drink at the bar at the far end of the room. Once his glass was full, Gino walked toward his father.

"Father, I want to know what you plan to do now that old man Mancini is dead."

"What do you think I plan to do? Take the company right from under his boys."

Gino sat down on the sofa across from the fireplace. "Father, I am asking you to please be fair."

Carlo laughed. "Fair? I am always fair."

"You know what I mean. I know you didn't order that bomb to be placed in the car, but you didn't speak out against it, either."

"That bomb was your brother's doing. Not mine. And when I heard about it, I addressed it with him directly. He will not 'go rogue' again, so the issue is settled."

"For now. But I don't want any more 'gifts' sent to Justin, either. That walking stick and movie tickets was a sick joke. We don't need to degrade other people -- or ourselves -- like that."

"And I spoke to Marco about that, too. Just as you asked."

"Now that the Mancini boys are officially owners of the company, I just have a bad feeling in my gut. Like something bad is going to happen. And I don't want our family causing more trouble."

"Gino, the Mancinis will get what they deserve." Carlo sipped the wine he had been holding in his hand. "And now there are apparently four of them."

"They were all caught by surprise by that revelation at the reading of the will."

"I'm sure," Carlo said. "It's a complete surprise to everyone."

"I talked to Justin. They don't even know where to begin searching for this person."

"You care a lot about him, don't you?" Carlo asked.

"Justin? Yes, I do, Father. I'm sorry if that upsets you."

"Gino, you know I have always supported you and your lifestyle. I love you and I'm proud of you. But please be careful. I don't say that because Justin is a Mancini. I say that because I see behaviors in him that aren't trustworthy. I don't want you to get hurt."

"Thank you, Father. I appreciate that. He is a complicated man. But I think I know him better than anyone. I know to keep my eyes open around him. But I do love him, too."

"You take people as you find them, son. Flaws and all," Carlo said. "Just remember who your family is and don't get caught in the middle."

"That sounds more like a threat than advice, Father."

"Maybe it's both."

Gino took another sip from his drink. "I can take care of myself. Now I have to go. I have a meeting and then I'm having dinner with Justin." Gino finished his drink and put the empty glass on the table in front of him. "I'll see later."

As Gino was leaving the room, Marco entered it and the two nearly collided.

"Whoa," Marco said. "Where are you off to so fast?"

"I have a meeting," Gino replied. "What's with the hair? Trying to look even more good looking like me?" Gino laughed and disappeared down the hallway.

Marco smiled. "Hardly."

"Where have you been?" Carlo asked Marco.

"Just meetings in the city, Father," Marco lied.

"Have you made any progress at all on the Mancini search? Now that the secret is out, they will be scrambling to find their new brother, too."

"Still working on it, Father. I'm doing the best I can."

"Well, do better."

"I have a feeling that I'm going to learn something very soon," Marco said with a smile as headed over to the bar to pour himself a drink.

At the same time in Chicago, Derek and Emmett were having coffee at Boystown Blend. They were seated in a corner of the coffee house talking privately.

"Are you sure you're okay?" Emmett asked his brother as he took a drink from his coffee cup.

"I'm fine," Derek said. "It was a long trip."

"I'm sorry I couldn't be there to help you," Emmett said. "But I just couldn't go."

"I understand," Derek said. "It's not a problem. You and our dad had your problems. Hell, Dad and I had our problems, too. But after the visit we had a few weeks ago, I thought I should go. And I'm glad I did. Especially for the will."

"I know. We have a brother out there somewhere."

"Still trying to wrap my head around that one," Derek said with a sigh.

"Like I told Max, I'm surprised there aren't even more out there with the way Dad cheated on Mom."

Derek smiled and rolled his eyes. "Exactly."

"Poor guy doesn't even know he's about to inherit a quarter of a huge corporation."

"Speaking of which," Derek said, "we are now officially and legally heads of Mancini Global. How do you feel about that?"

"You know how I feel, Derek. I wanted no part of it before and I don't want any part of it now."

"Well, whether you like it or not, you are a part owner now."

"Then I'll give my share to you," Emmett said. "You'll have fifty percent and I won't have to worry about it."

"Is that really what you want to do? Think about it a bit. Talk it over with Max. It's a big decision."

"I can talk it over with Max for sure, but my mind is made up. I don't want any part of it. Not sure why you do, either. That company has caused so many problems for all of us. Sell it and be rid of it."

"We can make it our own now. Take it in any direction we like."

"You maybe. But not me," Emmett said, drinking more coffee. "But I will talk to Max first."

"I think that's a good idea. You two will be married soon -- you should talk those major decisions out."

"Wow," Emmett said. "Now you're a marriage counselor, too?"

Derek laughed. "Me? Doubt it. Speaking of which, I should probably get home to Joyelle. I'm sure she's eager to see me and hear how things went in California."

"Sure," Emmett said, standing up and pulling on his coat.

"Thanks for the ride. And the coffee," Derek said, also putting on his jacket. Then he gulped down the rest of his coffee.

As they headed toward the door, Michael Martinez and Keith Colgan were coming through the door of the coffee shop.

"Hey, guys," Emmett said with a smile.

"Oh, wow," Keith replied. "Funny seeing you here."

"We were so sorry to hear about your father," Michael said. "How are you guys doing?"

"We're okay. Thank you," Derek said.

"Derek just got back from California," Emmett added.

"You must be wiped out," Michael said.

"Hey, we were thinking of hosting a dinner for you two," Keith said. "We all want to see you and offer our support and condolences."

"That's kind of you," Derek said. "Sure."

"Great," Keith said with a smile. "I'll be in touch about dates."

"And let us know if you need anything at all," Michael added.

"Thank you," Emmett said, hugging Keith and then Michael.

"Bye," Derek added as Emmett and he left the coffee shop.

Michael and Keith approached the counter to place their coffee orders. "This has to be rough for them," Michael said.

"Of course," Keith replied. "Even though they were not close with their dad."

"That doesn't matter. It still impacts you in ways you don't even anticipate. Believe me, no one knows that better than I do."

"True," Keith said.

"Are you okay? You've been kind of quiet lately."

"Me? Naw, I'm fine. Come on; let's order." Michael and Keith got the attention of the girl behind the counter and placed their coffee orders.

To their left, in the far corner of the coffee shop, Jesse Morgan and Ben were seated at a small table.

"I appreciate you meeting with me," Jesse told Ben. "Sincerely."

"Well, you certainly got my curiosity."

"I'll be frank. I don't like you and I will never forgive you for what you did to me on New Year's Eve."

"What I did to you? I think you have it backwards. You set that entire trap up for me."

"Regardless. I don't want to rehash that. There's no point."

"What is the point?" Ben asked.

"The point is that we need to get along, for Mom's sake. She's pregnant and she needs to take care of herself and not be stressed out."

"That is something you and I finally agree on. In fact, I just signed a lease on an apartment for us here in the city."

"Great," Jesse said. "I'm sure she'll like that."

"Yes," Ben said. "I have pics of it right here on my phone." Ben pulled out his phone and pulled up some photos. Then he handed this phone to Jesse, who looked at the photos. "It's a pretty cool place; I think she'll like it."

"Nice," Jesse said, scrolling through the photos on the phone.

"Excuse me a moment," Ben said, getting up from the table and walking to the bathroom.

Jesse watched Ben do into the bathroom. Then he quickly took out his own phone and pressed a few buttons on it. He touched his phone to Ben's and then pressed a few buttons on Ben's phone as well. Putting his phone back into his pocket, Jesse mumbled, "You sick fuck."

Ben returned to the table. "Well, thank you for this little visit, but I really do need to get back to work."

"I understand," Jesse said. "Please take good care of my mother. And please give her my best."

"Absolutely," Ben said, turning and leaving the shop.

Jesse stood up and pulled on his coat. As he did, he said to himself, "Next time I'll get you away from her for good."

Jesse left Boystown Blend as Cole O'Brien and David Young were walking through Maggie Daley Park, having just finished ice skating. Their ice skates over their shoulders, they left the ice skating ribbon and walked through the park toward Michigan Avenue. The park was crowded, as usual, with people walking in all directions.

"Who knew you were such the skater?" David asked with a wide smile.

"I'm a man of many talents," Cole said, jokingly. "You only know the tip of the iceberg."

"Well, I'm looking forward to knowing more."

When they reached Michigan Avenue, they turned south and headed toward the Art Institute. The winter Chicago wind propelled them forward.

"So you and Tyler are getting along well as roommates?" Cole asked.

"Great, thanks," David replied. "We both lucked out. And we're really grateful to Emmett and Max for letting us live in that condo. It's great."

"Cool," Cole said. "You're like Jesse and me."

"Well, not quite. Jesse and you have a much longer history of friendship. But Tyler and I are certainly building one. It's fun."

Cole smiled. "This is fun, too."

David stopped walking and turned to Cole. "Really? You're having a good time?"

"Of course. I always have fun with you."

David took Cole's hands into his and pulled them to his chest. Then he leaned in and kissed Cole. The kiss grew deeper and more passionate. When it ended, Cole looked around to see if anyone walking on the street was watching them. David, however, remained focused on Cole.

"I'm sorry -- I shouldn't have--"

Cole smiled and put his gloved index finger on David's mouth. "Shh. You don't have to apologize. It's okay."

"But I know you and Derek--"

"Stop. Today is about you and me. And I'm enjoying it." Cole kissed David again.

"Thank you," David said.

"Come on, let's get out of this cold." Cole and David trotted up the stairs to the main entrance of the Art Institute, passing the building's iconic green lion statues as they did.

David and Cole headed into the Art Institute to continue their day as Max rushed into Boystown Bistro to meet Logan, who was already seated at a table with a half-full glass of wine in front of him.

"Sorry I'm late. Construction issues," Max said, kissing Logan on the cheek and taking a seat across the table from him.

"No problem," Logan said. "I'm in no rush."

"Good. I want to hear everything you have decided for the fundraiser. I think construction will pretty much be on time."

Logan patted his hand on the folder next to his plate. "I have everything right here."

Their server Dustin Alexander approached the table. His thick, dark hair hanging a bit over his stunning, blue-green eyes, Dustin recognized Max. "Good evening and welcome back to Boystown Bistro. I'm Dustin; we met the last time you dined with us. Can I get you a cocktail or drink?"

"Thanks, Dustin," Max replied. "Sure, I'll have a vodka soda, please."

"Another glass of wine for you?" Dustin asked Logan.

"Yes," Logan replied.

"I'll be right back," Dustin said as he turned and left the table.

"You might want to slow down a bit," Max said to Logan.

"Max, please don't do that. We're not together anymore. You don't get to say things like that."

"Together or not, I still love and care about you. And God knows your boyfriend Jesse isn't going to look out for you like I did."

"He's not my boyfriend anymore," Logan said.

"Did something happen?"

"I don't want to talk about it," Logan said. "That's not why we're here."

"Logan, we're friends. You can talk to me." Logan didn't reply. "Look, I know something must have happened between you two. Look how you're drinking lately. You only drink like this when you're upset or

217

depressed. I know from experience. What did that kid do to you?"

"I said I don't want to talk about it."

"You're still working with him -- at the office and on this fundraiser. But something just isn't right. Maybe I can help?"

Logan laughed. "With Jesse? I doubt it. You two will never get along."

Dustin returned with the drinks. He placed a glass of wine in front of Logan and removed the empty one. Then he put Max's drink in front of him.

"Can I get you started with an appetizer or salad?" Dustin asked.

"How about the grilled calamari?" Max asked Logan, who nodded in approval.

"Great," Dustin said, smiling at Max. "I'll put that order in and then come back and we can discuss entrees." Dustin left the area.

"That kid likes you," Logan said about Dustin. "Did you see that smile he gave you?"

Max ignored the comment. "Logan, please," Max said. "I want to help you. Even if it means helping you with Jesse. I want you to be happy."

"Let's talk about Emmett," Logan said. "How is he? With his father's death and all."

"He's coping. They weren't particularly close, but I think it's still affecting him."

"I'm sure," Logan said, drinking his wine.

"So you're not going to tell me what happened between you and Jesse?"

"Let's discuss the fundraiser," Logan replied, opening the folder on the table next to him. "We have a lot to finalize here." Logan turned the folder around and handed it across the table to Max.

Later that evening, Cole and David were walking down Roscoe Street toward Cole's apartment. Holding hands, they paused at the front gate of Cole's apartment complex.

"Thanks for a great day," Cole said. "I really had a great time."

David smiled. "I'm glad. We usually seem to have a good time together."

"We do," Cole agreed. "Well, it's getting late so I better head inside."

"I need to get home, too. Thanks again."

Cole and David hugged and then stood facing one another. David leaned in and kissed Cole, who welcomed the kiss. They wrapped their arms around each other and embraced as their kiss continued. Eventually, they pulled apart.

"Good night," Cole said, smiling widely and then heading inside the gate.

"Night," David replied.

Cole entered the front door of his apartment building and David continued to walk down Roscoe Street, both of them unaware of Derek watching them from the living room window of his condo building across the street.

As the next morning dawned, it brought bright sunshine which glistened on the snow piled up along sidewalks and streets. The sunshine streamed into Max and Emmett's bedroom window above the restaurant and club.

Emmett was just waking up and rolled over toward his sleeping fiancé. He softly kissed Max's chest and ran his hand down the side of Max's body. Pulling the sheets out of his way, Emmett got between Max's legs. He licked his way up Max's leg.

Max began to wake up from his deep sleep. He looked down at Emmett, his dick growing immediately hard. Max smiled at Emmett and placed his hands on the back of Emmett's head. Pushing down, Max forced Emmett's mouth further down on him.

Digging his fingers into Emmett's shoulders, Max prepared to shoot. Emmett wrapped his hand around Max's thick tool and continued to suck the head. Max squirmed more, moaning loudly. "Oh, Emmett..." Max let out another loud moan as he shot down Emmett's throat.

"Thanks, babe," Max said with a smile.

Emmett laughed. "Good morning."

"Sure is," Max replied as he put his arm around Emmett and held him tightly.

"Derek wanted me to talk something over with you. About the family business."

"What's that?"

"I want to turn my quarter of the company over to him."

"Okay..."

"And he said it's too big of a decision to make without thinking more about it and talking with you."

"Well, he does have a point. That's a lot to give up."

"I wanted nothing to do with the business before. Why should that change now?"

"I'm not sure it has to change. However, before you weren't a part owner and now you are. There's a lot more at stake. Financially and otherwise."

"What would you do if you were me?"

"Emmett, you know I would never tell you what do to. I'll back whatever decision you make."

"You're my fiancé, I want your opinion."

"Maybe there's a middle ground? I'm just thinking out loud here, but what if you gave Derek your proxy to make decisions and vote for you, but you still maintain your ownership. It might be nice to have a share of the profits since we're just starting a business out, which is always risky."

"Interesting idea. Handsome and bright – no wonder I love you."

"It's just a thought. Seems like a nice middle-ground, for now. You can always sign over your quarter at any time in the future if you still want to."

"I agree," Emmett said, kissing Max's chest. "I'm sure I'll hear from Justin either way. He won't be happy about this."

"It's your decision to make, not his."

"I know," Emmett said, glancing at the clock. "We should get downstairs; the crew will be here soon."

Max rolled over and got out of bed, the sun shining through the window on his hard body. He picked up his phone from the night table. "Hmm. Message from Jacqueline. She wants to meet me for lunch. Says it's urgent."

"Urgent?" Emmett asked as he stepped out of bed. "Wonder what that's all about?"

"You okay with me meeting her? Can you handle things downstairs while I'm gone?"

"Of course, no problem. Sounds like it's important."

"You're the best." Max said with a smile. "Want to shower with me?"

"I'm in," Emmett said, following Max into the bathroom.

While Emmett and Max showered, Jensen woke up in the basement store room of the restaurant below them. Wrapped in a blanket and lying along the wall, Jensen stretched out his arms and wiped his eyes. Then he sat up and looked around the dark room.

At the same time, Cole was seated at a table at the Walnut Room in Macy's State Street store. His server poured him another glass of water and then walked away from the table as Jacqueline arrived.

"Mrs. Morgan," Cole said, rising from his chair to greet Jacqueline with a kiss on the cheek. "Thanks for coming."

"How could I say 'no' to á breakfast invitation from such a handsome man?"

Cole smiled. "Well, thank you." Jacqueline took her seat and then Cole sat back down. "Remember the last time we were here? Thanksgiving weekend."

"I do," Jacqueline said, putting her napkin in her lap. "That was fun."

"This room seems so empty without the Christmas tree."

Jacqueline looked in the direction of where the large tree once stood. "It does."

The waiter returned to the table. "Good morning. May I bring you something to drink?"

"I'm okay with water for now," Jacqueline replied. "Thank you."

The waiter nodded and walked away.

"I'm sure you're wondering why I asked you here to breakfast."

Jacqueline smiled. "I am."

"It's about Jesse."

"Is something wrong?"

"Actually, yes. You two aren't speaking. And that's wrong."

"That's between my son and me, Cole."

"I know, Mrs. Morgan." Cole leaned forward. "I know what happened and what you saw in that hotel room on New Year's Eve."

"It was disgusting."

"I'm sorry. But you have to understand Jesse's motives. He didn't know what else to do to get you away from Ben."

"How about telling me the truth? Would that have been so hard?"

"He didn't think you'd believe him. He wanted you to literally see the kind of person Ben is."

"Oh, I did. But I saw my son as well."

"What he did, he did out of love for you. You are the most important person in his life. He was desperate to get through to you."

"I'm sorry he had so little trust in me that he couldn't just tell me what was going on."

"Like I said, he didn't think you'd believe him." Cole took a sip of water. "You are his only parent. And he's your only child, at least for the next few months. Do you really want to live without him in your life?"

"What he did was unforgivable."

"You're his mother. And I know you, Mrs. Morgan. You have a huge heart and a large capacity to love. He said you texted a short sentence to him the other day. That shows you still care about him. Reach out to him again. Talk to him."

"I'm sorry, but I can't. It's just too hard. I can't get those images out of my head."

"Maybe if you talk to Jesse. Tell him how you feel. He's been trying so hard to reach you."

"I feel betrayed and I can't get over it."

"Mrs. Morgan, my mother is very sick. Every day is a struggle and a blessing. I know how special a relationship with a parent is, because I could lose it any day. Don't waste time being separate from Jesse. You two can get through this together -- and come out of it closer than you have ever been."

"I appreciate what you're trying to do," Jacqueline said, forcing a smile. "I really do. But this is between my son and me. No one else."

"Please just think about that I said."

"I will try, but I can't promise anything. Now tell me more about how your mother is doing."

The waiter returned to the table and Jacqueline and Cole placed their breakfast orders.

Cole updated Jacqueline on the health of his mother as Derek entered David's office in St. Joseph Hospital's wellness center.

"Derek," David said, looking up from this desk. "How are you?"

"I'm fine, thanks," Derek said, closing the office door behind him. "Do you have time to see me?"

"I don't have you in my appointment calendar for today."

"This isn't a professional visit; it's personal."

"Oh?" David said, gesturing Derek to take a seat.

"I'm fine standing," Derek said. "I want to ask you a question. What's going on with you and Cole?"

"Excuse me?"

"I saw the two of you last night out in front of his apartment. What is going on with you two?"

David stood up. "I'm not really sure it's any of your business, Derek."

"The hell it isn't. You know that Cole and I are involved."

"Involved? How so? Maybe you need to explain that more clearly."

"You know what I mean. You saw that video like everyone else did."

"So it's true? Does Joyelle know?"

"You know she has amnesia. Don't play games with me."

"Games aren't my style, Derek. But they certainly seem to be yours. I am free to spend my time with whomever I choose."

"I don't care who you play with as long as it's not Cole."

"Because he's yours?"

"Yes. Because we are working things out between us. They are complicated."

"Well, of course, they are. Because you are married to Joyelle, who has no memories of the night that your supposed love for Cole was exposed. And because you refuse to make a decision about who you really want to be with."

"I--"

"Derek, what you do with your free time is your business, not mine. Just like my free time is my business. And I'll spend it any way I want…with anyone I want."

"I'm telling you to stay away from Cole."

"Cole's a big boy. He doesn't need your protection…or your dysfunction. If he wants me to stay away from him, he can tell me himself. Now I think you should leave; this conversation is over and I have a patient waiting who actually has an appointment with me."

"Just stay away from him," Derek repeated as he left the office. David shook his head in disbelief and sat back down at his desk.

When lunch time approached, Max headed to The Drake Hotel to meet Jacqueline. As he entered the Coq d'Or lounge in the hotel's lower level, he saw Jacqueline already seated at a table. He walked over, greeted her with a kiss on the cheek, and sat down across from her.

"It's good to see you," Max said. "It's been too long. How are you?"

"I apologize for the cryptic message, but I have to be very cautious these days."

"Cautious? Why?"

"That's the reason for this lunch. I wanted to warn you about Shawn…Ben."

"What about him?"

"He's dangerous. You need to be careful."

"Dangerous? He's been doing great work on my new restaurant. What are you talking about?"

"He's a dangerous man. You don't really know him. I want you to release him from the construction project…for your own safety."

"Jacqueline, forgive me, but you're not making sense. Is there something you're not telling me? Because I have found him to be a responsible worker."

"Something happened. On New Year's Eve."

"Tell me," Max said.

"It was horrible. I can't believe Logan didn't tell you."

"Logan? What's he got to do with this?"

"He was there."

"Where?"

"With me at the hotel room."

"What hotel room? Jacqueline, please. You're not making things clear."

"On New Year's Eve during the party, I received a text that Jesse needed to see me right away in one of the hotel rooms. Logan had been looking everywhere for Jesse and happened to be standing with me when the text came through. We thought something might be wrong, so we went to the hotel room together."

"Okay..."

Jacqueline's eyes filled with tears. "When we arrived, the door to the room was unlocked. We went in...and..."

"And?"

"And saw Ben and Jesse having sex."

"Wait, what?"

Jacqueline wiped the tears from her eyes. "It's true. When Logan and I walked in, my husband was on top of my son. And then security arrived telling us to vacate the building."

A waiter walked over to their table. "Good afternoon. Welcome. May I get either one of you drink to start?"

"A club soda, please," Jacqueline said.

"I'll have a vodka on the rocks."

"Thank you," the waiter said. "I'll be right back with those." Then he walked away.

"My God, Jacqueline. Why haven't you told me this sooner? Why are you still with Shawn?"

"That's my business," Jacqueline said.

"Of course," Max said. "I didn't mean to over step." Max paused a moment. "Have you two talked about it?"

"Yes, several times. He blames it all on Jesse."

"How so?"

"Apparently, Jesse and Ben were lovers before I met Ben. When Jesse broke up with him, Ben took it really hard. He came after me as an act of revenge against Jesse, but says he wound up actually falling in love with me."

"Do you believe him?"

"I don't know what to believe." The waiter returned and placed the drinks on the table in front of Jacqueline and Max. Jacqueline took a large sip of her drink before continuing to speak. "Jesse set up the whole scene in the hotel room to prove to me what kind of person Ben really is. There were cameras and everything."

"Cameras?"

"Oh, yes. In fact, Ben made me re-watch the whole nightmare to prove to me that he was the victim of Jesse's set-up."

"And was he?"

"It is true that Jesse set up the whole thing. Cameras and all. But it only worked because Ben went along with it, rather than leaving. So they're both responsible. I haven't spoken to Jesse since."

"I don't believe this."

"I haven't spoken to anyone about this, except Ben. I know I can trust you. And I want to protect you as well. He's reckless and unstable. Don't put your new business in his hands."

"You want me to fire him?"

"I think it's best."

"But you're staying with him? Has he done something to you? Is he holding something over you?"

"I'm carrying his child," Jacqueline said. "I don't like him right. And I don't trust him. But he is the father of my child."

"I'd never judge you, Jacqueline. Only you know how you feel. But this story has me scared for you. God knows what he is capable of. And Jesse? How could he do that to you?"

"Cole had breakfast with me this morning. He says Jesse did it out of love. It was the only way he could think of to show me what kind of person Ben is."

"Why didn't he just tell you?"

"He didn't think I'd believe him. And honestly...I probably wouldn't have. He's right about that."

"Wait a minute. You said Logan was with you?"

"At the hotel. Yes. In fact, he's the one who got me out of there and back to my hotel."

"And he saw everything? Jesse and Ben going at it?"

"Yes," Jacqueline replied.

"Then that explains it. His break-up with Jesse. His drinking and depression. Damn that bastard."

"That 'bastard' is my son."

"Who you're not even speaking to," Max added.

"I told you -- that's between us."

"I warned him not to hurt Logan," Max explained. "Or he'd answer to me."

"This isn't about them; it's about you. I just want you to protect yourself. Ben is volatile and can turn on you in an instant. I wouldn't want anything to happen to you. Or Emmett."

"What would Ben have against Emmett?"

"You are both Ben's employers. Just be careful."

"Jesse brought this man into all of our lives. If it weren't for him, none of us would even know Shawn...Ben."

"I'm having his child. And that's a gift that he can't take a way. Once he's a father, he'll focus on that. You don't know how being a parent can change a person."

"Maybe not," Max replied. "But I know what it means to protect people I love. And I intend to do that."

"Good," Jacqueline said. "You'll do what you need to do regarding Ben. I just wanted to make sure you keep your eyes open with him."

"Thank you. For everything you have shared with me."

As Jacqueline and Max finished their lunch together, Marco was alone on the balcony off his bedroom at the Ciancio estate. With the pool and hillside in the distance, Marco had his focus not on the beautiful scenery, but on the diary in his hands. Having broken the lock on his mother's diary despite his Aunt Connie's warning, Marco was carefully reading page after page of his mother's distinct handwriting.

Occasionally taking a drink from the wine glass on the table next to him, Marco carefully made his way through his mother's past as revealed by the pages of her diary. When he reached one point in the book, the warning words of his aunt became a painful reality. He looked up from the book and looked out over the vineyards.

"My God, Mother. What have you done?"

Meanwhile, in Chicago, Emmett made his way down the stairs from his condo to the restaurant below. Because workers had not yet arrived, the space was quiet. Emmett walked through the area, checking out certain design elements as he headed toward the kitchen.

Upon arriving at the kitchen area, the door from the basement storage area opened and Jensen emerged. Coming face to face with Emmett, Jensen bolted toward the front door.

"Wait!" Emmett yelled, running after Jensen. "Stop!"

Jensen raced through the space as Emmett followed. Then Emmett leapt toward Jensen who tripped over a wooden saw horse. Emmett pounced on him, pinning him to the ground. Jensen struggled to get free from Emmett, who asked, "Who the hell are you?"

At the same time, Keith was pacing back and forth at the front gate of Chicago's Graceland Cemetery. His hands shoved into his pockets in an effort to keep warm,

Keith was looking in every direction as he waited for the person who demanded to meet there.

After a moment, a taxi pulled up to the front of the cemetery and Rachel got out of the car. It quickly pulled away and Rachel walked over to Keith.

"Why did we have to meet here? It's freezing outside today."

"There's a very specific reason," Rachel said.

"A cemetery is melodramatic, even for you. What do you want?"

"The last time we spoke, I thought I knew everything about your terrible past. But as luck would have it, fate revealed a piece of information that surprised even me."

"What are you talking about?"

"We both know what I'm talking about," Rachel said with a smile. "The man you killed so many years ago in that accident is buried right here in this cemetery."

"So what?" Keith asked.

"You're right. The location of his burial doesn't matter. However, his identity does. Even I could never have imagined that the man you killed was none other than your boyfriend's father."

"How do you know that?"

237

"I watched you both the other day -- right here. When he brought you to 'meet' his father on his birthday. Such a touching moment. I was just as surprised as you were that the man you killed in accident was your boyfriend's father. And I saw the pain in your face as you stood at the grave."

"I don't know what you're talking about."

"Oh, you do. But don't worry; your secret is safe with me. Like I told you last time we met, there are only two people who know what you did back then -- you and me. And your police officer boyfriend will never need to know the truth...as long as you follow instructions."

"What do you want?"

"Just a small task, really." Rachel reached into her pocket and pulled out a small, brown glass bottle with a black cap on it. She handed it to Keith.

"What is that?"

"What it is doesn't matter. What you're doing to do with it does." Rachel paused a moment. "It's simple. You're going to poison your ex-boyfriend Emmett for me."

As Keith stood in the cold wind staring at the bottle in his hand, Jesse was in his apartment watching television.

Wearing only a pair of sweat pants, Jesse had his feet up on the coffee table and was on the phone with Cole.

"No problem, bro. Take your time; I'll see you when you get home." Jesse ended the call and put his phone back into his sweatpants pocket as a loud knock came to the door. The pounding on the door didn't stop. "One sec, I'm coming."

Jesse got up from the sofa and opened the door to his apartment. Instantly, Max lunged through the door and punched Jesse hard across the face. Jesse fell backwards and blood from his mouth splattered across the wall and floor.

"You son of a bitch!" Max yelled, pouncing on Jesse and continuing to punch his face. Jesse struggled futilely as Max's punches sent blood in several directions. "I told you not to hurt him. I told you to leave him alone!"

Max continued to pound Jesse whose body went limp and showed no signs of defending itself. Jacqueline rushed into the open door of the apartment and saw Max beating Jesse.

"Max, stop!"

"I'm going to kill the bastard!"

"Max, stop! He's your son!" Jacqueline yelled as she struggled to push Max off of Jesse's motionless body. One's identity may change in a moment.

Episode #27

One's memories define her character and purpose. As Jacqueline Morgan Donovan hovered over the bloody body of her son Jesse, memories of him as child flooded her mind. She recalled giving birth to him, witnessing his first steps, hearing his first words, taking him to his first day of school, celebrating his birthdays, attending his graduations, enjoying Christmases and other holidays, and even seeing him in the hotel room with her husband Ben Donovan.

"You're going to be okay," Jacqueline whispered while she held a towel to his face to stop the bleeding. His eyes were already swollen and bruised. She looked over at Max Taylor who was rinsing a towel in the kitchen sink. "Why isn't the ambulance here yet?"

"It will be. It's only been a few minutes." Max returned to Jacqueline and swapped towels with her. Max mumbled to himself. "My son. My God."

"I can't believe you did this to him."

'Why didn't you tell me? How could you keep that from me?"

"Not now, Max," Jacqueline said. "Not now."

Suddenly, Cole O'Brien rushed into the apartment. "What the hell is going on? There's an ambulance pulling up outside and--" Cole stopped upon seeing Jesse on the floor and the blood all over the room. "What the hell happened?"

Before anyone could answer Cole's question, two paramedics entered the apartment. Without wasting any time, they knelt down next to Jesse and checked his vitals.

"He's my son," Jacqueline said as Cole helped her up from the floor.

"Please step back, Ma'am," said one of the paramedics. "We'll do all we can to help."

With his arms around Jesse's mother, Cole looked over at Max. "Did you do this to him? Did you?" Max didn't reply. "I asked you a question."

"Sir," a paramedic said to Cole, "we could actually use your help getting him on the stretcher and into the ambulance.'

"Sure," Cole said, focusing his attention on the paramedics. He stood up and assisted the paramedics as they instructed.

While the emergency team got Jesse into the ambulance, Emmett Mancini was standing in front of

Jensen Stone, who was seated in the corner of the restaurant.

"You got nothing on me," Jensen said to Emmett. "You can't keep me here."

"We'll see about that when Officer Martinez arrives," Emmett replied.

Just as Emmett checked his watch, Michael Martinez entered the front door of the restaurant.

"Hi, Michael," Emmett said. "He's right here."

"Well, well," Michael said with a smile, immediately recognizing Jensen. "We meet again." Jensen didn't say a word. "What's your name?"

"Jensen Stone."

"Good to see you again, Jensen Stone. So who were you soliciting this time, my friend Emmett here?"

"I didn't do anything," Jensen said.

"I found him here in the restaurant this morning."

"Trespassing, eh?" Michael said. "What were you doing in here this morning?"

"Nothing."

"Why do I find that hard to believe?"

"Believe what you want," Jensen said, "but it's the truth."

Michael turned to Emmett. "Did he steal anything? Notice anything missing?"

"I haven't had a chance to really look. I've been standing right here with him until you arrived," Emmett explained.

"Why don't you take a look around and see?"

"I promise you – nothing is missing," Jensen said.

"You know, one of our workers said someone stole money from his wallet recently."

Michael looked at Jensen. "Do you know anything about that?" Jensen shrugged his shoulders. "You're not quite as talkative today as you were that day on the sidewalk when you were grabbing your crotch."

"If you want to get out of here and have a good time together, I'm game," Jensen said.

"I'll pass," Michael replied. "So where do you live?"

"Here and there," Jensen said. "With friends mostly."

Michael turned to Emmett. "Do you want to press charges?"

"I don't know. What do you think I should do?"

"Check the basement and see if anything is missing; we'll go from there."

244

"Okay," Emmett said, heading down in to the basement storage area.

Michael's cell phone rang and he pulled it from his belt. "And you stay right where you are," Michael said to Jensen. "I have to take this."

Jensen watched Michael walk a few steps away and answer his cell phone. Sitting quietly, Jensen refocused his attention on the basement door. A few moments passed and then Emmett came through the basement door.

"Find anything missing?" Jensen asked.

"Nope," Emmett said.

Jensen smiled. "I told you."

Michael walked back over to Jensen and Emmett. "What did you find down there?"

"Everything is there, just like I said."

"Lucky for you," Michael said, smiling at Jensen. "So I'm assuming no charges are being pressed."

Emmett shook his head. "No, Michael. But I would like to speak with Jensen privately if that's okay."

"Of course," Michael said. "I need to get going anyway. Just got a call about an attack close by."

"Thank you for coming over, Michael," Emmett said.

"No problem," Michael said. "And, Jensen? I hope we don't cross paths again anytime soon."

"That makes two of us."

Michael gave Jensen a wide grin and grand eye roll before leaving the restaurant. Then Emmett sat down on the floor next to Jensen.

"What do you want to talk to me about? Or do you just want a piece of me?" Jensen asked, running his hand between his legs.

"You were right about there not being anything missing downstairs. But you also know what I found down there, don't you?" Jensen's face grew stern as he clearly tried to force back tears. "How long have you been living down there?"

Jensen forced a laugh. "Living? What are you talking about?"

"I saw the blankets and the clothes in the corner. What's going on?"

"Look, I'm not some homeless person, okay? I got locked out of my apartment last night and needed a place to stay. The back door was open."

"It's okay, Jensen. I understand what's going on."

"I told you--"

"I know what you told me -- that you locked yourself out of your apartment. But there isn't any apartment, is there?"

"No...I...." Tears began to stream down Jensen's face and his whole body started to shake as he completely broke down.

Emmett moved closer to Jensen and put his arms around him. As Jensen continued to sob, his head fell onto Emmett's shoulder. Emmett quietly held and rocked Jensen, whose tears rolled down his upset face.

While Emmett consoled Jensen, Michael made his way to St. Joseph Hospital. Once he arrived at the medical center, he entered the emergency room area where he found Jacqueline and Cole seated next to one another and Max standing alone in the corner looking down at the floor. Upon seeing Michael, Cole stood up from his seat.

"How's Jesse?" Michael asked Cole.

"I was just going to ask you if you knew. We haven't heard anything," Cole replied.

"I'm just arriving." Michael looked toward Max. "Sounds like we need to have a chat."

"I'm sure," Max said, walking closer to Michael.

Michael approached Jacqueline. "I'm sorry about all this. I hope your son is okay."

"Thank you," Jacqueline replied softly.

Michael looked at Max. "Follow me. There's a private office around the corner where we can talk."

"Sure," Max replied. Then he turned to Cole and Jacqueline, asking, "You'll come and get me if there's any news?"

Jacqueline nodded as Cole put his arm around her. They watched Michael and Max leave the room together.

"Do you want me to call your husband?" Cole asked.

"He's on his way," Jacqueline replied.

"I should probably let Emmett know so he can be here for Max."

"Good idea," she said. "And please call Logan, too. Go on. I'm okay."

Cole got up and walked out of the room. Sitting alone, Jacqueline started to cry when her attention was diverted by Joyelle Mancini entering the room. Jacqueline stood up to greet her.

"Mrs. Morgan, I'm Joyelle Mancini, a friend of your son and a nurse on staff here at the hospital."

"Good to meet you. How is Jesse?"

Joyelle smiled. "He's going to be fine."

"Oh, thank God."

"His face has some swelling and bruising and he has slight concussion, but he's going to be fine. No damage to his teeth or jaw. They are taking him to a room because we want to keep him here over night, just to be safe. I can walk you up there and Dr. MacMahon will be in to speak with you as well."

"Thank you so much," Jacqueline said, following Joyelle out of the waiting area.

Joyelle walked Jacqueline to Jesse's room while Rachel Carson and Keith Colgan continued their conversation near the entrance to Chicago's Graceland Cemetery. Keith held the bottle that Rachel had given him.

"Poison Emmett? You've got to be kidding me."

"Do I look like I'm joking?"

"Why would you want to do that to him?"

"My reasons aren't your business. All you need to worry about is slipping some of that into his drinks occasionally over the next few weeks."

"Absolutely not."

"I'd re-think that decision quickly, unless you want me to tell Michael your little secret. Your relationship will be over, he will never speak to you again, and you may go to jail. Would you prefer that scenario?" Keith didn't reply. "Didn't think so." Rachel paused. "Oh, and one other thing. I have a written statement about your accident and your secret attached to my will now. So if anything should randomly happen to me, your story will become public immediately. Just so you understand that."

"You bitch," Keith said.

"I'm just protecting myself. And you, of course, too."

"You're just like your brother. You don't give a damn about anyone other than yourself."

"And don't you forget it." Rachel rubbed her gloved hands together. "It's cold out here and I have to go now. I'll be in touch in a few days to see how things are going. Oh, and please give Michael my best. He's a keeper." Rachel smiled and headed toward Clark Street to catch a cab as Keith stared down at the bottle in his hand.

At the hospital, Derek Mancini made his way down the hallway toward the nurse's station. He looked into several rooms as he passed them and finally reached the station where he found Tyler Bennett.

"Tyler," Derek said.

"Hey, Derek. Joyelle is down on two. I can page her for you if you'd like."

"No, thanks. I actually came to see you."

"Me?"

"Got a minute?"

"Sure," Tyler said, walking around from behind the desk. "What's up?"

Derek looked from side to side to make sure no one else was around. "What are you doing telling Joyelle about Cole saving her from the explosion?"

"What?"

"She told me that you have been talking to her about the explosion and Cole trying to save her."

"I mentioned it, yes. It was hardly a lengthy discussion."

"That doesn't matter. You know the doctors said not to pressure her. You shouldn't be discussing that with her."

"I wasn't pressuring her. I just assumed that you, her husband, would have told her what happened."

"Like you just said, I am her husband. I'll tell her things when I think she's ready to hear them."

"Who made you God?" Tyler asked. "And when do you think she'll be 'ready' to hear about that video and your love affair with Cole?"

"You son-of-a--" Derek stopped himself. "Just stay out of our lives."

"Sooner or later, she's going to remember. Then what?"

"We will work it out between ourselves, with no input or interference from you or anyone else. Understand?"

"I understand the situation better than you think, Derek. Now, if you'll excuse me, I have work to do." Tyler walked away from Derek, who stood watching him. Then the elevator door opened behind him and Joyelle got out.

"Derek," she said, greeting her husband with a kiss. "What are you doing here?"

"Just looking for my lovely wife," Derek said with a smile.

"Oh, really?" Joyelle asked, smiling and kissing Derek again.

"Maybe you can leave a bit early?"

"They just brought Jesse in -- our neighbor from across the street. He was beaten pretty badly."

"Mugged or--?"

"No. It was Max."

"Max? Why would Max beat up Jesse?"

"I don't know. Michael Martinez is questioning Max now."

"Well, does Emmett know? Is he here?"

"He just got here. He's in the waiting room."

"Okay, I'll go down and talk with him."

"I'm going to check back in on Jesse and then we can head home," Joyelle said. Joyelle walked away down the hall and Derek got into the elevator when the doors opened.

At the same time in California, the Ciancios -- Marco, Gino and their father Carlo -- were having dinner in the smaller of the mansion's two dining rooms. Carlo sat in his usual place at the head of the table with one son on each side of him.

"Father, I intend to set up a meeting with the Mancinis in the next week or so. Would you like to attend?" Marco asked.

"Of course. We need to present a united front and make clear our expectations."

"Okay," Marco replied. "I'll make the necessary arrangements."

Gino took a sip of his wine before speaking. "I want this to be civil. Let's make a deal that works out for everyone and be done with it."

"Not so fast," Marco said. "They owe us."

"They owe us money, that's all. Let's get back the money they owe us and the appropriate interest and that's it. This war between us needs to end."

Carlo spoke up. "Gino, I appreciate your request for peace. But I intend to get what we deserve from them. Not for me, but for you boys. You are going to inherit Ciancio International when I'm gone and you deserve to have it at its best and strongest."

"Father," Gino said, "we have more money and property than anyone deserves. We don't need more."

"It's not about money and property," Carlo replied. "It's about justice."

"Don't worry, Father," Marco declared. "We'll get all we deserve and more." Marco turned to his brother. "Just be sure you don't get caught in the crossfire."

"And you just be sure you stay on message," Carlo said to Marco. "No moves that aren't pre-approved by me."

"Yes, Father," Marco said, taking a drink of wine. "Father, I have been meaning to ask you something."

"What's that?" Carlo asked.

"It's about Mother's art collection."

"My God," Carlo said. "What made you think of that?"

"It contained so many amazing pieces that she worked hard to collect. It's a shame that you got rid of them all."

"I didn't 'get rid' of them; I auctioned them. Seeing them in this house was a painful reminder of her absence here. You know that."

"I remember," Marco said. "But there were some amazing paintings and sculptures in it."

"That auction funded the foundation we started in her honor. It was worth it and helps a great number of people with cancer."

"Oh, absolutely, "Marco said. "She would be very proud of the foundation's work."

"Why are you asking about the collection all of sudden?" Gino asked.

"Maybe I'm just in a sentimental mood lately," Marco replied. "Keeping a few of the pieces may have been a nice memory of her. But it doesn't matter, I guess."

"There are many other ways to remember your mother. There are still reminders of her throughout this house."

"I know," Marco said. "Which firm ran the auction? I can't remember."

"Strauss's, why?"

"Just curious."

"You are never 'just curious,'" Gino said. "What are you up to?"

"What, I'm not allowed to miss our mother?"

Gino smiled. "I know you."

"And I know you. Okay? We're even," Marco said, laughing. "Now finish your dinner." Both Gino and Marco looked down at their plates as Carlo drank more of his wine.

As the Ciancio men finished their supper together, Michael walked Max back into the emergency room waiting area where Emmett and Derek were seated.

"Thanks for being so forthright in your responses to my questions," Michael told Max.

"I have nothing to hide," Max said.

"I'll be in touch," Michael said. Then he looked at Derek and Emmett. "Hey guys."

Emmett and Derek greeted Michael and then Emmett hugged Max. "I have been so worried about you."

"Excuse me," Michael said. "I'm going up to see Jesse." Michael left the room.

"What happened?" Emmett asked.

"I snapped. I just lost it," Max said, sitting down on a chair.

Emmett said down next to him. "What do you mean?"

"I found out some terrible things that Jesse did to Logan and I went over and beat him up."

"Beat him up?" Derek said. "You nearly killed him."

"And then Jacqueline came in and saw me punching Jesse and yelled out that I am his father."

"His father?" Emmett asked.

"Jesus," Derek mumbled.

"Trust me; I am as shocked as you. I've been trying to wrap my brain around it since I heard it."

"Have you seen Jesse or Jacqueline?" Derek asked.

"Not since arriving here, no. I've been with Michael."

"Are they pressing charges against you?" Emmett asked.

Max shook his head. "I don't know. Has anyone called Logan?"

"Jacqueline had Cole call him," Emmett replied.

"Okay, good," Max said. "I'm sorry for all of this."

Emmett hugged Max. "Don't worry; we'll get through all of this together."

On the hospital's second floor, Ben Donovan walked down the hallway until he reached his wife standing at the other end. Deep in thought, she was staring out the window looking over Lake Michigan. When Ben touched her arm, he startled her.

"Oh, it's you," Jacqueline said, turning to face her husband.

"How are you? How's Jesse?"

"He's going to be okay," Jacqueline said.

"Good," Ben said, hugging his wife. "I'm happy hear that."

Jacqueline looked into Ben's eyes. "I told him the truth."

"What are you talking about?"

"I told Max the truth. He knows Jesse is his son. And I'm sure Jesse heard, too.

"You told them? Why?"

258

"It was the only way I could stop Max from killing Jesse. He was beating him so hard."

"How did he take it?"

"I don't know. Things happened so fast. I haven't had a chance to talk to him more."

"It'll be okay," Ben said.

"Yes, it will," Jacqueline said sternly. "Because your hold over me is gone. You can no longer blackmail me because there is nothing to blackmail me with."

Ben smiled. "Baby, that's behind us. I thought we had stepped forward from all of that."

"Stepped forward? After what you did? After you forced me to stay married to you? No, Ben. We are finally done. I'm finally free of you."

"You're carrying our child. You'll never be free of me. And I'll never let you go."

"You don't have a choice. Your power over me is gone. As of this moment, we are finished. As far as I'm concerned, you can go straight to hell." Jacqueline slapped Ben hard across the face and hurried away from him down the hallway.

Ben put his hand to his cheek and then back down to his side. "It won't be quite that easy, my dear wife."

Then he walked down the corridor, stopping outside the doorway of Jesse's room.

When he looked inside, he saw Logan Pryce sitting next to Jesse's bed; he was holding Jesse's hand. Jesse was sound asleep and Logan was staring at him as if in a trance. Ben observed the two for a moment and then headed to the elevators.

While Ben waited for the elevator, Jacqueline got out of one on the main level of the hospital and followed the corridor to the emergency room waiting area where she found Max with Emmett and Derek. The men stopped their conversation and focused on her.

"How's my son?" Max asked. He shook his head and continued. "My son. I can't believe I'm even saying that."

"He's going to be fine. They gave him a heavy sedative to sleep through the night. He won't be awake any time soon."

"Can I see him?"

"I don't think that's a good idea right now. Logan is up there with him. Jesse's going to be fine; that's what matters."

"Are charges going to be pressed?" Derek asked.

Emmett elbowed his brother.

"It needs to be asked," Derek persisted. "If there are, you two probably shouldn't be speaking."

"No," Jacqueline said. "There won't be charges pressed."

"Even when Jesse is awake?" Derek asked. "Ultimately, he gets to decide."

Jacqueline smiled. "You have my word."

"Thank you," Max replied.

"Why don't we leave these two alone?" Emmett asked Derek. "Let's go get some coffee or something." Derek nodded and followed his brother out of the area.

Jacqueline sat down in a nearby chair. "I'm sure you have a lot of questions."

"How could you keep this from me? For all these years? I will never understand that."

"We were so young, Max. And no longer together. And you were beginning a whole new lifestyle."

"So what? I still had a right to know."

"I did what I thought was best."

"For you, maybe," Max said. "My God, Jacqueline. You denied me so many things. And even more recently, when we re-connected, you said nothing. And you sat back

261

and watched my ex Logan try to build a relationship with Jesse and still you said nothing."

"Watching you two interact and not get along only reinforced my decision. Jesse had lived this long without knowing his father; I didn't think he needed to know now. But when I saw you beating him, it just came out. I didn't know how else to stop you. And--"

"And...what? What aren't you telling me?"

"Ben knows."

"Wait, you told Ben and not me? How could you?"

Jacqueline shook her head. "I didn't tell him. He figured it out all on his own. He had DNA tests run and everything."

"DNA tests? And he didn't tell me? Or Jesse?"

"No," Jacqueline explained. "He used the information to blackmail me...into staying married to him."

"Damn," Max said. "That's why you stayed with him. When we talked earlier today, I couldn't figure out why you would stay with him."

"Now you know."

"That bastard. I'm sorry," Max said.

"And now you know why I want you to be very careful around him."

"No more warnings needed," Max said. "I'll let him go the next time I see him."

"Just be careful."

Max let out a sigh. "What do we do now? About us and about Jesse. I have so many emotions running through me all at once...and yet I feel numb."

"I'm sorry. This is a lot for you to take in."

Max put his face into his hands and Jacqueline put her arm around him. They sat together quietly in the waiting room.

Outside of the waiting room, Emmett and Derek hadn't made it far down the hallway before stopping to talk.

"I'm worried about you being with him," Derek said.

"With Max?"

"Look what he did to Jesse. Doesn't that scare you? Have you ever seen that angry side of him?"

"Derek, I appreciate your concern. It means a lot to me. But Max would never do anything like that to me. You just have to understand all the occurred between him and Jesse. They were on bad terms."

"And if you and Max ever argue and end up on bad terms? What will happen to you then?"

"You're being ridiculous."

"Am I?" Derek asked. "And what's going to happen now that he's a father?"

"I don't know. We'll have to figure all that out."

"Figure it out? Emmett, this is going to change your whole relationship."

"Derek, stop. If you want to focus on a relationship, focus on your own. Mine will be just fine."

"I'm sorry," Derek said. "I am just looking out for you."

"I know, but I'm okay."

"Okay, but if he hurts you in any way--"

"He won't. He loves me."

Derek and Emmett began to walk down the corridor again. "There's another matter we need to discuss. The family business."

"Not now, Derek."

"Justin is coming back to town so the three of us can talk and make some decisions."

"I told you -- I don't want to be a part of it."

"Did you discuss that with Max?"

"Yes. I think I am going to sign over my voting rights to you; that way you can make decisions for the company on my behalf but I'll retain ownership."

"Sounds like a good plan. But I'd still like you to meet with Justin and me. So you can tell him that yourself. And that I had nothing to do with it. It's entirely your decision."

"That's fine. Just tell me when and where and I'll be there."

"Great," Derek replied, putting his arm around Emmett as they continued toward the cafeteria.

Later that evening, Tyler arrived home from the hospital and found his roommate David Young sitting on the sofa in their living room. He was drinking a beer and watching television.

"Hey, hey. You're home," David said. "Long day."

"Really long day," Tyler replied, removing his hat and gloves and putting them into the closet. "And I have to be back early in the morning."

"Everything okay?"

Tyler walked into the kitchen and grabbed a beer, then returned to the living room and took a seat across from David, who switched off the television.

"I'm not sure," Tyler said. "I had the strangest confrontation with Derek earlier. He accused me of trying to force Joyelle's memories back."

"He what?"

"He said he didn't want me talking to Joyelle anymore, to stay away from her."

"You two work together. How is that even possible?"

"I know, right?"

"But it's funny you say that, because I had a run-in with him earlier today, too."

"Is he on tour today or what? What was your run-in about?"

"Cole," David replied, taking a drink of his beer. "He said he saw Cole and me hanging out and he wants it to stop. Cole belongs to him."

"What the fuck? Where does he get off saying that to you?"

"I told him that I would hang out with whoever I want. And if Cole has a problem with me, he can tell me himself."

"Good. Derek really needs to stay out of other people's business."

"He likes to control things, I guess. He won't commit to Cole himself, but he sure doesn't want Cole with anyone else, either."

"Like you said...it's up to Cole, not him."

"Exactly. And I have no intention of not seeing Cole again. We have a good time together."

"I told you before: we would both be a lot better off if Derek weren't around."

David raised his beer bottle. "Cheers to that."

Tyler touched his bottle to David's and they both drank their beers.

While Tyler and David finished their beers, Keith and Michael were getting ready for bed in Michael's bedroom. Coming out the bathroom after showering, Michael walked up behind his naked boyfriend and wrapped his arms around him.

"Penny for your thoughts, Stormy," Michael said as he kissed Keith's neck. "You've been so quiet tonight."

"Just tired, that's all," Keith replied.

"Long day for both of us, I guess," Michael said. "First the break-in at Emmett's restaurant and then Jesse."

Keith turned to face Michael. "I know. I still can't believe all of that with Max and Jesse."

"Well, Jesse is going to be fine and there are no charges being filed against Max, so that's all good news."

Keith forced a smile. "I'm glad."

"And even better news is that we're here alone together and I have you all to myself." Michael kissed Keith.

Keith got into bed and Michael followed. They wrapped their bodies together in a warm hug, Keith putting his head against Michael's chest.

"Everything okay?" Michael asked.

"Just tired," Keith replied. "But everything's always better when your arms are wrapped around me."

Michael kissed Keith on the forehead. "I'm glad."

Keith closed his eyes and tried to fall asleep, his mind remaining on his earlier conversation with Rachel.

As Michael and Keith dozed off to sleep, Emmett and Max were in their bedroom talking and getting ready for bed as well.

"You're sure you're okay with Jensen staying in the guest room tonight? I know this is a lot for you take in after everything else that's happened today."

"I trust your instinct," Max replied as he pulled off his clothes. "If you think it's okay, I'm okay with it, too."

"Well, I didn't know what else to do. After my long talk with him this morning and finding out he has no home, I couldn't just kick him out."

"Where's he been staying?"

"When not in our club basement, you mean? He said he bounces from friend to friend and even stays overnight with his...clients."

Max laughed. "Clients? That's a nice way to put it. The boy is a stripper and a prostitute."

Emmett pulled off his pants and underwear and crawled into bed. "He's also 19 years old and homeless. Kicked out when his parents found out he's gay. He puts up a tough front but he's just a scared kid."

"We still need to be careful. He's admitted to stealing, among other things. And now he's staying in our home," Max said as he got into bed next to Emmett.

"I'll take responsibility for him tonight since I told him he could stay. In the morning, we can all talk together."

Max put his arm around Emmett. "The only thing that makes today bearable is having you by my side."

"Aww, babe," Emmett replied. "There's no place I'd rather be." There was quiet for a moment and then Emmett spoke again. "How are you feeling about all of this?"

"You mean finding out I'm a father?" Max said with a chuckle. "It's going to take some getting used to. It's hard to process over twenty years of lies in one night. I still can't believe she kept him from me. I had a right to know."

"Yes, you did. But you know now. That's what we have to deal with."

"Thank you for being so understanding and supportive."

"I don't approve of what you did to Jesse. You have to somehow make that right."

"I don't know what came over me. As soon as she told me what Jesse did to Logan -- and to her -- I just lost it. I went into a rage."

"Well, we need to work on that, too. It can't happen again."

"It won't. I promise."

"We have a lot to sort through here. Let's just take one day at a time."

Max kissed Emmett. "I love you."

"I love you, too. Everything will be okay."

Emmett and Max fell asleep quickly and slept soundly through the evening. As the next day arrived, they were up early, immediately heading to the kitchen for their morning coffee. Both dressed in sweat pants, Emmett poured two cups of coffee and placed one on the counter in front of Max, who was checking his cell phone.

"I need to get downstairs to talk with Ben as soon as he arrives."

"Do you want me to be there, too? It may not be pleasant."

"No, thanks," Max said. "I'll handle Ben on my own. I brought him into our lives and I'll get him out. Besides, you have to meet with your brothers."

"Okay," Emmett said. "But my offer stands, in case you change your mind."

Jensen then entered the kitchen wearing nothing but his tight underwear. "Good morning, guys."

"Hi, Jensen," Emmett said. "Did you sleep okay?"

Before Jensen could answer, Max said, "Um, in this house you should probably cover up a bit. Put some clothes on. We're not two of your tricks."

"Oh, sorry," Jensen said. "Most of my clothes are still in the dryer."

"You're fine," Emmett said. "Do you want some coffee?"

"No, thanks. I'm not a big coffee drinker."

"Well, there's other stuff in the fridge. Help yourself."

"I really appreciate you guys letting me stay here last night. And for being understanding about staying in the basement."

"It's fine," Max said. "You and Emmett can discuss more arrangements today. I have to head downstairs and then to the hospital." Max got up from the counter and left the room, his coffee cup in hand.

"I don't think he likes me very much," Jensen said.

"It's not you. He's dealing with a lot, that's all. Don't take it personally."

"If you say so." Jensen added, "I should probably get my clothes and go."

"No," Emmett said. "Stay and have breakfast with me and we'll talk more."

Jensen laughed. "I'm never going to turn down food. Done."

"Well, you're going to help me make it. This isn't a hotel," Emmett said with a smile.

"Great," Jensen said. "Let me go pull on some pants first."

"Good idea," Emmett replied. He watched Jensen leave the room and began removing items from the refrigerator.

Downstairs, Max was moving some chairs around the restaurant when Ben finally arrived.

"Sorry, I'm late," Ben said. "I had something important to take care of first."

"Sit down," Max said sternly, offering Ben a chair.

"What's up, man?" Ben asked, sitting down.

"Your time working for me, that's what." Max handed Ben an envelope. "Here's the money I owe you, plus a little extra. Consider it severance."

"Severance? What are you talking about?"

"Our business relationship is done, Ben. You knew Jesse was my son and, for whatever reason, didn't say a word to me. And then you used the information to blackmail Jacqueline into staying with you. Sorry, I don't associate with people like you, let alone work with them."

"Come on," Ben said. "That's not true."

"It is. And I'm not going to argue with you. Let's try to part on as good of terms as possible."

"But I'm not finished here. There's a lot more work to be done."

"There is. And it'll be finished with me overseeing it. Not you. Look, I have to get to the hospital to see my son. So this conversation is over. I wish you the best."

Ben stood up from his chair. "You can't do this to me."

"I just did. What you and Jacqueline decide to do about your baby is your business. But you had no right to withhold information about my son and use it to blackmail his mother. Now get out of here."

"You won't get away with this."

"Goodbye, Ben."

Max ushered Ben to the door and pushed him out onto the sidewalk. Then he locked the door behind him and headed toward the back of the restaurant.

Later that morning, Derek was hosting a meeting with his brothers Emmett and Justin in his office in downtown Chicago. He sat behind his desk while his brothers sat in chairs across from him.

"I'm glad to see you getting around better, Justin," Derek said. "That's good news."

"It is what it is. I'm learning to live blind as best I can," Justin said. "But it doesn't mean I still don't have a perfect vision of what I want for this business."

"Well, that's why we're all here today. To sort through it and make some decisions."

"Before we get into any serious talk, I want to say something," Emmett said. "I have thought long and hard about this -- and discussed it with Max, too -- and I've decided to turn over my voting rights and decision-making power to Derek."

"What?" Justin asked. "How can you do that? It disrupts the balance that Dad created in his will."

"Come on, Justin. You know I have never wanted to be a part of this. I left it all a long time ago and I have no interest in it now. I am not going to let our father manipulate me from the grave. I've made my decision."

"But that gives Derek control."

"It gives him fifty percent for decision-making; that's all. And I may revoke it if I ever want to. But right now I trust Derek completely."

"Well, I intend to have my say in things one way or another," Justin said.

"Of course," Derek replied. "The whole point of this meeting is to unite us. Get us all on the same page."

"So what do you have in mind?"

"A couple of things," Derek said. "First, we need to pay back the debt you incurred to the Ciancios. I know your agreement entitled them to a large chunk of the business if you missed the payment deadline, which you did. I suggest we offer them full repayment of the loan, plus the appropriate interest, plus eight percent of the company -- two percent from each of our four shares."

"You think they'll go for that?" Emmett asked.

"They will have to. Otherwise, we will keep them mired down court cases forever trying to settle this. They won't like that any more than we would."

"I know them better than either of you. They won't just roll over and play dead."

"Neither will we," Derek replied. "And we'll show them that."

"You said you had a couple of ideas..."

"Yes," Derek continued. "I want to move the company headquarters here to Chicago."

"Why?" Justin asked. "The company's roots are in California. Literally."

"Because I think we need a fresh start. It will be a grand gesture to the public that things are changing and it's not business as usual. Plus, Emmett and I have no intention of moving. Chicago is our home."

"Yes, but moving the headquarters will be expensive."

"We'll do it gradually -- one division at a time -- and help employees with the move, if they choose to make it. Of course, the wine division will remain in California. That only makes sense."

"And what about our other brother?" Justin asked. "What's he going to say about all of this?"

"We have to locate him first," Emmett replied. "That's no easy task."

"I've hired an investigator," Justin said. "That should help."

"Regardless, we have to move forward," Derek said. "So I'm going to set up a meeting with the Ciancios. We'll invite them here and share our offer with them. I'd like you both to be there, too. Again, to present a united front."

"Of course," Emmett said.

"I still hold them responsible for the loss of my children. I don't plan to lose any more because of them," Derek declared.

Justin stood up from his chair. "We'll work it out with them. I'll do whatever I can to help. You have my word on that." Suddenly, Justin lost his balance and stumbled.

"Hey, are you okay?" Emmett asked, standing up and reaching out to Justin.

"Yes," Justin said. "I just stood up too fast."

"You sure?"

"Yes," Justin said, forcing a smile. "I'm fine now."

"Okay, I have something else I need to take care of," Derek said, getting up from his chair. "As soon as I know when the meeting will be, I'll let you both know."

"Sounds good," Emmett said.

Derek grabbed his coat from the back of his office door. "Come on, I'll walk you guys out." The three brothers left the office and each headed in his own direction once they were outside the building.

While her husband headed on to his next task for the day, Joyelle was finally waking up in her bed. Having worked so late the night before, she slept in later than usual to try to catch up on some rest. Rolling over and finding that Derek had gotten up much earlier, Joyelle got out of bed.

Wearing a scrubs top and sweatpants, she followed the smell of fresh coffee into the kitchen. When she arrived and found the freshly brewed coffee, she also found a note from her husband: "Enjoy your day off. xo." She smiled at the note and then filled a coffee cup with the dark coffee.

After taking sip, she pulled her recipe book from the shelf and gathered ingredients from the cabinets and refrigerator. With all the ingredients assembled, Joyelle began to prepare a batch of her famous chocolate chip cookies.

At the same time in his office in San Francisco, Marco was on the phone. Sitting behind his desk, he waited for someone to answer his call.

"Mr. Strauss," Marco said when someone finally answered. "It's Marco Ciancio. How have you been, my friend?" Marco paused as he listened to the response to his question. "Good, good. Glad to hear it. Listen, I need a bit of a favor from you. Years ago, you ran an auction of my mother's art collection. Do you remember?" Marco paused again. "Yes, exactly. It was quite a collection.

What I need is a copy of the sales documents. I need to know who bought each piece in the collection." Once more, Marco paused. "Yes, I realize it'll take some time, but I hope to have the information as soon as possible. It's of great importance to me. Thank you. I knew I could count on you." The two men concluded the conversation and Marco hung up the phone.

"What as that all about?" Rachel asked as she entered the office.

Marco stood up from his desk. "Just a family matter. When did you get in?"

"Just now. I came straight here from the airport. I wanted to see you."

"Good," Marco replied, wrapping his arms around her. He kissed her deeply and she put her hands on his chest.

"Are you sure I'm not interrupting?"

Marco smiled. "Not at all." Marco walked over to the door of his office and locked it. "I always have time for you," Marco added, returning to Rachel.

"I was hoping so," Rachel replied, unbuttoning Marco's shirt and running her hands over his chest. "I've missed you."

"I've missed you, too," Marco said, kissing Rachel and opening her blouse. "Let me show you just how much."

Marco kissed Rachel's neck and shoulders, eventually working his way down to her breasts. Rachel removed Marco's shirt completely, digging her fingers into his back. He slowly lowered her onto the sofa in his office and climbed on top of her.

While Marco and Rachel made love in his office, Cole opened the door to his apartment. Derek rushed past him and into the living room, not noticing that Cole was wearing the Michigan t-shirt that Derek had given him when he was in the hospital.

"What a great surprise," Cole said, closing the door behind Derek.

"I needed to see you," Derek said. "I know Jesse's at the hospital and Joyelle is sleeping in because she's off today, so it's the perfect time."

"Cool," Cole said. "You know I love seeing you. So what's up?"

Without responding, Derek powerfully threw Cole up against the wall, pinning him there. He raised Cole's hands above his head against the wall and kissed him deeply. Cole wrapped one leg around Derek, pulling him even closer.

Derek's mouth moved to Cole's jaw line, neck, and shoulders as he pulled the Michigan t-shirt off of Cole. Pressing his crotch into Cole's, Derek looked into Cole's eyes. "You're mine. Not David's. Not anyone else's. Mine."

"Yes," Cole whispered.

Derek released Cole's hands and pulled off his own shirt, baring his muscled chest to his lover. Cole grabbed the back of Derek's head and pulled him close, kissing him deeply. Derek pulled down Cole's sweatpants, revealing the underwear that was barely containing his erect cock.

Derek attempted to remove Cole's underwear, but Cole pushed him backwards onto the couch. Losing is balance momentarily, Derek ended up on his back on the sofa. Cole crawled on top of him and massaged him through his pants. Putting his hands on the back of Cole's head, Derek pushed his face deeper into his crotch. Then Cole opened Derek's pants.

The corners of Cole's mouth curled up in a partial smile as he sucked Derek's cock. Wrapping his legs around Cole, Derek thrust in and out of Cole's soft lips. When Cole pulled Derek's pants and socks off, Derek used his feet to pull Cole's underwear off. Neither of them noticed when Derek's wallet fell out of his pants onto the floor.

Both completely naked, Derek stood up and lifted Cole from the sofa. He placed his hands firmly on both sides of Cole's face and kissed him deeply, passionately. His hands then slid down Cole's back to his firm ass. Slapping Cole's butt several times, Derek lifted Cole off the floor and Cole wrapped his legs around Derek's hips.

Carrying Cole into the bedroom and their mouths never parting during the short walk, Derek then pushed Cole onto the bed. Grabbing Cole's ankles, Derek pulled Cole's legs over his shoulders. He spit into Cole's hole a few times and then shoved himself into Cole's welcoming ass.

His toes curling, Cole took Derek deep inside of him. Still standing, Derek pumped into Cole deeper and harder as he bit Cole's calves. Cole dug his fingers into the bed sheets and then reached up to grab Derek's chest instead. He grabbed the back of Derek's neck, pulling his face close to his and kissed him deeply.

They continued to kiss as Derek forced himself deeper. Then he put his hands on Cole's shoulders and pushed him back down onto the bed. Cole struggled to get free as Derek vigorously stroked Cole. Before he could do anything to stop it, Cole was spewing cum all over himself.

Derek reached down and scooped up some of Cole's cum, applying it to his own cock as lube. Then he spread Cole's hips wider and prepared to shoot inside of him.

With a powerful thrust that forced Cole to yell out, Derek exploded inside of Cole. He pushed further and further, ensuring that every drop made its way into Cole. Then he leaned forward to kiss Cole one final time before pulling out of him.

Derek rolled over onto his back next to Cole and both men rested for a moment, looking up at the ceiling.

"It gets hotter and hotter each time," Cole said, wiping the sweat from his forehead.

"No one is ever going to take you from me."

Cole rolled over and kissed Derek's chest. "You have nothing to worry about. I've been yours since that first night in Boston."

Derek smiled and said, "That's as it should be." Then he kissed Cole and wrapped his arm around him.

A few blocks away at Boystown Blend, Keith took the two cups of coffee he had ordered from the counter and walked to a table in the back corner of the coffee shop. He sat down and then looked around at the other customers in the room. Then he removed the small bottle from his pocket and poured some of its contents into one of the coffee cups. Returning the bottle to his pocket, Keith pushed the poisoned coffee across the table to where Emmett would be sitting.

A few moments later, Emmett came into the shop. He scanned the place looking for Keith and, upon seeing him, walked over to the table. Keith stood up and they hugged each other before both taking a seat at the table.

"I got you some coffee," Keith said, nodding toward the cup.

"Great, thanks," Emmett said. "It's so cold out."

"I know."

"So what's up? You said you had something you wanted to talk about."

"I do, but first I wanted to see how you are...with everything that happened yesterday."

"Oh, I'm okay, I guess," Emmett said, taking a drink from his coffee cup. "It's crazy but I'm coping."

"Max is a father. It's almost unbelievable."

Emmett took another drink of his coffee. "No, it's real. Jacqueline kept it from him all these years.

"Well, if you need anything, I'm here for you," Keith said.

"Thank you; I appreciate that. Now what else did you want to ask me about?"

"I heard all about the fundraiser you guys are hosting and I would like to help out with whatever you need. Sounds like a great cause and Michael and I want to support it in any way we can."

"Oh, great. Logan and Jesse have really been the ones planning it. Max and I are just providing the venue. But I'm sure they could use the help, especially since Jesse is hurt. I'll let them know."

"Sounds good," Keith said, watching Emmett drink more of his coffee. Emmett finished his drink quickly as Keith took a sip from his own cup.

Keith and Emmett wrapped up their conversation as Joyelle finished loading her freshly-baked cookies into two large, round tins. Then she grabbed some ribbon and tied it around each tin, topping them off with large bows.

She walked over to the closet and removed her winter coat, scarf, hat, and gloves. Bundling up for the cold weather outside, Joyelle picked up one of the cookie tins from the counter and headed outside to deliver the treats.

At the hospital, Logan and Jacqueline got out of the elevator and headed down the hallway toward Jesse's room.

"Fate really has thrust the two of us together lately," Jacqueline said with a smile.

"That's for sure."

"Maybe this is an unfair question, but do you think you'll ever be able to forgive my son for what he did?"

"No one knows better than you how horrible it was seeing him in the hotel room that night."

"It's been hard to completely put out of my mind," Jacqueline admitted. "But he is my son and I'm realizing now that shutting him out wasn't probably the best way for me to respond. He's a good person with a good heart."

"And how many second chances do we get in life?" Logan asked. "So, yes, I am trying to forgive him and move forward. I'm just so grateful that he's going to be okay."

"Navigating all of this isn't going to be easy. For you or me or Max."

"Or Emmett. But we'll have to figure it all out. The main thing is that we get to take Jesse home today. He's safe and he's going to be fine."

When they reached Jesse's room, they entered it. The room was dark and there was no sign of Jesse. His hospital bed was empty and the window blinds were closed. Jacqueline and Logan exchanged glances of confusion.

Logan turned to the bathroom door and opened it. Looking inside, he saw Tyler lying on the floor unconscious. Wearing only his underwear, Tyler's mouth was covered with duct tape and his hands and feet were bound with duct tape as well.

"Oh, my God," Logan said, kneeling down next to Tyler's body. "Call the nurse."

Jacqueline stepped into the hallway and yelled for a nurse. One rushed from the nurse's station to the room.

"What is it?" she asked and then saw Tyler on the floor. "Oh, no. What happened?"

"Where's my son?" Jacqueline asked. "My God, where's Jesse?"

While Jacqueline panicked over her son's whereabouts, Derek was sitting on the end of Cole's bed, pulling on his pants, socks, and boots. With his arms wrapped around Derek, Cole sat behind him kissing his neck and massaging his chest, as he did on the very first night they met in Boston so long ago.

"Thanks for coming by," Cole said. "Great surprise and great way to start the day."

"We needed to talk," Derek replied.

"I'm not sure we did much talking."

Derek turned around and kissed Cole. "True. But we did clarify who you belong to. Nice shirt, by the way."

"Mmm," Cole said with a smile. "You're the only one who could ever get me to wear a Michigan shirt."

"Well, don't expect me to start wearing a Notre Dame one just yet," Derek said. "And you can tell David and anyone else to back off. You're with me."

"No arguments from me," Cole said, getting up from the bed and pulling on his t-shirt and underwear while stepping into his flip flops. "But you need to handle things with your wife."

"I'll handle all of it," Derek said, standing up and pulling on his shirt. "Now I have to get back to the office."

Derek got up and walked back into the living room with Cole following him. Cole helped Derek put on his overcoat and then kissed him.

"We'll talk soon," Derek said, heading out of the apartment after giving Cole one final kiss.

Cole closed the door behind Derek, smiling at all that had just occurred between them. Then he looked down and noticed Derek's wallet lying on the floor. "Oh, shit." He grabbed the wallet and headed out the door to catch Derek.

As Derek emerged from Cole's apartment building, Joyelle exited her condo building across the street. Cookies in hand, she took a few steps down the walkway and stopped when she noticed Derek on the apartment stairs. She was about to call out to him when Cole ran out, carrying the wallet. She noticed the Michigan t-shirt, which she had delivered to Cole's hospital room months before at Derek's request.

"Wait, you forgot this," Cole said, handing the wallet to Derek.

Derek took it from Cole. "Oh, thanks, stud."

Joyelle watched as Cole kissed Derek. Suddenly, her mind flooded with images. One by one, they raced across her mind's eye. Cole jumping on her as the limousine exploded. Derek racing after her as she rushed from the New Year's Eve party. The video of Derek telling Cole that he loved him. Being held in Tyler's arms and kissing him. Tyler telling her that Cole had Derek's wedding ring. Delivering the Michigan t-shirt to Cole in the hospital.

Cole turned and went back into his apartment as Derek continued down the stairs and turned onto the sidewalk. Joyelle dropped the cookie tin, which popped open sending cookies in all directions. And Joyelle stood silently in the cold, tears streaming down her face. One's memories define her character and purpose.

Episode #28

The search for a missing person often leads to unexpected discoveries. During the course of his career, Officer Michael Martinez had investigated numerous incidents involving missing people. From worried parents whose children were simply late arriving home from school to hostages being held for ransom, the situations that Michael had examined during his career were varied and often challenging as well.

Beginning his newest investigation, Michael stood in the corner of the hospital office with his arms folded, the Chicago skyline visible through the window behind him. He was questioning Tyler Bennett, who sat dressed in scrubs and holding an ice pack to the back of his head. Jacqueline Morgan Donovan and Logan Pryce stood off to the side, their eyes focused on Tyler.

"Why don't we start with what you remember?" Michael asked. "Take your time."

"I went into Jesse's room to check on him and prepare him for his release. The room was dark and the blinds were closed. He looked like he was asleep. I gathered his clothes and other items that we had taken off him when he was admitted to the hospital and placed them on the counter. Then I went into the bathroom to pour the juice that was left in his cup down the drain. I felt something hit the back of my head. And that's the last thing I remember until you found me on the bathroom floor taped up."

"You didn't see or hear anyone else in the room with Jesse and you?"

"No," Tyler said.

"And what are you missing besides your scrubs?"

"Just my hospital name badge and card key."

"Do you have any idea where my son could be?"

Tyler looked at Jacqueline. "I'm sorry; I don't."

"What about tracking the use of Tyler's card key?" Logan asked.

"We did," Michael said. "It was used to access a restricted elevator and exit about half an hour before you found Tyler in the bathroom. They also found an abandoned wheel chair near that hospital exit. Jesse's belongings, some sedatives, and some syringes are missing from his hospital room as well. And we have checked the hospital's security cameras. They don't provide a clear view of that part of hallway for us."

Tyler put the ice pack into his lap. "I wish I could be of more help."

293

"You've been very helpful," Michael replied. "One of my guys can get you home if you need a ride. Assuming the doctor has cleared you to go."

"He has. It's just a small bump on my head. I'll live," Tyler said with a smile. "Just need to get my clothes from my locker downstairs."

"Get some rest," Logan said.

"And if you think of anything else, please let me know," Michael added.

Tyler stood up from the chair. "Of course."

"What do we do now?" Jacqueline asked. "I'm sure Ben has something to do with this. He has to. You've got to find my son."

"We will. I know it's not easy, but you need to try to stay calm. We are trying to locate your husband. You can help us by continuing to call him. But until we have more definite evidence, we have to cast a wider net. We can't focus on your husband alone."

"Tyler, thank you," Logan said.

"Sure," Tyler replied. "Good luck to all of you."

As Tyler was leaving the room, Max Taylor passed him and stopped in the doorway. "What is going on? I just came from Jesse's room. It's full of cops."

Jacqueline walked over and hugged Max. "Jesse's gone."

"What are you talking about?"

"Tyler was attacked earlier in Jesse's room," Logan explained, "and Jesse is missing. We think he has been kidnapped."

"Well, where's the security around this place?" Max asked angrily as Jacqueline stepped back from him.

"Don't go getting all upset," Michael said. "Your temper has gotten you in trouble before, remember?"

"Don't worry about my temper," Max said. "Worry about finding my son."

"You saw my team in Jesse's room. They are on it."

"Like you were when Emmett disappeared? We found him on our own, no thanks to you."

Clenching his fists, Michael took a few steps toward Max. "Look, Max--"

Logan interrupted Michael. "Max, why don't we take a walk and get some coffee?" Logan put his arms on Max's shoulder and turned him toward the door.

"That sounds like a great idea," Michael said. "I'll stay here until my team reports back."

Logan escorted Max from the room and walked him down the hall.

"You need to calm down," Logan said. "Otherwise, you're not helping."

"He's my son," Max said.

"So I've heard," Logan replied. "Do you think that fact is going to magically change things between the two of you?"

"What do you mean?" Max asked, as they reached the elevator.

"You two can't stand each other. You practically killed him. Now you're referring to him as 'my son.'"

"I'm trying to wrap my head around it, I guess."

"You and me both," Logan said. The elevator doors opened in front of them and they got inside.

"I supposed it's good we have some time alone to talk about this. You must be just as freaked out by the news as I was."

"Not nearly as upset as I was when I heard about you beating Jesse. What the hell were you thinking?"

"What was I thinking? What were you thinking when you started dating that little shit? I heard what he did to you and his mother on New Year's Eve. No wonder you have been upset and drinking. Why didn't you tell me?"

"I didn't tell you because it's none of your business. And I knew you'd try to 'fix' it for me because you always think you have to be my hero."

"Your hero?"

"Like you always did during our entire relationship. Logan can't do anything right so Max has to fix everything for him."

The elevator doors opened; Max and Logan walked out and headed toward the cafeteria.

"Is that what you really think?" Max asked.

"What I *think*? I *lived* it for all the years we were together," Logan said as they entered the cafeteria. "So, no, I wasn't going to tell you what happened on New Year's Eve because I was trying to prevent something like this from happening. But it happened anyway, didn't it? You were on a crusade."

"Wow," Max said. "That's quite an opinion you have of me."

"It doesn't matter. The damage is done."

"Well, we need to work it all out."

"Jacqueline and I have realized that maybe we were too hard on Jesse. He did what he did to get her away from Ben. And while his plan was completely misguided, he was right about Ben."

"That's true."

"So maybe we should have been more understanding. He's stubborn and he's cocky but he's a good person with a big heart, too."

"He got that last part from his mother," Max said with a smile.

"And his father," Logan added. "You're a very good man, Max. There's no question about that."

"Thank you," Max said as they two approached the coffee counter. "So do you love him?"

"Jesse?" Logan asked. "I can't talk about that with you. You're my ex and now you're his father, too. Besides, I'm not sure what I feel right now."

"Fair enough. Let's get some coffee and get back upstairs. I feel like I owe Michael an apology, too."

"You want to keep that one on your good side," Logan said, jokingly. "He carries a gun."

Max laughed as they placed their orders before heading back upstairs to Michael and Jacqueline.

At the restaurant, Emmett Mancini was showing Jensen Stone some of the designs for the restaurant signage. Seated at a small table together, Emmett flipped through the design options, soliciting Jensen's feedback.

"That one's really cool," Jensen said. "Classic and retro."

Emmett smiled. "I like it, too. Max and I ranked them separately to see how our choices overlapped. Glad you agree with mine."

"Speaking of which, I should probably get out of here before he gets back. You guys have enough going on without having to deal with me."

"Where are you going to go?"

"I have to work at the bar tonight. Then I'll stay with a friend."

"Stripping?"

Jensen corrected Emmett. "Dancing."

"Haha, okay. Dancing. In any event, you still need a place to stay that's more permanent. And I've been thinking. We're in the process of hiring staff for the restaurant. Would you be interested in working for us? It'd certainly be more stable than what you're doing now."

"Wow, I hadn't even thought about that. Would Max be okay with it?"

"Well, I'd have to talk to him about. But you seem trainable to me," Emmett said, jokingly.

"Even a dog is trainable," Jensen added with a smile.

"Exactly."

A knock came to the front door and both Emmett and Jensen looked up from the table to see Dustin Alexander pushing the door open.

"Can I help you?" Emmett asked.

"Hey guys," Dustin said, stepping inside the restaurant. "I'm Dustin. Remember me from Boystown Bistro, Emmett?"

"Oh, yes," Emmett replied, getting up from his seat. "How are you?"

"I'm good, thanks. I don't want to interrupt but I have been passing by this place often and watching the progress you're making. It looks fantastic."

"Thanks," Emmett said.

"I'm just wondering if you are looking for any help. Servers, greeters, bartenders?"

"All of the above," Emmett said, smiling.

"I have a lot of experience."

"Don't you like working at the bistro? You seem to be doing well there."

"I am," Dustin said. "But they can't give me more hours and I need to be working as much as possible."

"This is Jensen, by the way," Emmett said, introducing the young man to Dustin.

"Nice to meet you," Dustin replied.

"It's funny; we were just talking about staffing and hiring," Emmett added. "From the few times I've seen you in action at the bistro, you seem like a great worker. Why don't you leave me your contact info and I'll have Max get back to you and set up an interview? He's taking the lead on hiring."

"Sure," Dustin said, handing Emmett his resume. "This has all my work history and contact information on it."

Emmett took the resume from Dustin and glanced over it. "Impressive. Thanks. We'll be in touch."

"Great, thanks. Sorry to interrupt," Dustin said, turning to leave the restaurant. "And nice to meet you, Jensen."

"Same," Jensen replied as he watched Dustin leave the restaurant.

"Nice guy," Emmett said.

"Seems like it. Cute, too" Jensen added. "Well, I need to get going. You talk things over with Max and let me know what he says."

"Sure thing. I'm going to call him now. Not sure what's keeping him."

"See you later," Jensen said, heading out the front door.

Emmett pulled out his phone and called Max.

While Emmett tried to get a hold of his fiancé, Joyelle Mancini was in her bedroom frantically stuffing a suitcase with clothes. She rushed to the closet, grabbed a few items, and returned to the bed on which the suitcase was sitting.

She stopped to look at her wedding picture sitting on top of the dresser. Running her fingers over the top of it, she paused a moment. Then she picked it up and threw it against the wall, watching as the glass shattered and fell to the floor.

Derek ran into the room, still dressed in his overcoat and scarf. "What was that?" He looked down at the glass on the floor, then at the suitcase on the bed, then at his wife. "What are you doing?"

"What does it look like I'm doing? I'm leaving."

"Leaving? Where are you going?"

"Anywhere but here."

"What happened?"

"You and Cole, that's what happened. I remember. I remember everything."

Derek reached out to grab Joyelle, but she stepped backwards. "Wait, Joyelle. Let me explain."

"Explain what? The lost wedding ring? The video at the party? The kiss you two shared this morning on his front steps? And God knows what else."

"It's not like that. I love you."

"No, you love him. You said it yourself in that video."

"That video was taken out of context. Edited."

"I seriously doubt that," Joyelle said, zipping her suitcase closed.

"Joyelle, you're upset. Let's sit down and talk about this."

"You must think I'm a fool," she said, grabbing her purse and hat. "There's nothing to talk about. You made your choice." She removed her wedding ring and tossed it onto the bed. "You can have that. Cole already has one -- now there's an extra. In case you 'lose' one again."

"I did make my choice -- you. You're the one I married."

"Clearly, it's all been a lie."

"That's not true."

"Save it, Derek," she said, lifting her suitcase from the bed. "Clean up the glass. At least that's one mess you *can* clean up." She left the room and moments later, the front door slammed loudly.

"Fuck," Derek said, kicking the broken picture frame across the floor.

At the same time, Gino Ciancio was in his office in San Francisco reviewing some paperwork. His secretary buzzed in through his phone.

"You have a call from Rome waiting on the line."

"Rome? Okay, thanks." Gino picked up the telephone. "Hello?"

"Hello, Gino," his Aunt Concetta said in a soft voice.

"Aunt Connie? My God, how are you?"

"I'm good, dear. How are you?"

"I'm great, thanks. Wow, it's good to hear you voice. It's been such a long time."

"It hasn't been so long," Concetta said. "Only a few days, really."

"A few days?" Gino asked.

"I am calling to see what you decided to do with the diary."

"The diary? Aunt Connie, I'm not exactly sure what you're talking about."

"Your mother's diary that I gave to you the other day."

Gino paused for a moment, puzzled. "Aunt Connie, is everything okay?"

"I'm fine, thank you."

"I'm only asking because I haven't seen you in years. You never gave me any diary. And certainly not recently."

"But we just met -- oh, dear God!"

"What is it? What's wrong?"

"What have I done? What have I done?"

The call suddenly ended. "Aunt Connie? Aunt Connie, are you there?"

Gino put the phone down and got up from his desk. He walked out of his office and knocked on his brother's office door. When there was no answer, Gino opened the door to look inside. It was empty.

He pulled his cell phone from his pocket and dialed a number. "It's me. Please bring the car around. I need to get home right away." He walked back into his office, grabbed his coat, and headed out of the office toward the elevators.

Meanwhile, Emmett was opening the door to the restaurant to welcome his brother Justin. Emmett helped Justin into the restaurant and over to a chair near the front window. Once Justin was seated, Emmett sat down as well. Several workers were also present, finishing up work on the space.

"Thanks for coming by," Emmett said.

"I wanted to feel out the place, since I've heard so much about it," Justin said. "And I want to talk to you, too."

"Any time."

"I just wanted to tell you that I understand why you are giving your voting rights in the company to Derek. You two are very close and it's cool. I didn't want you to worry about it or think that I feel any resentment."

"Thank you," Emmett said. "I appreciate you saying that."

"I do, however, hope that you'll remain connected to the business. You have a good head on your shoulders and we could learn from you. And vice versa, of course."

"You know how I feel about the company. But if there is anything specific that you ever need help with, I'd be happy to share my thoughts."

"Good. It is a family business, after all." Justin stopped for a moment and began to turn his head in different directions. Then he blinked and shook his head.

"Are you okay?" Emmett asked.

"I'm not sure, I--" Justin put his head down and blinked again.

"Justin?"

"Oh, my God," Justin said, extending his hand toward Emmett. "It's you."

"Me?"

"I can see you." Justin turned to his right. "And the table. And the chair."

Emmett jumped up from his chair. "Holy shit!"

"It's like...shadows," Justin explained, pointing in different directions. "Coming in and out of view."

"Let's get you to the doctor," Emmett said.

Justin slowly stood up, his walking stick falling onto the floor. "Hold on." Justin put his hand to his head and steadied himself.

"You okay?"

"Just a bit dizzy, but I'm okay. Things are focusing in and out."

"Here," Emmett said, putting his arm around Justin. "Let me help you."

The two brothers slowly walked out of the restaurant to Emmett's car and then drove to the hospital.

As two brothers headed toward St. Joseph Hospital, two other brothers came face to face in the Ciancio mansion. Naked, Marco Ciancio stood at the foot of his bed looking at Rachel Carson, also naked, who was lying in the bed.

"Are you sure you don't want round two?" Rachel asked, smiling.

"I need to get to the office to actually get some work done today," Marco said.

"You're the boss; you don't need to be at the office all the time."

"My brother might argue with you on that one," Marco said, pulling on his underwear. "Go on, get dressed."

Rachel reluctantly got out of the bed and walked into the bathroom. As the bathroom door closed, Gino pounded on the bedroom door before opening it and rushing it into the room. Lunging at Marco, Gino pinned him against the wall.

"What have you done?" Gino asked.

"Whoa, brother," Marco said. "What is going on?"

Gino put his hands around Marco's throat. "What did you do to Aunt Connie? Tell me!"

"Aunt Connie?"

"Don't bullshit me, Marco. I just got off the phone with her. Now tell me!"

Rachel emerged from the bathroom, dressed in a robe. "What is going on?"

Both Gino and Marco looked at her and Gino released his hold on Marco.

"I didn't realize you were on the clock," Gino said. "Get dressed and get down to the library. You have five minutes." Gino left the room, slamming the door behind him.

Marco rubbed his throat. "Don't worry; I've got this."

"I sure hope so," Rachel replied. "He looks furious. It's kind of hot, actually. Maybe I'm with the wrong brother."

Marco grabbed Rachel and kissed her violently. "I'm the one who's in charge. Don't forget it." Marco released Rachel, picked up his clothes from the floor, and went into the bathroom.

Making sure the bathroom door was closed, Rachel pulled her phone from her wallet and dialed a number.

Walking over to the large window, Rachel waited for Keith Colgan to answer her call.

"Hello?" Keith asked as he stood in the St. Joseph Hospital cafeteria with a coffee cup in front of him on the counter.

"It's me," Rachel said. "Just checking in to see how things are coming."

"They're coming," Keith replied.

"And what, exactly, does that mean?"

"It means that I'm taking care of things as I said I would," Keith replied.

"Good, good," Rachel said. "Because I have your boyfriend Michael on speed dial. And we both know how he'd hate to know the truth about you."

"I understand," Keith said. "Don't worry about it. Now I have to go."

Keith put his phone back into this pocket and looked around the cafeteria, which wasn't crowded. Then he pulled the brown bottle from his pocket, poured some of its contents into the coffee cup, and put the bottle away.

He left the cafeteria and took the elevator up several floors. Exiting the elevator, he walked down the corridor where he found Emmett pacing back and forth.

"Hey," Emmett said. "Good to see you."

"I thought you might like some coffee," Keith said, handing Emmett the cup. "Between Justin and Jesse, I know you're sort of doing 'double duty' here."

"Thanks," Emmett said, taking a sip of the coffee. "Justin is in with the doctor now. I think his vision has returned."

"That's fantastic," Keith said. "It's nice to have some good news for a change. Seems like you two have gotten a bit closer lately."

"It's complicated," Emmett said. "But we're trying. Derek is, too."

"I'm glad," Keith said, as Max approached them from down the hall.

"Hey," Emmett said to Max. "Any word on Jesse?"

"No," Max said. He looked at Keith. "Michael is doing his best, though. He's a good man."

"Thank you," Keith replied. "How's Jacqueline doing?"

"She's hanging in there. Logan is with her."

"Good."

"Thanks for offering to help with the fundraiser. Emmett told me," Max said. "That's great. We can use all the help we can get now."

"Is it still on?" Keith asked. "With Jesse missing, I didn't know..."

"It's been crazy today, so I don't know. I'll talk to Logan about it later. I'm sure it can be rescheduled, if need be."

"Maybe that's best," Emmett said.

"You okay?" Max asked Emmett. "You look tired."

Emmett smiled. "Well, there's been a lot going on. For all of us."

"Agreed," Keith added.

"Everything go okay with the kid?"

"Jensen? We can talk about him later," Emmett said, drinking more of his coffee.

"Who's Jensen?" Keith asked.

"Long story," Emmett replied. "I'll tell you later. I need to check on Justin."

"I'll go with you," Max said.

"I'll catch you guys later. Let me know about the fundraiser," Keith stated.

"Thanks for the coffee."

"No problem," Keith replied as he watched Max and Emmett walk away down the hallway. Then he turned and walked toward the elevators.

At the same time, Marco entered the Ciancio estate library, where Gino, standing behind the bar and making himself a drink, was waiting for him. Marco had his mother's diary with him and placed it on the table in front of the fireplace.

"Sorry to have interrupted your love in the afternoon," Gino said.

"You were like a crazy man up there," Marco declared. "What is wrong with you?"

"What is wrong with me? What the hell did you do to Aunt Connie?"

"I met with her last week, that's all."

"But she thought she was meeting with me," Gino said. "Didn't she?"

"Her eyesight isn't what it used to be."

"What the hell are you up to? First all the questions about Mother's art collection and now this? I want to know and I want to know now!"

"Okay, okay," Marco said, walking over to the bar and making pouring himself a glass of wine.

"Start talking," Gino stated.

"I have been searching for the fourth Mancini brother."

"And?"

313

"Father and I were discussing it and I asked him if there was any possibility that our mother had a child by old man Mancini."

"What?"

"Of course, Father got upset and denied that possibility, but I wanted to check things out for sure. So I contacted Aunt Connie. After all, Mother spent all that time with her in Rome after her affair."

"And what did she say?"

"She denied any knowledge of a child. She said Mother was in Rome for cancer treatments."

"Isn't that true?" Gino asked, walking closer to Marco.

"It is, partially. A few days later, Aunt Connie called me back. Well, actually she called you."

"I never got any calls from her," Gino said.

"I know. But I did. She said she was coming to California to meet with me and give something important to me."

"You mean, she was coming to California to meet with *me*."

"Technically, yes."

"You son of a bitch."

"Mother kept a diary the entire time she was in Rome. She left it with Aunt Connie and told her to save it and give it to you whenever she felt it was appropriate."

"And you stole it."

"No," Marco said. "I just previewed it for you."

"Mother intended it for me."

Marco walked over to the table and picked up the diary. "And now you'll get to read it."

Gino took the diary from Marco. "You have a lot of nerve posing as me and stealing that diary. From an old nun on top of it."

"You're the one worried about going to heaven," Marco joked. "I prefer warmer climates."

"What's in here?"

"Read for yourself," Marco said. "But I'll give you the same warning that Aunt Connie gave me. If you choose to read what's in that book, your view of this family will never be the same. And she was right. Happy reading." Marco finished his wine and left the room.

Gino watched his brother exit. Then he sat down in the leather chair next to the fireplace. He opened the diary and began to read.

Outside the library in the hallway, Marco paused and removed two sheets of paper from his pocket; they

315

were two pages of his mother's diary that he removed prior to turning the book over to Gino. Marco looked back at the library door and smiled. Then he tucked the pages back into his pocket and continued down the corridor.

As the sun rose over Lake Michigan, the skyscrapers of Chicago glistened in its rays. With most of the winter snow melted, Spring was taking hold in the Windy City. Joggers ran along Lake Shore Drive and others opted to walk to work instead of taking a cab or a bus.

In his office, Derek paced back and forth behind his desk while talking on the phone with his brother Emmett.

"Thanks for letting me know, Emmett," Derek said.

Cole O'Brien entered the office and Derek indicated for him to come in and take a seat, which he did.

"That's good news. I'll see him later on today," Derek told Emmett. "No, no. She didn't come home last night. I'm sure she stayed at her mother's." Derek paused to listen to Emmett. "Listen, I have to run. I have a meeting, but I'll check in with you later on today. I'm sorry you're not feeling well. Get some rest."

Derek ended the call and put his cell phone down on his desk.

"Good morning," Cole said with a smile. "I was excited to get your call. Always love seeing you."

"Me, too," Derek replied, walking around the desk and standing in front of it. "That was Emmett. My brother Justin's vision has returned."

"That's great."

"And that's not all that's returned. So have Joyelle's memories."

"Oh," Cole replied. "How did that go?"

"Not well," Derek said. "She saw me leaving your apartment and us kissing when you gave me my wallet. Apparently, that triggered everything coming back."

"Is she okay?"

"She yelled at me and didn't come home last night. I'm assuming that she stayed with her mother."

Cole stood up in front of Derek. "I'm sorry." He wrapped his arms around Derek. "But now we can be together."

"One step at a time. I still have to talk to her and try to make her understand all that's going on. I don't want to hurt her."

"I think we already have," Cole said, running his hands up Derek's chest. "I feel bad about that, but we have waited so long to be together. And now we can be."

Derek pulled away from Cole and walked over to the window. "I have an idea for us."

"I'm listening."

"You know that I have taken over my father's company. Well, we have decided to move the headquarters to Chicago, so we can run it from here. It'll be a long process, but worth it."

"That's great. Less travel for you."

"And an opportunity for you as well. I want you to come work for me."

Cole's eyes widened. "Wait, what?"

"I know you just started your current job, but I want you to join my company. In fact, I'd like you to head up our public relations department."

"Wow."

"What do you say?"

"Derek, that's a huge job."

"I know, but you can handle it. I've seen your work. Our current department head is retiring and doesn't want to make the move here to Chicago. He'll work with and mentor you until his retirement so there will be a smooth transition. And, yes, there will be a significant pay increase for you, too. So what do you say?"

Cole walked over to Derek. "What do I say? To working with you? Yes, yes, yes." Cole kissed Derek, who wrapped his arms around Cole.

"Happy?"

"And surprised," Cole said, kissing Derek. "Honestly, I often wondered if we would ever really be together. But I trusted your word and now it really feels like it's happening. Thank you."

"I told you -- you're mine," Derek said. "It's going to be a lot of work, but exciting at the same time."

"Thank you. I'll give my notice at work this afternoon."

"Good," Derek said.

"The only thing that would make this better is if I knew Jesse was safe."

"Has there been any word?"

"Unfortunately, no. Jacqueline stayed with me last night. I didn't want her alone at a hotel."

"That was nice. Please give her my best."

"I will," Cole said, kissing Derek again. "Now I should probably run. I need to give my notice at work and to check in on her as well."

"Okay, I'll see you soon."

"Good luck with Joyelle. Let me know how it goes -- and if I can help."

"Will do," Derek said.

"I love you," Cole said, grabbing his coat.

"Love you, too," Derek replied, watching Cole leave the office.

Derek sat back down at his desk, picked up his cell phone, and dialed Joyelle's phone. The call went right to voicemail, so Derek ended the call and dropped the phone onto his desk.

After concluding his phone call with Derek, Emmett walked into his living room where Max was seated on the sofa. He sat down next to his fiancé and grabbed his hand.

"You okay?"

"Yes," Max replied. "Just thinking."

"They'll find him," Emmett said with a smile. "And he'll be okay."

"Thank you," Max said, putting his arm around Emmett. "I could never get through all this without you."

"You don't have to."

"How are you feeling?" Max asked. "You still look pretty pale."

"Not so great, but I'm okay. Just sort of nauseous."

"You need to take it easy and rest today."

"I'll be fine," Emmett replied.

"I'll take care of the meeting with Logan and Keith to discuss the fundraiser. And I'll interview Dustin, too. It'll get my mind off Jesse and you can stay here and relax."

"Our sign is going up outside today. It's a big moment for us and the restaurant. I'm not going to miss that."

Max laughed. "Okay, you can come downstairs for that, but then you need to promise me you'll rest."

"We need to talk about Jensen."

"What about him?"

"How do you feel about him staying here for a while? Just until he can afford his own place."

"You really feel for that kid, don't you? Even after all he's done."

"Max, when my father threw me out of the house for being gay, I had Derek to look out for me. Jensen has no one. He's stripping and hooking for a living and he's basically homeless."

"He's not as lucky as you were."

"Every time he hooks up with a client, he puts himself at risk. His health and his safety. And after being raped by Nick, I know how scary that can be. I feel like we can give him a new start. A job and a chance to stand on his own."

Max smiled. "Do you know how much I love you? You are one of the most selfless people I know. If you want to help that boy out, then let's do it."

"Really? You're okay with it?"

"I'll be honest -- I don't entirely trust him. Not just yet. But if you feel good about him and want to give him a chance, then I'm on board."

Emmett smiled and kissed Max. "Thank you."

"All right. Now, you promised you'd rest today. So until they come to install the sign later today, I want you lying down."

"Yes, Sir."

Max stood up and Emmett reclined on the couch. Max covered him with the blanket and Emmett closed his eyes. Max kissed him softly and then quietly left the room.

While Emmett fell asleep, Marco entered Gino's office. Gino was seated on a sofa with his mother's diary in his lap. Marco closed the door behind him and sat down in a chair across from his brother.

"I wanted to meet here so there was no chance of Father overhearing us."

"I understand," Marco replied. "I'm assuming you read the diary."

"I will never forgive you for tricking Aunt Connie. You knew that diary was meant for me and you stole it anyway."

"I did what I thought was necessary," Marco said.

"You manipulated a kind woman and you stole something very special from me. It's clear after reading this diary that Mother intended it for me and me only."

"And you think that was fair?"

"Fair or not, it's what she intended. And you violated her wish."

Marco rolled his eyes. "So you have read the whole thing?"

"Cover to cover," Gino said. "And Aunt Connie was right -- things will never be quite the same."

"Our mother had quite a few secrets," Marco added.

"Since you have read the diary as well, we may as well work together on some of these issues. That is, if I can trust you."

"You'll have to decide that for yourself."

"My understanding from reading this book is that Mother initially lied about having cancer as a way of going to Rome to hide her pregnancy. She secretly gave birth to a son and gave him away for adoption."

"Yes. She told Antonio Mancini that she gave birth to his son and that he would never, ever know the child. I guess that was her revenge against him for the affair. And then, as she was preparing to return to America, she was diagnosed with cancer. Aunt Connie said Mother thought that was God punishing her for the affair."

"That's what she says in the diary, too. And Aunt Connie had no other information about the child?"

"According to Aunt Connie, Mother told her nearly nothing. She gave birth to the boy and then put him up for adoption. She didn't tell her sister any of the details; instead, she put everything in the diary and locked it."

"It sounds like she wanted the boy to be raised to be a nurse, just like her."

"Or at least in health care to serve others, as she did," Marco added.

"And now I know why you were asking Father about the art collection."

"We have to get our hands on that painting. All the details about our half-brother are in that painting."

"Have you made any progress?" Gino asked.

"I contacted Strauss, who ran the art auction. He is putting together a report of who bought all the paintings. We'll have to go from there once I receive the list."

"It could be anywhere," Gino said. "And it's important that we recover the rest of the collection as well."

"Once I hear back from Strauss, we can plan our next steps. It goes without saying that Father can't know about any of this yet."

"Exactly," Gino said. "And what do we do about the other matter she wrote about in the diary?"

"One thing at a time," Marco said. "One thing at a time."

"I'm putting you on notice, Marco. No more lies. No more tricks. And no more going behind my back. This situation is too important and delicate for that."

"You have my word," Marco replied.

"Whatever that's worth," Gino mumbled.

As Gino and Marco finished their conversation, Tyler was drying off after taking shower. He looked into this bathroom mirror, turning his head to the right and left to look for signs of a lump where he had been hit on the back of the head.

A knock came to his front door, so he wrapped his towel around his waist and headed into the living room to answer the door. When he opened it, he saw Joyelle, who was carrying a tin of cookies.

"Joyelle," Tyler said, smiling.

"I heard what happened to you at the hospital. I wanted to make sure you are okay."

"Thank you."

"I made some cookies. May I come in?"

"Oh, of course. Come on in," Tyler said, opening the door wider. "David's at work and I was just showering. Obviously." Tyler took the cookie tin from Joyelle and placed it on the counter near him. "Give me a minute and I'll pull on some clothes."

Joyelle's eyes filled with tears. "Oh, Tyler..."

Tyler walked back over to Joyelle. "What is it? What's wrong?"

"I remember. I remember...everything."

Tyler smiled. "That's a good thing, right? It's what you were hoping for."

Joyelle shook her head. "I remember what you said about my wedding ring. And the New Year's Eve party. And the video."

"Oh, God," Tyler said softly, folding his arms around her. Joyelle continued to cry and put her head against his chest. "It'll be okay. It'll be okay."

Joyelle lifted her head and looked into Tyler's eyes. "I - I can't..." Without saying another word, Joyelle kissed Tyler. He pulled her closer and kissed her softly.

Stepping back a moment, Tyler looked at Joyelle. She looked up into his eyes and kissed him again as she took off her overcoat. He pulled her to him, kissing her deeply and unzipping the back of her dress. She ran her fingers over his lightly-hairy chest and then held the back of his neck as their tongues met.

She let her dress slip off and fall to the floor. Then her hands explored the muscles in his back until they reached the towel wrapped around his waist. She pulled it from him, revealing his fully erect penis, which pressed up against her panties.

Kissing her neck and her shoulders, Tyler lifted her off the floor. She threw her head back as his tongue explored the top of her breasts. His arms around her lower back and under the backs of her knees, Tyler cradled Joyelle as he carried her to his bedroom.

His bed still unmade, Tyler put Joyelle onto the bed and knelt down beside it. She leaned forward to watch

Tyler remove her underwear. Then he kissed his way up her body, his nipples tickling her stomach. She ran her fingers through his hair, pulling his face to her and kissing him. Her legs spread widely beneath him as he seduced her vagina with the swollen head of his cock. He looked into her eyes and wiped the tears from them as he pushed himself inside of her.

Joyelle let out a moan as Tyler entered. She dug her fingers into the small of his back as he drilled deeper inside of her. His mouth sucked her hard nipples, first one and then the other. His thrusts grew stronger and more rapid as her hands slid from his back to his firm ass.

"I have wanted this for so long," Tyler whispered. Joyelle kissed him and ran her feet up the backs of his legs. Tyler pushed up and looked into Joyelle's eyes as he released inside of her. She moaned loudly as Tyler spewed more and more inside her.

He pulled out of Joyelle and rolled over onto his back, breathing heavily. Joyelle put her head against him and he held her in his arms. As he kissed her forehead, she quietly cried, her tears rolling onto his chest.

Across town, Jacqueline opened the door to Jesse's apartment and greeted Max and Michael. They entered the living room and closed the door behind them.

"I'm sure you understand how anxious I've been since getting your call, Michael," Jacqueline said.

"We got here as quickly as we could."

"Have you found Jesse?"

"Unfortunately, no," Michael said. "However, we have found this." Michael held up an evidence bag containing a cell phone.

"A phone?" Jacqueline asked.

"When my team was searching Jesse's hospital room, they found this on the floor under the toilet in the bathroom."

"They are hoping that maybe you recognize it," Max added.

"You mentioned that your husband could be involved with Jesse's disappearance. We believe this is his cell phone."

Jacqueline took the bag from Michael and examined the phone through the bag. "That's Ben's. I recognize the cover and the small crack at the top."

"That's what our tech guys said as well, but I wanted to show it to you, too."

"What does this mean?" Jacqueline asked.

"It means your hunch may very well be correct," Max said. "We're pretty confident that Ben is the one who took Jesse."

Jacqueline's eyes filled with tears. "Well, what do you intend to do to find him? Ben's a crazy man. And when he's desperate, he'll do anything."

"You need to remain calm," Michael advised.

"Calm? My son is in the hands of a lunatic. For all we know, he could be dead by now."

Jacqueline broke down crying and Max put his arms around her, saying, "It's going to be okay. We're going to find our son."

While Max tried to comfort Jacqueline, Ben Donovan woke up lying on a bed wearing only his underwear. His hands were wrapped together with duct tape and his feet were bound together with tape as well. He looked around the room, which had no windows and only one door.

Ben rolled himself off the bed, landing hard on the floor. Then he struggled to make his way across the floor to toward the door. After a short amount of time, Ben made it to his destination. His back against the door, he slowly stood up, his bound hands reaching for the door knob.

He tried over and over to open the door, which was locked from the outside. He attempted with all his muscle to pull the door open but, losing his balance, fell onto the floor. "Let me out of here!" he yelled. "Let me the hell out of here!"

As Ben screamed for help, two nuns in Concetta's convent in Rome made their way down the hallway toward her room. The dim light fixtures along the corridor threw the women's shadows in several directions as they walked.

"No one has seen Sister Concetta for at least two days. She hasn't come down to any meals," one woman told the other.

"I wish someone had told me sooner," the other nun replied. "I would have checked on her right away."

When the ladies arrived at Concetta's room, they knocked on her door several times. When no answer came, one of the women pulled out a key and unlocked the door. They opened it and entered the room.

Upon entering, the women were greeted by a breeze coming from the open window at the far end of the room.

They turned on the lights and saw Concetta's bed in an odd position beneath the window.

"Concetta? Concetta?" one of the nuns called out loudly. The other approached the bed and the window. She noticed a rope tied to one leg of the bed and running through the window. When she looked out of the window, she let out a horrible scream. Immediately, the other woman rushed over to the window and looked through it.

Looking out the window, the women saw the limp body of Concetta hanging from the rope by the neck and swinging slightly in the wind. Both women yelled out as the breeze rippled through the dress that clung to Concetta's dead body. The search for a missing person often leads to unexpected discoveries.

Episode #29

Complete satisfaction is often elusive. Because of unforeseen circumstances or shifts in focus, people often adjust their goals as they work toward them. Even the most carefully planned strategies often require revision or fine-tuning. And sometimes the path to success is a long and bumpy one.

As the Ciancio jet circled the city of Chicago, all three Ciancios -- Carlo, Gino, and Marco -- discussed strategy for their meeting with the Mancini brothers. Carlo and Marco spoke of a specific endgame, but Gino advocated for flexibility and compromise.

"This meeting is what we have worked so hard for," Carlo said. "It's time to take from them what we deserve."

"Father, as I have said before, we need to be careful," Gino said. "And fair."

"Fair?" Carlo asked. "Don't forget your loyalty to this family, Gino."

"I am thinking of our family. And I'm thinking it's better in the long run for all of us if we can resolve this situation peacefully."

"No one's advocating violence," Marco said, pouring himself another glass of wine at the bar. "We just want what Justin originally agreed to give us."

"We all know the situation has changed since then. Their father is dead and the Mancini brothers are united."

"Well, three of them are," Marco remarked. "No one knows yet where the fourth one is."

"We'll track him down sooner or later," Carlo said. "Before they do."

A voice came over the speaker in the cabin: "Mr. Ciancio, we have been cleared for landing. Please be sure you're seated."

Marco returned to his chair. "Have you heard anything else about Aunt Connie, Father?"

"Nothing," Carlo replied. "I still can't get over it. Suicide. Why would she ever do such a thing?"

Gino and Marco exchanged glances. "I have no idea," Marco said. "Something was clearly troubling her."

"Your mother loved her very much," Carlo said. "They spent a lot of time together, especially during your mother's treatments."

"Now they are together again," Gino said.

"That's right," Carlo agreed. "One day we'll all be together again. But until that day, there's work to be done."

"Father, I plan to go to Rome to see her grave at the convent," Gino said. "You are both welcome to join me. Regardless, I feel like it's something I need to do."

"You're a good boy, my son," Carlo said with a smile. Marco and Gino exchanged glances again as the plane made a smooth landing onto the Chicago runway.

As the Ciancios exited their jet and got into the limousine that was taking them into the city to their hotel, the sound of the bedroom door being unlocked woke Ben Donovan, who had spent the night on the floor. Startled, he sat up as Jesse Morgan stepped into the room carrying a small tray.

"Good morning," Jesse said as he placed the tray on a table near the bed. His eye and cheek were still badly bruised and swollen, although his mouth appeared to be healing more quickly.

"What the fuck are you trying to do to me?" Ben asked, as Jesse grabbed his arm and helped him get up from the floor.

"I'm bringing you something to eat. I'm not sure you'd be so kind to me if the roles here were reversed. This tape around your feet isn't necessary anymore," Jesse said as he sat Ben on the edge of the bed. He reached into his pocket, pulled out a small pocket knife, and cut Ben's feet loose from the tape. "I found this knife in your kitchen. Comes in handy."

"I should never have told you about this place."

"Why not? It's where you intended to live happily ever after with my mother. And my half-brother that she's carrying."

"So you decided to lock me up here? You won't get away with this."

"Oh, I don't intend to," Jesse said with a smile. "That's part of my plan. I'm counting on Michael finding us here."

"What the hell are you talking about? And what did you do to your wrists?" Ben asked, looking at the bruises on Jesse's arms.

"It has to look like you kept me here against my will. These tape marks will help."

"Jesus."

"No one knows you like I do, Ben," Jesse said, putting his face close to Ben's. "We were meant to be together, remember? That's what you wanted."

"I told you. I love your mother. We are working things out."

"We'll see about that. She knows what kind of a man you really are."

"And now that you know who your father is, you should concentrate on him."

Jesse slapped Ben hard across the face. "Don't you ever bring him up again. Ever!"

Ben smiled widely. "You can't deny biology. He's a part of you and you're a part of him. There's no escaping it."

"And there's no escaping here," Jesse said. "Don't worry; they've found your phone. They'll be here soon."

"What are you talking about?"

"You're not the only one who knows how to install apps. My mother told me you were monitoring my phone. I decided to use that to my advantage," Jesse said. "Why don't you have something to eat? You're going to need your strength where you're going." Jesse walked toward the door.

"Wait, please," Ben pleaded.

Jesse smiled at Ben, left the room, and locked the door behind him. Ben angrily kicked over the table, sending the food on the tray in every direction.

While Ben's food flew all over the room, the waiter at the Signature Room atop Chicago's John Hancock building placed two plates of food on the table in front of Justin Mancini and Gino. The two men looked out over the city from their table beside the large window.

"Is there any better place than this to celebrate the return of your vision?" Gino asked.

Justin smiled. "I guess not. The city looks amazing from up here. We don't have anything nearly this spectacular in San Francisco."

"Well, then maybe it's a good thing you'll be moving here permanently."

"Moving here? Who said anything about that?" Justin asked, taking a sip of his champagne.

"With the Mancini headquarters moving here, you're going to have to, right? You'll want to be here with Derek and Emmett."

"We have been getting closer."

Gino smiled. "I'm glad. Family's important. No one understands that better than I do."

"Gino, I don't want you to get caught in the middle of our families fighting."

"Isn't that what *I* normally tell *you*?"

"I'm serious. Tomorrow's meeting could be rough. I don't want your feelings for me to get you in trouble. I understand that you need to do what's best for your family. As I do for mine."

"I'm my own man, Justin. My father and Marco don't think for me -- and they don't speak for me, either."

"I just want you to be careful. Maybe it's my turn to look out for you for a change."

Gino raised his champagne glass. "I'll drink to that."

"Gino--"

"Come on, Justin. This is supposed to be a celebration. Let's not talk business. There will be plenty of time for that. Let's talk about us."

"Is there an 'us'?"

"I'd like there to be," Gino said. "I love you -- you know that."

"Gino, you know I can't commit to anything right now. I have so much going on. And a few scores to settle, too."

"You're talking about Rachel."

"She nearly destroyed my relationship with Derek. And she ruined his marriage in a horrible way," Justin said. "Oh, I know I'm partially to blame. I'm the one who filmed the video in the first place. But she's dangerous and reckless."

"Why are we even talking about her? I want to talk about us. I want to be with you, Justin. I know you have feelings for me, too -- buried under that thick skin of yours."

"I do love you...in my own way," Justin admitted. "But I can't promise anything will come of it."

"How about one day at a time? Can you at least give me that?" Gino asked.

Justin smiled. "Sure."

"Then that's all I'm asking for right now." Gino raised his glass again. "To us?"

Justin touched his glass to Gino's. "To us."

Gino and Justin drank their champagne and continued their lunch conversation against the backdrop of the magnificent views of the city far below them.

Just north of the John Hancock building stood St. Joseph Hospital. Inside the hospital cafeteria, Joyelle Mancini and Tyler Bennett were seated at a table near the window overlooking Lincoln Park. Joggers enjoying the Spring weather could be seen making their way through the park's paths.

"I thought we should talk about the other night," Joyelle said.

"Okay," Tyler replied tentatively.

"I shouldn't have come over to your place in such an emotional state," Joyelle said. "It wasn't smart of me. Or fair to you."

"Fair to me?" Tyler asked with a smile. "Are you kidding? I'm glad you came. It was an incredible evening."

"I don't want to put you in the middle of my marriage."

"Joyelle, we both know that your marriage is over. Derek cheated on you and is in love with someone else. He has been for some time."

"I know," Joyelle said softly. "But that's something I need to work through and accept on my own."

"We're friends and I'm here for you. You don't need to do it on your own. You can lean on me."

"That wouldn't be fair," Joyelle said. "Especially knowing your feelings for me."

"The feelings, I believe, are mutual. And what happened between us showed that. It was special...wonderful."

Joyelle shook her head. "Tyler, I can't jump from one thing to the next like that. I need time to wrap my head around all this."

Tyler grabbed Joyelle's hand. "I understand. And there's no rush. We can take our time together."

Derek Mancini entered the cafeteria, pausing at the entrance to look for his wife. Spotting her at the table with Tyler, Derek rushed over and grabbed Tyler by the shirt, lifting him out his chair.

"I told you to stay away from my wife!" Derek said angrily, punching Tyler and sending him tumbling backwards onto the floor.

Joyelle jumped up. "What the hell are you doing?"

Tyler lunged forward toward Derek, pushing him backwards into several chairs.

"Stop it!" Joyelle yelled, stepping in between the two men. Then she looked directly at Derek. "You're making a scene and I work here. Haven't you caused enough damage already?"

"I came here to talk to you," Derek said, standing up and adjusting his coat.

"You call this 'talking'?" Joyelle asked, helping Tyler up from the floor.

"You're way out of line, buddy," Tyler said angrily. "Next time you come at me, you better finish what you start; otherwise, I will."

"Tyler, can you please give us a moment?" Joyelle asked.

"Of course," Tyler replied. Then he looked directly at Derek. "You don't deserve her."

Tyler walked toward the exit of the cafeteria and Derek yelled toward him, "She's my wife."

"Only technically," Joyelle clarified as she returned the disturbed chairs to their proper places. "Now what the hell did you want to talk about?"

"Us," Derek replied.

"There is no 'us' anymore. Apparently that label is reserved for Cole and you."

"He's not a bad person, Joyelle. He saved my life -- and yours, too."

"This isn't about him. It's about you cheating on me and lying about it."

"Joyelle, I love you. We can get through this."

"You have an odd way of showing it. Have you been gay this entire time?"

Derek lowered his voice, looking around to see if diners in the cafeteria were still looking at them. "I'm not gay. I won't see Cole again; I promise. I'll send him away from both of us, I swear. Just give me a chance to prove myself."

"You know, I will never, ever get over the loss of our children. But right now I can't think of anything worse than raising any children related to you."

"Joyelle, don't say that."

"I have to get back to work. I'll be in touch, through my attorney." Joyelle turned and began to walk away.

"Please stay and talk. I know we can work this out." Joyelle kept walking away and left the cafeteria. Derek violently pushed a chair out of his way. "Dammit."

Just up the street in his apartment bedroom, Michael Martinez pushed deeper into Keith Colgan, who spread his legs wide beneath him. Michael kissed Keith deeply, his tongue probing his mouth, his neck, his shoulders. Keith ran his fingers through Michael's hair and down his back as he held tightly to his boyfriend.

Wrapping his arms around Keith, Michael flipped them both over so that Keith could ride him. Looking up at

Keith, Michael continued to thrust while massaging his chest. Keith reached back to grab Michael's powerful legs and threw his head back as Michael's thrusts increased in strength and frequency.

Leaning forward, Michael kissed Keith's chest. As Michael adjusted his legs, Keith grabbed the back of Michael's head and kissed him deeply. He dug his fingers into Michael's shoulders as their tongues moved in and out of each other's mouths.

Gritting his teeth, Michael prepared to cum. Pumping hard into Keith, Michael released his load, filling Keith. Keith moaned with pleasure, stroking his dick against Michael's chest. Michael grabbed Keith's penis and continued to stroke it as he watched Keith's facial expressions. With a soft moan, Keith erupted.

Keith collapsed forward onto Michael who held him tightly and kissed him again. They wrapped their legs around each other and rested quietly for a moment.

"I love you, Stormy," Michael said.

"I love you, too," Keith replied. "I'd do anything for you."

Michael smiled. "Just being my other half is enough."

"I won't let anything ever come between us."

"Well, of course not," Michael said. "You're stuck with me."

"Do you want to come to that fundraiser meeting with me later on? We're going over the final details with Logan and Max."

"If I'm off duty in time, I'll be there."

"Perfect," Keith said, kissing his boyfriend.

Michael sat up. "Speaking of which, I should probably be heading in."

"Aww," Keith moaned. "We've had such a great morning."

Michael got out of bed. "And afternoon."

"I should get going, too, I guess."

Michael kissed Keith before heading into the bathroom. Once Keith saw the bathroom door close, he walked over to the chair over which his sweatshirt was draped. He reached into the pocket and pulled out the small brown bottle. He stared at it and then looked toward the bathroom door.

The conference room in Derek's office building featured floor to ceiling windows through which much of the Chicago skyline and the lake shore could be seen. Against the backdrop of the city view, Derek stood at the head of the long, wooden table; Justin and Emmett were seated on either side of him.

"Remember," Derek said, "no matter what our issues are among the three of us, we are united in front of the Ciancios. We are Mancinis, one and all."

"Are you sure you're okay?" Justin asked Emmett. "You don't look well."

"I'm okay," Emmett said. "I want to be here."

"Then I'm taking you right home afterwards so you can get some rest."

The door opened and Derek's secretary led Carlo, Marco, and Gino into the room. Then she departed.

"Welcome, gentlemen," Derek said, walking over to shake hands with the Ciancios as Emmett and Justin rose to their feet.

"Thank you for hosting us," Gino said.

The men all shook hands with one another and then took their seats. Gino sat next to Justin while Carlo and Marco sat opposite Derek.

"Again, thank you for coming to Chicago," Derek said.

"This office is very nice. Cozy, in fact," Carlo said. "But I'm not sure it's appropriate for an international company of the prestige you claim Mancini Global to be."

"When our new corporate headquarters open, they will be the envy of Ciancio International as well as every other company that wants to be like ours."

"I'm sure it will be," Gino said.

"Let's get down to business," Marco said. "We all know why we are here. To settle a debt."

"Of course," Derek said. He nodded to Justin who handed folders to the three Ciancios.

"Here is our proposed settlement for repaying the loan we obtained from you," Justin explained. "I'm sure you'll agree it's quite generous."

The Ciancios examined the paperwork contained in their folders. After a moment, Carlo spoke. "It's not what we agreed to, Justin. It's unsatisfactory."

Derek responded to Carlo's comment before Justin could. "The agreement that Justin made with you earlier was grossly unfair and was without the necessary approval of our father who was head of the company at the time. Justin acted without that proper authority, rendering the agreement null and void."

"Our attorneys would disagree," Marco said.

"If you want to take us to court, by all means do so. You won't win; it'll be dragged out as long as humanly possible and the negative publicity it brings your company will cost you in the court of public opinion," Derek said. "The offer we have given you here is more than fair. Full repayment of the loan, plus interest, and eight percent of our company."

"It's is a good offer," Gino agreed.

"It's not what we decided on," Marco said. "It's not our fault that you got in over your head. Justin was acting on your father's behalf and we simply want what we deserve."

"What you have in front of you is our final offer," Justin said.

Carlo pounded his fist on the table. "It's unacceptable. Not what we agreed to, Justin."

"It's a fair deal and a final one," Derek reiterated.

"Your father took my wife from me. You know what they say about sins of the father," Carlo continued. "You must pay for what he did."

Derek grew stern. "And you took my children from me -- something you must pay for, too!"

"What our father did was unforgiveable," Emmett said. "We all agree with that, Mr. Ciancio. But that has nothing to do with us -- or the business for that matter."

"Emmett is right," Gino said. "That's all in that past. We need to deal in the present."

Carlo looked angrily at his son. "The deal is unacceptable."

Gino looked to Derek. "Would the three of you please excuse us for a moment? I'd like to speak to my father and brother privately, if that's okay."

"Absolutely," Derek said. "We'll step outside."

Derek, Justin, and Emmett rose from their seats, nearly in unison, and left the conference room.

"What the hell do you think you are doing?" Carlo asked Gino.

"Father, I told you that I didn't want this to be hostile."

Carlo pointed at Gino. "And I told you to remember your loyalty to your family."

"I'm sorry, Father, but this fight cannot continue."

"That's not for you to decide," Marco stated. "I made that deal with Justin and he needs to comply with it."

"Their offer is a generous one," Gino insisted. "And we are going to accept it."

"The hell we are," Marco said.

"I told you that I was going to put a stop to this and it stops now," Gino said, looking directly at his twin. "Let me be clear. You caused that explosion that cost Derek his children and Justin his eyesight, at least for a while. Not to mention the life of the limousine driver. That is more than enough 'payback.' Either we take this deal or I go straight to the police."

"Are you out of your mind?" Marco asked.

"You would turn against your own family?" Carlo asked. "I raised you better than that."

"Father, you taught us to know right from wrong and to do the right thing. At least one of us learned that lesson. That offer is more than generous and still gets us a nice piece of their company."

"I can't believe I'm hearing this," Marco said. "Are you trying to destroy our family?"

"Actually, I'm trying to save it."

"That's your opinion."

"Would you both prefer to run our company from a prison cell? Father, if you ever trusted me, please trust me today," Gino said.

"We may not have a choice today but to accept their offer," Marco said. "But you can't hold prison over our heads forever. Our time will come."

"Let's take one thing at a time," Gino said. "All that matters today is that we are taking their offer and putting this entire loan issue to rest. It's over."

"For now," Carlo said. "Only for now."

Gino left the room to ask the Mancini brothers to return.

"This isn't over," Marco told his father. "Not by a long shot."

As Gino invited the Mancini brothers back into the conference room and signed the paperwork accepting their offer, Rachel Carson was in the bathroom of her hotel room. She stood in front of the mirror holding her home pregnancy test in her hand.

"Come on, come on," she mumbled, waiting for the results. She looked into the mirror and adjusted her hair. Then she looked back that the test, which was indicating a "negative" result. "Dammit," she said, throwing the test into the garbage can.

She walked out into the main area of the hotel room and picked up her phone. She dialed a number and waited for Keith to answer. Instead, she got his voicemail and left a message, "It's me. Call me back with an update." She threw the phone onto the bed, mumbling, "One way or another, I'm going to get what I want."

At the same time, David Young and Tyler were in their living room. David was getting ready for work while Tyler was sorting through some mail.

"Hey, are you going to be home tonight?" David asked. "I may invite Cole over for dinner."

Tyler looked up from the mail. "In other words, get lost."

David laughed. "You are more than welcome to join us."

"Naw, I don't like being a third wheel. Maybe I'll see if Joyelle wants some company."

"How are things going with her?"

"Depends who you ask," Tyler said. "I had another run in with Derek. He caused a scene in the hospital cafeteria."

"Oh, brother," David replied. "He really is a piece of work. I just don't understand what Cole sees in him."

"Especially when he can have you, the perfect man," Tyler said, jokingly.

"Well, duh," David added with a smile.

"Has Cole said anything to you since Joyelle got her memories back?"

"We have talked, just not about that."

"I'm wondering what Derek and he plan to do now."

David sighed. "Me, too. But I don't intend to give up."

"Good, you shouldn't."

"Things should be easier for Joyelle and you now, I'm assuming," David added.

"It's going to take time," Tyler replied. "But I'm optimistic. As long as Derek stays out of the way."

"Which you know he won't," David declared.

"Well, then I may have to be a bit more aggressive where he's concerned," Tyler said. "I just don't want to push Joyelle too hard. This is a lot for her to cope with."

"One day at a time," David said. "It'll work out."

"I like your optimism. And don't worry about tonight. I'll stay out of your way."

David smiled as he pulled on his coat to head to work. "Thanks."

Emmett was lying on the sofa in his living room with Joyelle seated at his feet. Joyelle pulled a blanket up over him.

"Thanks for coming by," Emmett said with a smile.

"I heard you weren't feeling well, so I thought I'd check on you. And I wanted to see how things were coming downstairs, too. Max showed me around. The place looks fantastic."

"Thanks," Emmett replied. "It's pretty exciting."

"Yes. So you need to rest up and get better." She put her hand on his forehead. "You don't seem to have a fever."

"No," Emmett agreed. "Just nauseous mainly. I probably shouldn't have gone to the meeting earlier today, but I needed to be there."

"Ah, yes," Joyelle said. "The big meeting about the family business."

"It went well."

"I'm glad...for your sake. You don't need any more stress in your life right now."

"Enough about me. How are you doing, Joyelle?"

"You mean how am I doing with your brother?"

"I know this is really difficult for you."

"That's an understatement. Do you know what it feels like when you realize that everyone around you knows things about you that you yourself don't? That's how it felt when my memories returned. Like I was the butt of a big joke."

"Not at all," Emmett said. "We would never think of you that way. We love you too much."

"Apparently your brother doesn't. He loves Cole."

"I don't know about that -- only you two can discuss that. What I can say is that you are and always will be my sister. You know how much I love you; we have been through a lot together. That will never change."

Joyelle smiled and kissed Emmett on the forehead. "And I love you, too. You've always been very dear to me."

"Thank you," Emmett said.

"You need to get some rest," Joyelle stated. "I just wanted to check on you. I'll check on you later, okay?"

"Great. Thanks again."

Derek quietly entered the room. "Knock, knock."

"Hey," Emmett said, as Joyelle turned around to face her husband.

"Hi," Derek quietly said to her.

"I'll let myself out," Joyelle said to Emmett, getting up from the sofa. "Take care."

"Joyelle, wait," Derek said.

Joyelle ignored him and left the room, heading downstairs into the restaurant space.

"Dammit," Derek mumbled.

"I'm sorry about all this," Emmett said.

"Thanks. You feeling any better?"

"I'm resting; I'll be fine."

"Good. I just wanted to see if you need anything."

Emmett smiled. "I'm good, thanks. Everyone's been checking on me."

"You're a popular man."

"Derek, I didn't say anything about this to Joyelle or Justin, but what are you thinking hiring Cole to work for the company? Are you crazy? When Joyelle finds out--"

"She won't," Derek said. "And it's not what you think. You have to trust me on this one."

"I've heard that before."

"How about you concentrate on getting well and I deal with my marriage, okay?"

"Okay," Emmett replied. Derek adjusted the blanket on his brother before leaving so that Emmett could rest.

Making her way downstairs and into the club, Joyelle found Max seated at a table talking with Jensen.

"Take care, Max," Joyelle said.

"How's he doing?" Max asked.

"He's resting," Joyelle replied. "Derek's with him now. I'll check on him again later."

"Thank you," Max said as Joyelle walked out of the restaurant. Max turned his focus back to Jensen. "Thanks again for meeting with me."

"Not a problem," Jensen replied. "I'm sure you have lots of questions."

"Emmett has told me a lot about you already. He's very fond of you."

"He's been great," Jensen replied.

"He told me a bit about your past as well as your living and economic situation."

"That all sounds so formal," Jensen said, smiling. "Emmett and I discussed a lot of possibilities. I just want to make sure you're okay with them."

"He told me you discussed living with us for a while. And you working here in the restaurant as well."

"Both were his ideas, not mine. I don't want to intrude or be a burden."

"I'll be honest. I was skeptical about you. But I trust Emmett's judgment so I'm okay with you staying with us for a while. And working here as well, if you want to."

"That'd be great," Jensen replied. "I'd really appreciate it."

"No more stripping, though. As a worker here, that's not appropriate anymore. We are trying to build a business as well as a reputation within the community."

"I understand."

"Then welcome aboard," Max said, extending his hand to Jensen, who shook it. "Just don't let me down."

"I won't. I'm very grateful."

"We'll get you trained quickly. The fundraiser we're holding here is right around the corner."

"Sounds exciting," Jensen said, as Dustin Alexander entered the restaurant.

"Dustin," Max said. "Come on in. We were just finishing up."

"I'll get out of your way," Jensen said. "Thanks again."

"There's no rush," Dustin stated.

"Your timing is perfect," Max said. "We just finished. Come on and sit down."

"I'll see you both later," Jensen said, leaving the restaurant.

Dustin sat down at the table in the seat Jensen vacated. "Thanks for meeting with me."

"Not a problem," Max said. "I was glad to hear you are interested in working for us."

"Very much so," Dustin added. "This is going to be a fantastic new addition to the 'hood."

Max smiled. "We think so, too."

"And you and Emmett seem like a great couple. It'd be my pleasure to work for you."

"Thank you," Max said with a smile.

"I look forward to getting to know you better," Dustin said, his handsome eyes focused on Max.

While Max and Dustin continued their interview, Gino and Justin were lying in the bed in Gino's room at the Park Hyatt Hotel. Both naked, Gino had his arm around Justin, who was running his fingers over Gino's chest.

"You were amazing today," Justin said.

"Are you talking the meeting? Or just now in bed?" Gino asked, jokingly.

Justin smiled. "Both, actually."

"Well, thank you. I'm glad you're pleased."

"That deal would never have happened today, except for you. You have no idea how grateful I am for that."

"I want this feud to stop. All the fighting and nonsense."

"How did you convince them to agree?"

"I have my ways," Gino said with a smile. "I can be pretty persuasive when I want to be."

"I know you can."

"I want us to be together, Justin. Minimizing the fighting between the families should help us."

"But what if they come after you now? You have put yourself in a strange place with your own family because of me."

"I can handle them, as I did today. They won't be a problem."

Justin kissed Gino's chest. "I hope you're right. For your own sake."

"Don't worry so much," Gino said. "Let's just enjoy our afternoon together."

Justin rolled on top of Gino. "Mmm, I like the sound of that." Justin leaned forward and kissed Gino, who ran his hands up Justin's chest.

"I'm not giving up on us," Gino whispered. "Not until I hear you say, 'I do.'" Gino kissed Justin deeply.

While Gino and Justin made love again, Marco and Carlo were having wine in the lounge of the hotel overlooking Chicago's water tower and Jane Byrne Plaza.

They were seated near the window, watching pedestrians pass through the park several stories below them.

"I can't believe his behavior this afternoon, Father," Marco said. "He betrayed us."

"No, Marco," Carlo said. "He just reined us in."

"But he defied you."

"No," Carlo declared. "He reminded me of what kind of man he is. He wants peace for this family and is willing to do anything to get it."

"Even threaten us with prison."

Carlo looked from the window to Marco. "Would you have done anything different to get something you wanted?" Marco didn't reply. "He made me proud today. He stood up to us, which took more guts than standing up to them."

"But we lost what we wanted, Father. All because of him."

"No, we just delayed what we wanted. And not because of him, because of them." Carlo sipped his wine. "We got eight percent of Mancini Global. That's more than we had yesterday. It's a start. And we'll get out hands on more over time. Don't lose focus, Marco. They are the enemy, not your brother."

"Yes, Father," Marco agreed. "One by one, we'll bring them all down."

"In time."

"I intend to cut the head off the Mancini dragon," Marco said. "Derek goes down first."

"Now *that* sounds like a plan," Carlo said, raising his glass and touching it to Marco's. "To Derek Mancini. And his quick demise."

Carlo and Marco toasted while Max was meeting with Logan, Keith, and Michael at the restaurant. They were seated around a table at the center of the restaurant and a few workers were on the far side of the restaurant fixing some wiring in the ceiling.

"Is there any news about Jesse?" Max asked.

Michael shook his head. "I'm afraid not."

"Are you sure you're okay having this meeting now?" Keith asked.

"Absolutely," Max said. "We need to proceed and it's good to have other things to focus on."

"This whole fundraiser was Jesse's idea," Logan added. "We need to make it happen. It's what Jesse wanted."

"Fair enough," Michael said. "Then we are happy to help."

"Where's Emmett?" Keith asked.

"He's upstairs resting," Max explained. "He isn't feeling well."

"I'll go up and check on him before we leave," Keith said.

"I made a checklist of things to run through to make sure that we are all on the same page," Logan said. "And to bring Keith and Michael up to date. We really appreciate your help."

"Our pleasure," Michael added. "The police department is going to make a donation and several of my team will be attending with their spouses."

"Fantastic," Logan said. "We are just about booked, which is awesome." Logan looked down at this list. "The decorations are set. Although we are so close to St. Patrick's Day, we are sticking with the 'classic Hollywood' theme to go along with the restaurant's design." Logan looked at Max. "The place looks amazing, by the way. I can't believe you pulled it together so beautifully and so quickly."

"Thank you," Max said. "Ironically, it's Ben who kept the workers on schedule."

"And you've heard nothing from him?" Michael asked.

"Not a word since I fired him," Max said.

"We have worked some green into the color scheme of the decorations, just for a hint of the holiday," Logan said. "So that's all set." Logan pointed to the front of the club space. "The silent auction will be set up over there. Jesse took care of that and we have some pretty fantastic donations."

"And entertainment?" Keith asked.

"Quite a coup, actually," Max said with a smile.

"We have booked Whiskey and Cherries as well as Amy Armstrong."

"Love them," Keith said. "Great job."

"And...our surprise guest is Steve Grand."

"No way," Michael said. "He rocks."

"I know," Logan said. "When we reached out to him, he accepted right away. Such a nice guy. It's really exciting."

"Wow," Keith said. "You guys have left no stone unturned."

"It should be a memorable night."

"And the food?" Michael asked.

"My chef will have that taken care of," Max said.

"Then there's not much left for us to help with," Keith added.

Michael's phone rang loudly and he pulled it from his pocket. "Excuse me," he said to the others as he rose from his seat and walked a few steps away.

"Actually, I do have a short list of things we could use your help with," Logan said to Keith, handing him a sheet of paper. "They're small but they're important."

Michael returned to the table. "That was Jacqueline. She said she remembered something and wants to meet me at the station."

Logan stood up from his chair. "I'm going with you."

"Me, too," Max said.

Keith stood up from his chair. "You guys go ahead. I'll stay here and check in on Emmett."

"He'd like that," Max said.

"Let's go then," Michael said. Max and Logan followed Michael out of the restaurant. Keith watched them go. Then he pulled the brown bottle from his pocket and headed upstairs.

As the men hurried to the police station, Jesse unlocked and entered the bedroom where he was holding

366

Ben. When he opened the door, he saw that the room was in complete disarray. The bookshelf was toppled over, books and clothes were scattered everywhere, and a table was knocked over. Ben was nowhere to be seen.

Jesse stepped into the room cautiously and suddenly Ben jumped out at him from behind the door. His hands still partially taped together, Ben put his arms over Jesse's head and pulled back violently against his neck, choking him.

Gasping for breath, Jesse elbowed Ben and kicked his leg. The two continued to struggle, Ben trying to strangle Jesse and Jesse fighting to break free from Ben's grasp. Jesse reached behind him and grabbed Ben's shoulders. Then, leaning forward, Jesse flipped Ben over him. The tape around Ben's wrists gave way and Ben landed on his back on the floor.

Jesse jumped on top of him, pushing his knees into Ben's chest, and grabbed Ben's neck. Ben reached to his right and grabbed a lamp lying on the floor. He quickly raised it and hit Jesse in the side of the head, knocking him to the ground.

Ben stood up and kicked Jesse in the gut. Then he lifted Jesse off the floor and threw him onto the bed. Jesse struggled with Ben, trying to get free of his tight hold; however, Ben climbed on top of him, pinning him down.

"Now, doesn't this look familiar?" Ben said with a smile. "I'll be damned if I'm going to go to jail for something I didn't do."

"You bastard," Jesse said.

"When are you going to learn, boy? You can't beat me."

Jesse spit at Ben and Ben punched him in the face. "Aren't you bruised up badly enough from your father? Do you really want more?"

"Let go of me."

Ben reached down and pulled some neckties up from the floor. He used them to tie Jesse's hands to the headboard.

"These aren't ideal, but I didn't come prepared like you did," Ben said. "They'll hold you long enough."

"You can't keep me here."

"Besides, you're used to this position, aren't you, pussy boy?"

While Ben tied Jesse to the bed, Jacqueline waited for Michael in his office at the police station. When he entered, she stood up from the chair to greet him.

"Michael."

"I got here as quickly as I could. Logan and Max are with me. I asked them to wait in the lobby." Michael held up Ben's phone in the evidence bag. "And I have Ben's phone with me as you asked."

"Good."

"So what's up?"

"I wanted to share something. I'm not sure it'll help at this point but I thought I'd tell you anyway. One time when Ben and I were arguing, he told me that he was monitoring Jesse's whereabouts on his phone."

"Oh?"

"He pulled out his phone and pressed a button or app or something and a map appeared. He showed me a dot on the map and said the dot was Jesse. I didn't mention this sooner because Ben is smart. With his phone lost, I'm sure he has probably disabled it by now. He'd never allow for it to lead us right to him."

"Let me get my tech guy in here. Be right back."

Michael left his office and Jacqueline sat back down in the chair.

Ben remained seated on top of Jesse, his knees pinning his chest down. Jesse struggled to free his arms from the ties holding them to the headboard. Ben looked down at Jesse's bruised face and ran his fingers across it.

"Such a handsome face. I fell it in love with it...once. That seems so long ago now."

"You don't know what love is."

"To think your own father distorted it -- and caused these bruises and scrapes."

"I told you never to mention him to me."

"And yet your body is still as hot as ever," Ben said, ripping open Jesse's shirt. He ran his hands over Jesse's chest as Jesse began to breathe more nervously. He leaned forward and kissed Jesse's nipples, tickling them with his tongue. "If only there were time for that. Time for some fun. One last time."

"Get off of me," Jesse demanded, kicking his legs violently.

Ben grabbed another tie and wrapped it around Jesse's head, gagging his mouth. "I always tell your mother that you talk too much." Ben leaned back and held down Jesse's legs. "I think it's time to silence you once and for all."

Jesse tried to yell out but his voice was muted by the tie gagging him. Ben picked up yet another tie and held it at both ends. Then he wrapped each end around his hands until about a foot of it remained between his hands. He pulled it tightly.

"Such a shame," Ben said. "We could have been so happy together. But you wanted something better, someone better. I wasn't good enough." Jesse continued to struggle to get free. "I have a child coming now. He's doesn't need to know about my past with you. And your mother doesn't need to worry about you anymore."

Ben lowered the tie to Jesse's neck and began to push down tightly. Jesse struggled as Ben continued to press harder and harder.

Then the sound of sirens in the distance caught the attention of both Jesse and Ben. They looked at each other for a moment before Ben leapt off the bed and fled from the room. Jesse breathed deeply and struggled to get free.

Moments later, Michael rushed into the room, his gun in his hand. He ran over to the bed and untied Jesse, first his mouth and then his hands.

"Are you okay?"

"Ben just ran out!"

"My men are outside. If he's still here, they'll get him."

Jesse sat up, rubbing his wrists and neck. "He was going to kill me."

371

"Well, you're safe now. We can talk about all that later."

Another police officer brought Jacqueline and Logan into the room. "Jesse!" Jacqueline rushed over, sat down on the bed, and hugged her son. She pulled back a moment, ran her hands over his bruised face, and then embraced him once more.

"I love you, Mom," Jesse said. "I'm so sorry for everything."

"Shh," Jacqueline said, holding her son tightly.

Logan approached the bed and Jesse looked up at him. Jacqueline finally let go of her son. Logan's eye filled with tears as he leaned forward and hugged Jesse.

Michael stepped back and walked toward the door as Max entered the doorway.

Seeing Max, Jesse began to yell. "You get out of here! Get the hell out of here!"

Michael looked at Max, then Jesse, then back at Max.

"Get out!" Jesse screamed again.

"Come on," Michael said, gently putting his arm around Max and escorting him from the room.

"Get him out of here!"

Later that evening, Marco and Rachel were dining in Chicago's famed Pump Room restaurant. Their waiter refilled their wine glasses and then stepped away from the table as they continued to enjoy their meal.

"So you now own eight percent of Mancini Global, is that correct?" Rachel asked, taking a sip of her wine.

Marco nodded. "No thanks to my brother, Gino."

"What?"

"Never mind about that," Marco said. "You are correct; we own eight percent of Mancini Global."

"Which means that each of the remaining four Mancini brothers owns twenty three percent."

"Clearly, you got straight A's in math," Marco said.

Rachel smiled. "Well, what if I told you that I am about to get control of one of those twenty-three percent shares?"

Marco put down his fork. "What are you talking about?"

"I am about to take twenty-three percent ownership of that company."

"How?"

"Never mind about that," Rachel said, repeating Marco's words from earlier. "The fact of the matter is that

I am. And that twenty-three percent combined with your eight would give you a majority vote at the company."

"It would. Thirty one percent to each of their twenty three."

"Clearly, you got straight A's in math, too," Rachel said, with a smile.

"Just what are you up to?"

Rachel took another sip of her wine. "Me? Nothing. Just putting control within your reach."

"And what do you want in return?"

"What's makes you think I want anything in return?"

Marco laughed. "I know you, Rachel. A missionary, you're not."

"Well, maybe I do want one little thing in return," Rachel said, smiling.

"What is that?"

"To be your wife. I want you to marry me."

Before Marco could reply, his cell phone began to ring. He looked to see who was calling and then stood up from the table. "Excuse me, I have to take this." Marco walked into the lobby of the restaurant and answered the call. "Mr. Strauss. How are you?"

"Good, thank you," the man on the other end replied.

"I gathered the information that you requested and emailed it over to you just now."

"Excellent. Thank you. And the one painting in particular that I asked about. Were you able to locate who purchased that one?"

"We keep very good records here. We had the information on all the artwork in the collection. The painting you asked about, called 'The Nursemaid,' was sold to someone named Todd Smith in Chicago."

"Thank you so much, Mr. Strauss. You have no idea how helpful you've been." Marco ended the call and put his phone into his pocket. "One step closer, Mother. One step closer."

Still not feeling well, Emmett was sound asleep in his bed. The bedroom was dark and quiet until Jensen discreetly opened the door. The light from the hallway entered the bedroom, dimly lighting it.

Jensen stood silently watching Emmett sleep. Then he quietly approached the bed. He carefully pulled the covers up over Emmett as he slept. Fluffing the pillow a bit, Jensen made sure that Emmett looked comfortable.

Then he knelt down next to the bed. He stared closely at Emmett's face, listening to him breathe. He gently ran his fingers through Emmett's hair and leaned forward to kiss Emmett on the lips. When the brief kiss ended, Jensen stood up and left the room, closing the bedroom door behind him.

While Emmett slept, his brother Derek was in bed with Cole in the corporate condo of Derek's company. The room was dimly lit and the lights of the Chicago skyline were visible from the window near the bed. Moonlight from outside the window highlighted the contours of Derek's and Cole's naked bodies as they made love.

Lying on top of Derek, Cole kissed him, raising his hands above his head. Cole's tongue explored Derek's neck and shoulders as well as his armpits, while Derek's hard cock pressed against Cole's abs. Derek's legs massaged Cole's as Cole buried his face in his lover's chest. He looked up at Derek's face as he bit his nipples and tugged on them. Derek lowered his arms around Cole, his fingers massaging Cole's back. As Cole's hips spread Derek's legs apart, Derek slapped Cole's athletic ass.

Cole pulled Derek's legs up and pressed the bulging head of his dick against Derek's hole. He looked into

Derek's eyes and pushed harder, trying to get inside of him. Derek clenched his teeth and dug his fingers into Cole's back as Cole's penis hit against him.

"Please, Derek," Cole whispered, adjusting his legs and pushing even harder against Derek.

Without responding verbally, Derek flipped over on top of Cole, pulling his legs over his shoulders. He kissed Cole deeply and pressed his erect penis into Cole's ass. Cole ran his fingers down Derek's shoulders and along his arms. The ring on Cole's chain sparkled in the moonlight against his sweaty chest.

Cole wrapped his legs around Derek, who pushed deeper into Cole. Holding the back of Derek's neck, Cole kissed him deeply, his tongue working its way deep into Derek's mouth. Derek's thrusts became more violent and Cole gripped Derek's back for support.

Finally, Derek let out a groan and filled Cole. Then Derek reached over to the dresser and grabbed the two glasses of champagne that were standing on it. He handed one to Cole, who immediately drank from it.

"Lots to celebrate," Derek said. "My successful meeting today. And you officially being on the Mancini payroll."

"And us," Cole added.

"Of course," Derek said, kissing Cole.

"Why did you want to meet here in the corporate condo?" Cole asked. "It's nice but we have never met here before."

"Just thought it would be someplace different," Derek replied, sitting on the end of the bed and pulling on his clothes.

"It's nice," Cole said, looking around the condo.

"You'll be able to stay here if you want whenever you return to town," Derek said, standing up and buttoning his shirt.

"What do you mean, when I return to town?"

Derek walked over to the window and looked out onto the city. "Well, you'll be moving to California now."

Still naked, Cole got up out of bed. "California? What are you talking about?"

"I told you that our public relations department is currently located in California and that you'd be working with the current department head until he retires."

"Yes, but you didn't say anything about California."

"I told you that moving the headquarters here would be a long process. Being done over time, department by department."

"Yes."

"Well, it turns out that public relations department will be one of the last to move. Hopefully within two years."

"Two years?" Cole joined Derek at the window. "I can't move there for two years. I just moved here."

"It's only temporary."

"Temporary? And what about us? We can finally be together."

"I told you it was complicated."

"Complicated? This is bullshit." Cole paused a moment. "Wait a minute. You did this on purpose. You knew about California all along. Even before you made me quit my job."

"Don't be ridiculous. It's an incredible job opportunity for you."

"You're trying to get rid of me, so you don't have to deal with us being together." Cole watched Derek turn and walk toward the condo door. "That's the truth, isn't it?"

"We can talk about this later. I have to go."

"You can't do this me," Cole said, walking over to Derek and grabbing him. "I love you. You said you loved me."

"I have to go," Derek said, shaking himself loose of Cole's grip and leaving the condo.

"You can't do this!" Cole walked back toward the window. Then he quickly turned toward the door. "You can't do this! I hate you!" Cole ripped the chain from his neck and threw it at the door. Complete satisfaction is often elusive.

Episode #30

The moon hung high over the city of Chicago, casting its warm glow on everything beneath it. In anticipation of St. Patrick's Day, Chicago buildings and landmarks bathed in green light as Chicagoans ventured outside to take advantage of the warm March evening.

Jesse Morgan and Cole O'Brien sat out on their back deck enjoying the night air and drinking beer. Jesse had his foot up on the deck railing and Cole was looking toward the downtown skyline.

"It's good to have you home, bro," Cole said.

"Cheers to that."

"You had everyone pretty worried."

"I'm sorry."

"You and I have been through a lot over the years together," Cole said. "And we've never kept secrets from each other. We both know everything about each other."

"What do you want to know, Cole?"

"I know what you told Michael about what happened. But I think there's more to it. I don't think you told him everything."

Jesse smiled. "You know me well."

"You know you can trust me."

"Of course," Jesse said, sipping his beer. "Ben didn't kidnap me. I kidnapped him."

"What?"

"I needed a way to get rid of Ben once and for all. Even if my mother and I never spoke again, I wanted her rid of him. So I came up with an idea to get him arrested for kidnapping me. I wasn't entirely prepared to do it just yet, but when he came to my hospital room the other day, I realized it was now or never."

"What did you do?"

"Remember when I told you that my mom had texted me about Ben monitoring me?" Cole nodded. "I checked his phone a while ago and, sure enough, he was. So I used the same feature to track his phone as well." Jesse paused to drink his beer. "When Ben came into my hospital room, I injected him with the sedative that the doctor was giving me through my I.V. Once he was out, I planted his phone in the hospital bathroom so it would be found there. I had to knock Tyler out to make it look like I had been kidnapped."

"And then you wheeled him out of the hospital using Tyler's card key just as Ben would have if he had kidnapped you."

"Exactly. I took him to the apartment he had just rented for him and my mom. I was able to tell when they found his phone in the hospital bathroom, so I knew it would only be a matter of time until they used that phone to track me down. Then he'd be locked up in prison where he belongs."

"But?"

"But he overpowered me at one point and tied me up. He was going to kill me. If Michael hadn't arrived when he did--"

"Well, thankfully, you're okay."

"But Ben got away."

"Do you think now maybe you'll stop with these crazy ideas? You're two for two -- and not in good way."

"I was desperate," Jesse said. "I needed to get Ben out of the picture. At least now there's a warrant out for his arrest. Once they find him, he'll be locked up."

"For a crime he didn't commit."

"You and I are the only two who know that," Jesse reminded Cole

"And him."

"Yes, which will make it even more sweet," Jesse said, smiling. "He'll know that in the end I finally brought him down."

"It'll just be good to know that he's out of our lives, so you can focus on the people who are in your life. Like Logan and Jacqueline. And Max."

"Aw, Cole," Jesse said. "Why do you have to bring him up?"

"He's your father, Jesse. You've got to acknowledge that sooner or later...for your own sake."

"Fuck that."

"I don't mean that you two have to be buddies or have any kind of relationship. But you yourself have to accept it as fact. It's like you're in denial."

"I really don't want to talk about this right now."

Cole reached over and put his hand on Jesse's arm. "Jesse, you're my brother. I can help you through this. So when you are ready to talk more, I'm here."

"Thank you," Jesse replied. "And how are things with Derek?"

"We're done."

"Just like that? All these months and months of saying you're going to be together and now you say you're done?"

"He's fucking with me, with my head. Just like you said he would. He wants Joyelle, not me. And now he's screwed up my professional life, too. I hate him."

Jesse laughed. "You don't hate him. You're upset with him, but you still love him. I know you, Cole."

"No," Cole insisted. "This time I'm serious. I am moving on and doing what's best for me from now on. I wish I never met Derek Mancini."

"Damn, I almost believe you."

"Believe me, because I'm completely serious. I'm not going to let him ruin my life anymore. He's done enough damage. I don't care what happens to him now."

"Does this mean a certain David has a chance?"

Cole smiled. "He certainly does. And when are you going to see Logan next?"

"We're going to hang out tomorrow."

"That's great. I hope you can get back on track. So much has happened."

"I'm optimistic."

"We both could use a little happiness and stability in our lives now."

"Agreed. All we need to do is get the toxic men out of our lives for good," Jesse said.

"Yes, permanently," Cole added, drinking his beer.

Down the block from Jesse and Cole's apartment, Tyler Bennett and David Young were leaving the Lakeview

Athletic Club after their workout. As they exited the gym, they walked north on Broadway passing many of Boystown's restaurants and businesses.

"I'm excited for you," Tyler said to David.

"I am, too," David said. "Cole really seemed upbeat when he called me. Like something had really changed."

"Maybe he's finally over the asshole?"

"Derek? I'm not sure. But I guess I'll find out tonight."

"He's better off with you," Tyler said.

"Well, thank you," David said, smiling. "And what's new with Joyelle?"

"Not sure. I know she met with her attorney about divorcing Derek, so that's a step in the right direction. Like I said, I don't want to pressure her."

"But you're still spending time together, right?"

"Absolutely," Tyler said. "I just wish we could get Derek out of the picture for good."

"Believe me -- no one would like Derek out of the picture more than me. But it sounds like maybe Joyelle is trying to do that with the divorce."

"Divorces take time. And Derek will stall it, I'm sure."

"Well, not much else we can do but wait and see."

"Maybe not," Tyler said. "You never know, though."

Tyler and David continued on their walk home, enjoying the unseasonably warm Chicago weather.

As Tyler and David walked, they passed right by The Boys and the Booze. Inside, Max Taylor was meeting with Dustin Alexander. Jensen Stone and several other staff members were seated in the club area in a training session reviewing the menu and wine list.

"Thanks again for this amazing opportunity," Dustin told Max. "I never imagined you'd be making me a manager."

"You have the experience and know-how. I'm glad to have found you," Max said. "You know how rough the opening of a restaurant and club can be. We need the best people we can find. And with you in charge of our team, I know they are in good hands."

"Thank you," Dustin repeated. "Today's training session seems to be going well. These guys you've hired are sharp. And the extra staff we're bringing in just for the fundraiser seem great, too."

"I tried to get people with prior experience; it makes a difference," Max said.

"Sure does." Dustin then added, "It's such a pleasure to be working with you."

Emmett Mancini emerged from the back stairwell and walked over to Max and Dustin. He looked really pale and disheveled, his hair pasted to his sweaty forehead.

"Hey, guys," Emmett said.

"Hey, babe, Max replied. "What are you doing out of bed? You need to rest."

"Stop telling me what to do," Emmett replied nastily. "I can take care of myself."

Jensen looked over from the table where he was seated.

"Whoa," Max said. "I just want to make sure you're okay."

"Stop trying to control everything and everyone," Emmett added.

"You do look like you could use some rest," Dustin said softly to Emmett.

"I don't need advice from the help, either," Emmett declared as he turned around and went back upstairs.

"I'm sorry about that," Max said. "That's not like him at all."

"He's just not feeling well," Dustin replied. "I'm sure that's all it is."

Jensen discreetly got up from the table and followed Emmett up the stairs. When he reached the top, he found Emmett in the kitchen.

"Hey," Jensen said as he watched Emmett make himself a protein shake.

"What do you want?"

"Nothing," Jensen replied. "Just seeing if you need anything."

"What I need is for people to get off my back."

"Okay, okay," Jensen said, raising his hands in the air as if he were surrendering. "I'll go back down." Jensen left the kitchen. Emmett watched him leave and then threw the tub of protein powder onto the floor, sending powder high into the air.

At the Park Hyatt Hotel just off Michigan Avenue, Carlo, Marco, and Gino Ciancio were having breakfast near a window overlooking the crowded street below.

"We received an invitation from the Mancinis this morning," Gino said, after taking a sip of his champagne.

"What kind of invitation?" Carlo asked.

"They are holding a fundraiser for cancer research and have invited us to join them as their guests. In addition, they have offered to donate a portion of the proceeds to Mother's cancer foundation. Isn't that great?"

"An olive branch or a white flag," Marco said.

"Maybe," Gino agreed. "But it's a nice gesture."

"I would agree with that," Carlo said. "It doesn't change anything as far as I'm concerned but your mother's foundation does amazing work. You two should attend. I plan to return home this afternoon."

"Very well, Father," Marco said. "I'll go."

"As will I," Gino added.

"Always good to keep your enemies close," Marco stated; Gino rolled his eyes.

"Excuse me a moment," Carlo said, getting up from the table and walking to the restroom.

"Now that he's gone," Gino began, "have you heard anything back from Strauss yet about the collection auction?"

"Yes," Marco said. "He called me to tell me that he needed a bit more time, but that he's working on it. There were so many pieces in the collection that it's taking longer to put together the report than he thought."

"Okay. But as soon as you get the report, I want to see it."

"Of course," Marco replied. "You'll be the first to know."

"Good," Gino said. "By the way, there's a press conference this afternoon. The Chicago mayor is formally announcing the move of Mancini Global's headquarters here to Chicago."

"I'm sure Derek is very proud," Marco said. "He should enjoy his moment in the spotlight. It won't last."

"You're impossible," Gino said, getting up from the table. "Tell Father I'll see him before he leaves." Gino walked away from the table.

Marco watched his brother leave and then pulled out his cell phone. He dialed a number and spoke, "It's me. I have a job for you."

The warm Spring breeze blew softly through Maggie Daley Park as Logan Pryce and Jesse slowly followed the park's winding path.

"Thanks for meeting me," Jesse said.

"Of course," Logan replied. "I thought this might be a nice place for us to start over together."

"Is that what we're doing? Starting over?"

"I think that's what we're here to decide," Logan said as a group of young children rushed past them.

"Let me start," Jesse offered. "I want to apologize for everything, especially New Year's Eve. I'm sure that must've hurt you very badly -- and Mom, too."

"It did," Logan admitted. "But I didn't handle it well, either. I went back to drinking and tried to shut you out of my life."

"Understandably. I'm sure I would have done something similar. Catching your boyfriend in bed with his mother's husband would drive anyone to drink."

Logan laughed. "It was horrible. But I know why you did it."

"I couldn't think of any other way to show my mother how bad Ben is. But, looking back, there were certainly other options. Cole tried to warn me about it all along, but I wouldn't listen."

"You do have a thick skull sometimes," Logan stated.

Jesse stopped walking and turned Logan to face him. "But I do love you. I still do. Very much."

"I love you, too, Jesse."

"Thank you for saying that. I appreciate your forgiveness."

"All is forgiven. When that maniac took you away, I realized that I hadn't handled this well at all. But that's in the past now. We need to focus on moving forward."

"I was hoping you'd say that," Jesse said, reaching into his pocket. He pulled out the ring that he had once given to Logan. "I'd like you to wear this again."

Logan looked at the ring. "I can't accept that. Not just yet."

"Oh," Jesse mumbled, disappointed.

"Not because I don't want to," Logan explained. "But because I think we need to talk more about us before we get to that place again. Even with New Year's Eve behind us, there are some issues we need to address."

"You're talking about Max."

"Among other things. Now that we know he's your father, we need to talk that through," Logan said. "And you need to accept it, too."

"Just because I don't like it, doesn't mean I haven't accepted it."

"You're angry about it."

"Wouldn't you be? The man tried to kill me. Look at my face. These bruises are constant reminders of it."

"The bruises will heal; they already are. Now you and Max need to heal, too."

393

"That's not going to happen," Jesse declared. "We are never going to get along. But that doesn't mean you and I can't be happy and build our relationship back up."

"We'll talk about this more; I promise," Logan said. "Now I have an appointment with a client and you should get back to the office."

Jesse smiled. "You're right."

"I will accept the ring back from you one day, Jesse," Logan added. "Just not today."

"Deal," Jesse said as he hugged Logan.

"I'll see you soon," Logan said and then he walked away down the path.

"Damn you, Max," Jesse mumbled.

Jesse left the park and walked north toward to the Boystown neighborhood, in the direction of St. Joseph Hospital where Joyelle Mancini was seated at a small table alone in the tiny break room on her floor of the medical center. She quietly ate some yogurt as she watched Derek's press conference on the small television suspended from the ceiling.

The press conference was being televised from in front of the skyscraper that was about to become the new Mancini Global headquarters. Derek was standing to the right of mayor of Chicago, who was celebrating the move of the corporation to Chicago. Justin stood to the mayor's left. After a moment, the mayor turned the podium over to Derek, who also shared upbeat comments about the economic benefits the city would receive from the Mancini Global move.

After listening to Derek speak a few moments, Joyelle began to cry and threw her yogurt container at the television. The container hit the T.V. and then fell to the ground, just as Tyler entered the break room.

"Hey," Tyler said, seeing Joyelle crying and walking over to hug her. "What's the matter?"

"I hate him," Joyelle cried. "I hate him so much."

Tyler looked up and saw Derek on the television. "Oh, Joyelle. I'm sorry."

"He ruined my life."

"No," Tyler said, still holding her. "You have a good life and now you have the chance to make it even better without him." Tyler pulled over another chair and sat beside Joyelle. "Everything is going to be okay."

"Thank you," Joyelle said, wiping her eyes. "I'm sorry. I didn't mean to get this upset."

"It's okay. You don't have to every hide your emotions from me."

"You're so good to me."

Tyler smiled. "It's my pleasure. Tell you what. Let's finish this shift and then I'm going to make you dinner.

"Oh, I don't know…"

"I'm not taking 'no' for an answer. I have a ton of food at home. It'll be fun."

Joyelle smiled. "Okay, okay."

Tyler turned off the television and picked up the yogurt container. "Great. We could both use a little fun in our lives." Tyler helped Joyelle up from her chair and the two nurses left the break room to return to work.

As Tyler and Joyelle tended to their patients, Michael Martinez was meeting with Jacqueline Morgan in the lobby of her hotel.

"Is there any news?" Jacqueline asked.

"Nothing, yet," Michael said. "I'm sorry. We will find him."

"Ben's a smart and dangerous man. I'm worried about my son's safety."

"We're concerned about your safety as well," Michael said. "I've spoken to hotel security here and they are working closely with us to ensure your safety as long as you stay here in town."

"I'm carrying Ben's child. As long as that's the case, I know I'll be okay. But I'm concerned about Jesse. Can you provide him with some extra security as well?"

"We already have extra patrols on his street and around his office as well. We are doing all we can."

"Meaning no disrespect, I'm not sure that's enough. Ben should have been found by now."

"I understand your frustration," Michael said. "I feel it, too. But we will find him. It's only a matter of time."

"Thank you."

"How long do you plan to stay in town?"

"Just until the fundraiser. Then I'm going home to meet with my attorney about a divorce."

"Okay. We'll be in touch with your local police as well so that they can keep an eye out once you return home."

"I appreciate that."

"Don't worry. We'll get him."

Jacqueline stood up from her seat. "Thanks again."

"You're welcome," Michael said, standing up and shaking her hand.

As Michael left the hotel to return to his office, Derek was returning to his own office after the press conference. Approaching the entrance to his office building, Derek was stopped on the steps by Jesse who called out to him.

"Derek, wait," Jesse said, walking up the steps behind Derek.

"Jesse," Derek replied. "It's good to see you. I'm glad you're okay after what Ben did to you."

"Thank you, but this isn't a friendly visit. I need to talk to you about Cole."

"Cole?" Derek asked, looking around to see if anyone else was nearby on the steps. "What about him?"

"He's my best friend and I don't like you fucking him over."

"What are you talking about?"

"Cole told me what happened. Making him quit his job to work for you and then trying to send him away? Are you out of your fucking mind?"

"I don't have to discuss this with you. It's between Cole and me."

Jesse persisted. "You know, ever since you two met in Boston, I have kept my comments to myself as you have manipulated my best friend over and over again. God knows why, but he loves you. And this is how you treat him? What the fuck is wrong with you?"

"It's really none of your damn business," Derek replied, turning to enter the building.

Jesse grabbed his arm and pulled him back violently. "The hell it isn't."

"Watch it, Jesse. You're making a scene."

"Who cares? This is my best friend we're talking about. He deserves the best."

"Look, I--"

"I'm warning you," Jesse said, pointing into Derek's face. "If you don't make things right with Cole, you'll answer to me. And if you don't think I follow through on threats...well, just talk to Ben Donovan!"

Later that evening, four dinner experiences were occurring simultaneously. The first was at Michael's home where Keith and he were hosting a small dinner party to formally offer support to the Mancini brothers for the loss of their father.

Michael and Keith sat at the ends of the beautifully decorated table and Keith, Max, Logan, Justin, Derek, and Emmett sat along the sides.

"Can we get your autograph, now that you're a TV star?" Max asked Derek.

Derek laughed. "I don't deal well with paparazzi."

"Well, you looked and sounded great today during the press conference. Well done," Michael said.

"Thank you," Derek said. "And thanks again for hosting us all tonight. This has been great."

"It's been a while since we all got together to just hang out," Keith said. "And we wanted to formally offer our condolences for the loss of your father since we couldn't be at the service in California."

"Why do you need to offer condolences?" Emmett asked. "Hell, I couldn't stand the old man and skipped his funeral, too." Emmett's comments got the attention of everyone. "He can rot in his grave for all I care."

Justin put his arm around Emmett. "It's okay."

Emmett shrugged Justin's arm off him. "I'm good."

"Well, regardless of each of your relationships with your father, we wanted to let you know that we are here for you and we love you," Logan said.

"We appreciate that," Derek said.

Keith stood up from the table and grabbed Emmett's glass. "Let me get you some more wine."

"Why don't you just bring the bottle to the table?" Michael asked. "It's easier."

"Sure," Keith said, somewhat ignoring Michael's suggestion and heading to the kitchen with Emmett's glass.

"So what was it like the meet the mayor?"

"Pretty cool, actually," Justin said.

"It was a landmark moment for the company," Derek added.

"And talk about landmark moments," Keith said, returning from the kitchen with a glass of wine in one hand and the bottle in the other. "How excited are you guys to debut your restaurant and club at the fundraiser?" Max reached for the glass of wine which Keith put in front of Emmett. "No, no. This glass is for Emmett. Here's the bottle for anyone else who wants more."

"I'll have some," Logan said, taking the bottle from Keith.

"We are pretty excited," Max said. "We can't believe this is finally happening. Emmett and I have been talking about opening a restaurant for -- well, forever."

"And Jesse has done a fantastic job preparing for the fundraiser. Along with Keith and Michael, of course."

"Our pleasure," Michael said. "And I thought it was really nice of you to include the Ciancios. Nice gesture."

"We're trying," Derek stated.

"Is Cole's mother coming?" Keith asked. Michael immediately shot him a glare.

"I thought we were leaving certain topics at the door tonight," Derek said.

"I'm sorry," Keith mumbled.

"Don't blame Keith," Emmett said loudly. "There are so many damn topics to avoid that it's like a field of landmines in here tonight. Jesse. Cole. It's ridiculous."

Max looked at his watch. "You know, it is getting late. We should probably be going."

"Fine with me," Emmett added as he got up from the table. "I'll get our coats." Emmett went into the bedroom to get their coats.

Derek looked at Max. "What is going on with him? He's been sick for days and now he's acting like this? He needs to see a doctor."

"I agree," Max said.

Keith interrupted them. "A doctor? I'm sure he just needs to get some rest. Something's going around. A lot of people in my office have been out sick, too."

"I'm sure they're not behaving like that, though," Justin declared. "Something is definitely wrong with my brother."

"Let's go," Emmett said, returning with the coats.

"I'll have everything checked out," Max assured Justin and Derek.

"Thank you," Derek replied.

Max and Emmett said goodbye to everyone and headed out into the warm Spring evening.

As the first dinner wrapped up, Joyelle and Tyler had finished eating their dinner and were seated on the sofa in Tyler's living room. Tyler poured Joyelle another glass of wine as she curled up on the couch beneath a blanket.

"Tonight has been amazing," Joyelle said. "So fun and relaxing. Just what I needed."

Tyler smiled. "I'm glad. I've had fun, too."

"I'd forgotten what it's like to relax and de-stress. Everything has been so crazy lately."

"I know," Tyler said. "Things will get better; I promise."

"They already are," Joyelle said.

"How'd things go with the lawyer earlier?"

"They went," Joyelle said. "The process has begun; that's what matters."

"You know I'm here for you throughout. Regardless of what develops between us."

"I know – and thank you."

Tyler hesitated a moment. "I know this may be a bit forward, but I'm wondering if you'd like to go to the fundraiser with me."

"That's not forward; that's wonderful," Joyelle replied. "Of course, I'd like to go with you. I was planning on going anyway, but with you would be even better."

"Derek will be there. And Cole, too. It may be awkward."

"It's going to be awkward regardless," Joyelle admitted. "I'd like having you there with me."

Tyler learned forward and kissed Joyelle softly. He pulled away slightly to see Joyelle's wide smile and then kissed her again. He carefully removed the wine glass from her grip and placed it onto the coffee table. Then he shifted his position, crawling on top of Joyelle and kissing her deeply. She ran her fingers up his back and pulled him closer to her.

While Joyelle and Tyler continued to kiss, Cole and David shared a kiss as well. Standing in Cole's kitchen, the two men kissed and then returned to cleaning the kitchen after their dinner. When the last of the dishes was in the dishwasher, Cole pulled two beers from the fridge and handed one to David.

"Thanks for helping with that," Cole said. "But I didn't invite you over here to clean my house."

David laughed. "It's not a problem. You made dinner, so helping to clean up was the least I could do. Everything was great, by the way."

"Thanks," Cole said, leading David back into the living room. They sat down on the sofa next to one another. "And I also want to thank you for being so patient with me."

"Patient?"

"Regarding Derek and everything. You knew I'd come around eventually. So thank you for not forcing things."

"Are you two really over?"

"We are," Cole said, sipping from his beer. "He made that very clear the last time we spoke."

"But that doesn't mean you're over him."

"I'm tired of being used. Look," Cole said unbuttoning his shirt and opening it to reveal his chest to David. "No more necklace or ring."

David leaned forward and put his hand on Cole's chest. "Mmm, I see that. And I see something else I like, too." David kissed Cole's chest. Then he kissed Cole on the mouth. The kiss grew more and more passionate as they embraced each other.

His hand behind David's head, Cole pulled David even closer to him. David then kissed Cole's neck and shoulders as his hands took Cole's shirt almost all the way off. Cole ran his hands down David's back to his butt. Cole grabbed David's firm ass while David continued to kiss him.

After a while, David sat up to catch his breath. "I should probably go before things get too hot to handle."

"Don't go," Cole said, kissing David again.

"I don't want to," David explained. "But I should. We'll have our moment, I promise."

"I look forward to it," Cole replied as David got up from the couch and re-buttoned his shirt.

"I really had a nice time. I'm wondering...would you like to go to the fundraiser with me?"

Cole smiled. "I'd love to."

"Are you sure it won't be uncomfortable for you?"

"Not at all. I'd love to spend the time with you."

"Then it's a date," David said as kissed Cole again. "See you then."

"Can't wait," Cole added.

Overlooking Millennium Park from their table in the restaurant in Jacqueline's hotel, Jesse was having dinner with his mother. Neither could remember the last time they had shared a meal alone together.

"Thank you for having dinner with me," Jacqueline said, adjusting the silverware on the table on front of here.

"Thank you for inviting me. It's good that we are sitting down to talk."

"I agree," she replied. "I want to apologize to you for ignoring all your attempts to reach out to me after New Year's Eve. I realize now that it was unfair of me."

"All I was trying to do was protect you. I'm responsible for bringing Ben into your life and I wanted to get him out of it."

"I know that now."

Jesse smiled. "There were probably a million better ways to do it, though. I caused you and Logan a great deal of heartache and you two are the last two people I wanted to hurt."

"We both know that," Jacqueline said. "And I'm glad you two spent some time together earlier today. He's a good man and he cares a great deal for you."

"We had a great talk earlier. I think we're going to be okay."

"I'm glad," Jacqueline said as she took a sip of her wine.

"So let's talk about the elephant in the room then," Jesse said cautiously. "Is Max really my father?"

Jacqueline nodded. "He is."

"How could you keep that from me? And how could you ever have slept with that man to begin with?"

"We were both much younger, Jesse. And we thought we were in love." Jesse rolled his eyes. "We did. But we broke up when we realized that Max was dealing with his own identity issues. By the time I found out I was pregnant, he was happily out of the closet. I didn't want to ruin his life."

"So you decided to ruin mine instead."

"No, of course not. I just made up my mind to raise you alone. And I think I did a good job."

"You denied me my father. And lied about it for my entire life. How is that a 'good job'?"

"I'm sorry."

"Too little, too late for that. While all my other friends were playing ball and camping with their fathers, I was wondering who mine was and why he didn't want me. And you refused to ever engage in a conversation about him."

"I did what I thought was best for us."

"Sounds like you did what you thought was best for Max." Jesse sipped his vodka. "And what's worse – just look at us now! We can't stand each other. He's just as disgusted by this revelation as I am."

"I'm hoping you two will be able to work things out."

"You'd have better luck bringing peace to the Middle East. It's not going to happen."

"You have to work at it."

"The way you worked to forgive me for what happened on New Year's Eve?"

"I have completely forgiven you."

Jesse sighed. "Now the question is….will I ever be able to forgive you?"

While so many other people were preoccupied with their dinner events, Ben Donovan drove a pickup truck down the alley behind Max's restaurant and stopped just past the back service entrance. His hair dyed blond and wearing a fake beard and glasses, Ben was disguised so that no one would recognize him.

He hopped out of the truck and unscrewed the light bulbs in the fixtures along the back of the restaurant. In the darkness of the alley, Ben unloaded several large kegs from the back of the truck. Then he opened the service entrance to the restaurant and carried the kegs inside one by one.

After carrying all the barrels into the club's basement, Ben connected them to one another with some tubing. He examined the pipes running across the ceiling above him, following several of them along the ceiling and walls. Determining which pipes connected to the restaurant's fire sprinkler system, he pulled a wrench from his pocket and opened one of the valves. He connected the first of the kegs to the pipe system, making sure the connection was secure.

Once finished with his work, Ben left the basement, returned to his truck, and drove away from the restaurant, leaving no trace of his ever having been there.

Saturday morning brought with it a spectacular sunrise. Chicagoans from every corner of the city flocked to the river walk for the annual St. Patrick's Day tradition of dying the river green. Thousands of people lined the bridges over the river as well as Wacker Drive and the sidewalks below it to watch as small boats dumped dye into the water. The river water quickly turned from its normal color to the same bright green as the shirts, scarves, and hats that the onlookers we wearing.

Standing along the Wacker Drive curve, David and Cole smiled as they witnessed the event together. Michael and Keith watched the festivities from the foot of the Michigan Avenue bridge and, further east along the river, Joyelle and Tyler also happily observed the changing of the water's hue.

"This is so cool," Tyler said. "Thanks for suggesting it."

"I thought you'd like it. It's truly a Chicago tradition. They say we're the greenest city in the world on this day each year."

Tyler laughed. "I believe it. Check out all these people."

"Three quarters of them will be drunk by noon," Joyelle added.

411

"I'm sure."

"Sorry to cut it a bit short, but I have to get to my doctor's appointment."

"Come on. I'll drop you off and then pick up my tux for tonight."

"Great, thanks," Joyelle said as the two made their way out of the crowd.

As the day progressed, the city continued to celebrate St. Patrick's Day with house parties, bar crawls, and other ways of enjoying the day. Those attending the fundraiser, however, busily prepared for the special event.

In their hotel room, Marco and Rachel were getting dressed. Rachel was in the bathroom with the door closed and Marco, half dressed, was on his cell phone.

"That's right. They will both be attending the fundraiser tonight so the apartment will be empty. Get in there and get that painting. Call me when it's done." Marco ended the call and continued dressing.

When Rachel emerged from the bathroom, she looked stunning in her gown. Shimmering in the light, the dress immediately caught Marco's eye.

"Wow," he said. "You look amazing."

"Well, thank you," she replied with a smile. "Amazing enough to finally accept my marriage proposal?"

"Is that what that was? I thought you were just thinking out loud that night at the restaurant."

"Not at all. I have something that you want. And you know what you need to do to get it."

"How about we wait until you actually have what I want in your possession? Then we can talk about marriage and whatever else." Marco kissed Rachel and then went into the bathroom, closing the door behind him.

Rachel's cell phone rang and she walked across the room to get it from her purse. "Hello."

"It's me," Keith said.

"What do you want?"

"I can't do this anymore. I won't do this anymore."

"You don't really have a choice."

Keith sounded anxious. "Have you seen what Emmett looks like lately? He looks horrible and he's acting weird. Max and Derek are talking about taking him to see doctors. Do you realize what that could mean? They will find out about us. And the poison."

"Would you relax?" Rachel asked, looking at the bathroom door to make sure it was still closed. "Calm down. Your friend will be fine. The medicine is untraceable doing exactly what it's supposed to do -- altering his mind and judgment a bit. That's all."

"Altering his mind? You're fucking crazy."

"No," Rachel said. "But your friend is...at least temporarily."

"I can't do this anymore."

"I have your boyfriend's phone number right here--
"

"How much longer?"

"Not long, I promise," Rachel said. "Now I have to go. I'll see you at the fundraiser." Rachel disconnected the call as Marco stepped out of the bathroom. "Hello, handsome."

"A business call at this hour?"

Rachel put her hands on Marco's chest. "Don't you worry about it, my handsome fiancé."

"Fiancé? Don't you think you're jumping the gun a bit?"

Rachel kissed Marco. "Not at all. We'll be married sooner than you think. And then you'll have the controlling interest in Mancini Global that you have always wanted."

Later that evening, the fundraising gala that had taken so much time and effort to plan finally commenced. Searchlights in front of The Boys and the Booze crisscrossed the partly cloudy Chicago sky guiding guests from all over the city to the event's venue. Cars and limousines formed a line outside the club dropping off guests, who stepped out of the cars eager to get inside, shed their overcoats, and show off their evening attire.

As guests arrived and checked their coats, they were greeted with a glass of champagne and the jazzy music of Whiskey and Cherries, the first performers of the evening. Servers worked their way around the room offering guests cocktails and hors d'oeuvres. Some guests inspected the layout and décor of the new restaurant while others made their way through the silent auction placing bids on their favorite items.

Max was speaking with Amy Armstrong, the singer scheduled to perform when Whiskey and Cherries concluded.

"You look amazing," Max told her, admiring her beautiful dress.

"Oh, you're sweet," she replied.

"We really appreciate you being here tonight."

Amy smiled. "My pleasure. How could I say 'no" to an event like this? And the place looks great, by the way."

"Thanks," Max replied. "Once the fundraiser is over and we get through our official opening, I'd love to sit down with you and talk about you performing here regularly."

"I'd like that very much."

"Great. Do you need anything else before you go on?"

"I'm good, thanks. I'm sure you need to talk to some of your other guests. Don't worry about me."

"Perfect. I'll catch up with you in a bit." Max turned and headed through the crowd toward the kitchen. On the way, he stopped to speak with Dustin. "Everything going okay?"

"Great," Dustin replied. "Appetizers are being passed, cocktails are flowing, and the staff is on top of things."

"All because of you," Max added. "Thanks so much. How's Jensen?"

"He's doing a great job. Everyone is. And the guests seem to be having a great time already."

"Looks like it," Max stated.

"And you look pretty handsome in that tux, I might add," Dustin added, winking at Max. "Just let me know if you need anything."

Max patted Dustin on the shoulder. "Thanks, Dustin. Let's just keep everything running smoothly."

As Dustin walked away, he passed Ben, who was still in disguise and wearing the same outfit as the rest of the wait staff. With a tray of appetizers in hand, he made his way through the crowd serving guests.

Dressed handsomely in a tuxedo, Justin searched the crowd to find his brother Emmett. When he found him, Justin hugged Emmett and then straightened his tie.

"Good to see you," Justin said. "How are you feeling?"

"Why does everyone keep asking that?" Emmett asked hostilely.

"Because we're concerned about you, that's why. You haven't been yourself lately."

"I'm just tired," Emmett declared. "I wish everyone would just get off my back."

"Let's get you checked out by a doctor on Monday, okay?" Justin asked as Keith walked over to the two men.

"I'm sure Emmett's just tired," Keith said, interrupting. "He'll be fine."

Justin raised his eyebrow. "Since when are you a doctor?"

"Don't talk to him that way," Emmett said. "He's right. I'm just tired."

"I don't think that's all it is," Justin said. "But I'm not going to argue with the two of you about it tonight." Justin walked away.

"Thank you," Emmett said to Keith. "I just want people to leave me alone."

"Of course," Keith said. "I'm sure you'll be feeling better soon."

After introducing Amy Armstrong to the crowd, Jesse stepped off the stage and walked over to the corner where Cole and David were talking with singer Steve Grand.

"I still can't believe you're here," Cole said to Steve. "This is so generous of you."

"We're both huge fans," David added.

"Thank you so much," Steve said as his signature smile widened.

418

"You have no idea how much you mean to so many people," Cole stated. "You're really a hero."

"I've been very fortunate," Steve said. "I'm glad to be able to help out wherever I can."

"Well, you being here tonight means so much to all of us," Jesse said. "Is there anything we can get you or that you need before you go on?"

"I'm all set, thanks."

"Thanks for donating your CDs for the silent auction, too. People are practically fighting over them."

Steve laughed. "I'm not responsible if any violence breaks out."

"I'm so excited to hear you sing," David said.

Cole added, "He's like a teenage girl at a boy band concert."

David put his arm around Cole. "That's how I feel all the time when I'm around you."

"Aww," Steve said as Cole blushed.

"On that note," Cole said, "I need another drink. Or two."

"Can we get you one?" Jesse asked.

Steve put up his hand. "I'm okay for now, thanks."

"Okay. I'll be introducing you as soon as Amy wraps up," Jesse explained.

"I'll be ready."

"See you in a bit," David said as he and Cole walked away toward the bar.

"Have you seen Derek anywhere?" Cole asked David as they walked.

"No, thank God," David said. "Why jinx it by asking?"

"Just seems odd that he's not here."

"I'm sure he is…somewhere."

David and Cole passed the silent auction area where Rachel was walking through the aisles browsing the available items. Justin spotted her and rushed over.

"Where the hell have you been?" Justin asked, grabbing her by the arm.

"Watch it," Rachel said. "You can't afford to replace this dress."

"You haven't returned any of my calls."

"So it is true. You can see again."

"Yes," Justin stated.

"That's good," Rachel said with a smile. "That way you'll be able to see me clearly when I walk down the aisle at my wedding."

"Wedding? What are you talking about?"

"You'll see soon enough."

"I don't even care who the loser is. What I do care about is that you betrayed me. Showing that video at my brother's engagement party?"

"I don't know what you're talking about," Rachel said, turning away from Justin.

"Don't walk away from me."

Marco walked up behind Rachel, slipping his arm around her waist. "Am I interrupting?"

Justin rolled his eyes. "Oh, for God's sake. Now it all makes sense. Your marriage? You two deserve each other."

"I won't say what you deserve," Marco replied. "Where's your brother Derek? I haven't seen him. Maybe he's doing another press conference."

"I'm sure he's around here somewhere," Justin said as he walked away from the couple.

"You okay?" Marco asked.

"Of course," Rachel replied. "You know I can handle myself."

"I sure do," Marco said with a smile as his cell phone began to ring. "Excuse me." Marco left the area and exited the club. Once on the sidewalk, he answered the call. "Got it?" Marco paused. "Excellent. I'll be right there." Marco put his phone away and hailed a taxi cab.

As Marco left the fundraiser venue, Ben was in the alley behind the restaurant. Working quickly, he applied locks to the rear exits of the club. He activated the locks and made sure they were secure so that no one could leave the fundraiser from the back doors. Then he walked around to the front of the club and joined a few other servers who were standing on the sidewalk having a smoking break. When they re-entered the club from the sidewalk, so did he.

Walking back inside, Ben passed right by Cole and David, who were talking as Justin approached them. He extended his hand to Cole to greet him.

"Hey, Cole," Justin said, shaking his hand. "It's been a long time."

"It has," Cole said uncomfortably.

"The last time was at the warehouse with Emmett," Justin said. "And the engagement party, of course."

"Of course," Cole said quietly.

David extended his hand to Justin. "I'm David Young."

"Oh, yes," Justin said, shaking hands. "Derek's physical therapist."

"Among other things," David said, as he wrapped his arm around Cole's waist.

Justin took note of David's arm. "I want to apologize for any stress that video caused."

"It's old news at this point," Cole said.

"We've moved beyond that," David added.

"I see," Justin stated. "I guess what I'm trying to say is that whatever is going on between Derek and you is between the two of you. I hope we can be friends regardless."

"Friends?" Cole asked.

"There's nothing between Derek and Cole anymore," David said. "Nothing to worry about."

"I was never worried," Justin said.

Jensen approached the three men with a tray of champagne glasses. "Champagne, gentlemen?"

"Thank you," Justin said, taking a glass from the tray.

"You," Jensen said when he looked at Cole.

"Do we know each other?" Cole asked.

"I'm Jensen," he said. "I just recognize you from the club where I used to dance."

David laughed. "Nice."

"Excuse me," Jensen said as he stepped away. When he walked a safe distance from the three men, he turned and looked back at Cole. He thought back to a chilly autumn day, when he saw Cole walking on Roscoe Street with his phone out; it was the day the Cole was trying to locate Derek's condo for the first time. Pulling his hood down over his head, Jensen lunged at Cole, hit him on the back of the head with a metal tool, and knocked him to the ground. Jensen took Cole's phone and ran off without being seen, leaving Cole bleeding on the sidewalk in front of Derek's home.

Jensen was startled from his daydream when Jesse took the stage. Standing in the spotlight, Jesse quickly got the attention of the fundraiser guests.

"Ladies and gentlemen, I just want to take a moment to formally thank you all for coming tonight. Planning this evening has been a great journey and I'm so pleased to see you all here tonight celebrating and raising money for a great cause. The inspiration for this evening was Maggie O'Brien, the mother of my best friend Cole. Maggie has been living with, and mostly beating, cancer for many years; she is an inspiration to all of us. Unfortunately, she could not make the trip to Chicago to be here tonight and she remains in our thoughts and prayers as she completes her latest round of chemotherapy."

The crowd responded to Jesse with thunderous applause. "I asked Cole to come up and say a few words but, for the first time in his life, he's being bashful. He just wanted me to offer his heartfelt thanks on behalf of his lovely mother." The crowd applauded again.

"Before I introduce our headliner tonight, I want to take a moment to thank a few people. First, I'd like to thank Logan Pryce, my dear friend who helped plan this evening. It wouldn't have been possible without him." Guests clapped to acknowledge Logan. "I also want to thank Emmett Mancini and Max Taylor for generously hosting this event in their beautiful new restaurant and club. We hope you all will come back once they are officially open." More applause from the guests. "Of course, we want to thank everyone who contributed items for the silent auction. We really appreciate your generosity. And finally, we'd like to thank our amazing entertainers. Brian, Meredith, and Danielle of Whiskey and Cherries. The amazing Amy Armstrong. And now, our very special guest and Chicago's very own all-American boy, Steve Grand!"

The crowd erupted in cheers as Jesse left the stage and Steve Grand walked forward into the spotlight. As Steve began to sing "Whiskey Crime," Jesse descended the stairs from the stage and was greeted with open arms by Logan, who kissed him.

"That was great," Logan said. "I'm so proud of you."

"Thanks, Logan," Jesse replied. "That means a lot."

"You mean a lot," Logan added. "To me." He took Jesse's hands into his and looked into Jesse's eyes. "I know we have a lot to discuss and work out -- and I know that we can do it together. I'm ready to start again. And I'm ready to wear your ring again."

Jesse's eyes welled up with tears as he hugged Logan tightly. "I love you so much."

"I love you, too," Logan said, kissing Jesse.

"And so do I," Jacqueline said as she approached the couple.

"Mom! You came," Jesse said, giving his mother a hug.

"I couldn't stay away," Jacqueline replied with a smile.

"Look at you," Jesse continued. "You look gorgeous."

Jacqueline smiled. "Thank you."

"You really do," Logan added.

From across the room, Ben watched Jacqueline and the others. "Dammit, Jacqueline," Ben mumbled. "You can't be here tonight."

Dustin walked over to Ben. "I need more champagne passed through," he told Ben.

"Sure thing," Ben replied, heading back toward the kitchen.

"Everything okay?" Max asked as he approached Dustin.

"You bet," Dustin replied. "You okay?"

"Great, thanks. You're doing a fantastic job. Thank you so much."

"That's what you pay me for," Dustin replied. "How's Emmett doing?"

"I haven't seen him," Max replied. "Or his brother Derek, either."

Max stepped away as Dustin returned to work. Cole stepped into Max's path to get his attention.

"Can I talk to you for a moment?" Cole asked. Reading Max's puzzled look, Cole added, "It's not about Derek, or the video, or anything like that."

"I really need to find Emmett."

"This will just take a moment," Cole persisted.

"Okay."

"I want you to know that I will help you mend fences with Jesse in any way that I can."

Max raised his eyebrows. "Really?"

"I know things aren't good between the two of you. And I know how stubborn and angry he can get--" Max interrupted Cole with a laugh. "--but you are his father and this much I know: he has spent his entire life wanting to know his father. It's going to be rough, but I know you two can work things out."

"Thank you for saying that."

"No matter what you think of me, I am here to help you. Jesse is a brother to me. I want him to be happy. And, in the end, having a relationship with his father is something I know he will cherish."

"I appreciate that, Cole," Max said. "And for the record, I have no hard feelings against you and neither does Emmett. What happened between Derek and you is between the two of you. No one else. And we are all very appreciative for the many great things you have done to protect the lives of people we all care about."

"Thank you," Cole said. "And you don't need to worry about Derek and me any longer. We are finished."

As Steve Grand continued to sing, Tyler and Joyelle danced to his music.

"Having fun?" Tyler asked.

Joyelle smiled. "The best time. Thank you."

"You're the best looking one here," Tyler added.

"You're sweet," Joyelle replied, putting her head against Tyler's shoulder. "And you feel good, too. You make me feel safe."

"You are safe with me, Joyelle," Tyler assured her. "Always."

"Thank you."

As they continued to dance, Joyelle spotted Cole and David talking at the edge of the dance floor. Joyelle stopped dancing and said to Tyler, "Please come with me. I need to do this." Taking Tyler's hand, Joyelle led him off the dance floor and over to Cole and David.

"Hello, Cole," Joyelle said as David stood behind him.

"Hello, Joyelle," Cole replied nervously. "You look great."

"Thank you," Joyelle replied. "I know how awkward this is for both of us, but I needed to talk to you. I want to thank you for trying to save me and my children in the explosion."

"You're welcome," Cole replied. "I'm so sorry for your loss."

"We both are," David added.

"You saved me that day on the sidewalk when I got mugged. I owed you one," Cole said, jokingly.

"Funny how our lives are so intertwined," Joyelle said. "But I appreciate what you tried to do on New Year's Eve."

"He's a good man," David said.

"I'm truly sorry for everything," Cole said. "I'm sorry for any pain this whole situation has caused you."

"Things work out as they're supposed to," Tyler said.

Justin saw the two couples talking and worked his way over to them. "You all look cozy."

"What do you want, Justin?" Joyelle asked.

"Have you seen Derek? I can't find him."

"Thankfully, no," Joyelle replied, turning away from Justin.

"What about you, Cole? Any sign of Derek?" Cole didn't reply. "Well, if any of you see him--"

"We won't," Tyler said.

"It's funny, isn't it, Joyelle?"

"What are you talking about?"

"Well, you gave me all that flack on the morning of your wedding when I asked you to marry me instead of Derek. I bet now you wish you had given me a chance.

You wouldn't be caught in this homoerotic mess, if you had."

"You're pathetic," Joyelle said.

Cole spoke up. "Justin, why don't you--"

"At least you would have known what it's like to be married to a real man. Instead you were just a closeted gay man's play thing."

Without hesitating, Tyler punched Justin in the face, sending him backwards onto the floor. As Tyler lunged forward to hit Justin again, David grabbed him and pulled him back.

"Easy, Tyler," David said.

"He isn't worth it," Joyelle added.

"You better watch your mouth!" Tyler yelled at Justin. "Stay away from her!"

Gino walked over and helped Justin up from the floor. "There you are. Making friends, as always."

Joyelle and Tyler returned to the dance floor to continue their dance. Cole and David walked away toward the bar.

"What was that all about?" Gino asked.

Justin brushed himself off. "I was actually looking for Derek. I can't find him."

"That makes two of us. I can't find my brother, either."

As Justin and Gino searched for their brothers, Marco was standing in his hotel suite with another man.

"You did well," Marco told the man. "No problems?"

"None," the man replied. "They were both at the fundraiser like you said, so there was no one in the apartment. It was a piece of cake."

"And you got the painting here without damaging it?"

"Right there," the man said, pointing to the covered painting leaning against the wall. "In perfect condition."

Marco removed an envelope from the breast pocket of his tuxedo jacket and handed it to his friend. "Good work. Thank you."

"Thank you. Have a good evening."

"I will," Marco said as he watched his man leave the room.

Then he walked over to the wall and removed the sheet covering the painting. He paused a moment and looked at the painting, which had hung on the wall of David and Tyler's apartment only moments earlier.

He turned the painting around and examined its back. He walked over to the desk and picked up a pocket knife. He carefully used it to cut open the back of the painting. Gently, he removed the layers of brown paper and matting. Then he found what he was looking for -- a small manila envelope.

He opened the envelope and carefully removed its contents. He quickly looked through the documents, skimming them one at a time. "My God, it's you." He looked back the papers in his hand. Then he began to laugh. "Who would have guessed that Emmett Mancini is his missing brother's landlord?"

While Marco savored his discovery, Emmett was in his bedroom above the club pulling clothes out of his closet and throwing them around the room. Carrying some papers in his hand, Jensen cautiously entered the room and watched Emmett in his frenzied state.

"Are you okay?" Jensen asked softly.

"What are you doing up here?"

"I came looking for you. We couldn't find you downstairs and they need your signature on these documents for the performers."

"Give me those," Emmett said, tearing the papers from Jensen's hand. He threw them onto the nearby desk, tore through the desk drawer to find a pen, and quickly signed them.

"Here," Emmet said, throwing the papers at Jensen.

Jensen knelt down to gather the documents. "I also wanted to see if you were okay."

"Does it look like I'm okay?" Emmett asked, throwing more clothes around the room. "I can't find it. I can't find it."

"What?" Jensen asked. "What are you looking for?"

"I can't find it!"

Jensen walked over to Emmett and gently grabbed his arm. "Emmett, you're not well."

"I'm fine," Emmett said, stopping and facing Jensen. "I just -- I just--" Emmett stopped his rant and looked into Jensen's eyes. He put his hands on Jensen's shoulders and kissed him.

Stunned, Jensen stood still as Emmett continued to kiss him. Then Jensen slowly folded his arms around Emmett and kissed him back. Their lips pressed against each other as Emmett ran his fingers through Jensen's hair.

Jensen massaged Emmett's back and lowered his hands to Emmett's firm ass.

Suddenly, Emmett collapsed in Jensen's arms. Jensen momentarily held the dead weight of Emmett's body in his arms and then let go, Emmett's body crashing into the floor. Jensen looked at the unconscious body at his feet and then pulled out his cell phone and dialed a number.

"It's me. I'm with him now. We may have a problem."

Derek walked out onto the back deck of his condo. As he began walking down the two flights of stairs to the ground level, a person watched him from the bottom of the stairs. Hiding in the shadows created by the moonlight hitting the stairs, the person remained unseen by Derek.

As Derek made the turn on the stairs and continued to descend the final flight, the person stepped forward. Raising a gun into the air, the person fired two shots directly at Derek. Blood splattered onto the stairs as well as the concrete below. While the shooter fled, Derek's body collapsed, falling over the railing and onto the ground. Motionless, his body rested at the foot of the stairwell, blood slowly spreading over the pavement.

Downstairs in the club, Jesse was thanking and saying goodbye to the entertainers. Jacqueline, Tyler, Joyelle were standing nearby as the members of Whiskey and Cherries as well as Amy Armstrong left the club.

"Thanks again," Jesse told Steve Grand. "You were amazing."

"My pleasure," Steve said. "This was an amazing night. I was I could stay longer but I have to catch a flight in the morning."

"No problem," Jesse said.

"You really were amazing," Joyelle added. "I think you made a bunch of new fans tonight."

"Thank you," Steve said with a smile as he left the club.

"What a sweetheart," Joyelle stated.

"You sure are," Tyler added, jokingly.

"I should be heading out, too," Jacqueline said to Jesse.

"Thanks so much for coming," Jesse said, hugging his mother. "You have no idea how much it means to me."

"I'm so proud of you," Jacqueline declared. "This was really a great event."

"I'll call you tomorrow," Jesse said.

"Good night," Jacqueline said to Tyler and Joyelle as she left the party.

Joyelle's phone began to ring. "Excuse me," she said as she removed it from her purse and walked away from the others.

From a distance, Ben watched Jacqueline leave the party. He smiled and mumbled, "Perfect. It's show time."

As Ben headed toward the basement, Joyelle answered her call.

"Hello?"

"Hello, Joyelle. It's Dr. MacMahon."

"Hello, Doctor."

"I'm sorry to bother you at night but we got the results of your tests back and I wanted to share them with you right away."

"Is anything wrong?"

"On the contrary," the doctor explained. "It's really good news."

"What news?"

"Congratulations, Joyelle. You're pregnant."

While Joyelle absorbed the doctor's information, Keith discreetly approached Rachel at the far end of the club.

"We need to talk," Keith said.

"Not here," Rachel said. "Do you want someone to see us talking?"

"Have you seen Emmett tonight? He looks terrible and is completely out of it. I'm done. I'm not doing this anymore.

"You know the consequences of that choice."

"I don't care anymore," Keith said. "I was engaged to Emmett once. I can't do this to him. I'm going to tell Michael my secret myself."

"Don't double-cross me, Keith. You'll wish you hadn't."

Keith left Rachel and searched for Michael in the crowd. As he did, he passed Gino and Justin.

"This is a special night," Justin said.

"It is," Gino agreed. "And you only got into one fight."

Justin smiled. "You're a very special man."

"Well, I won't argue with that."

"You are the one person in my life who always has my back. You see the good in me and overlook the bad."

"I try," Gino added. "You don't always make it easy."

"And I have come to realize lately just how much I really do love you."

"I love you, too, Justin."

Justin reached into his pocket and pulled out a small black box. "So I was wondering, Gino..." Justin opened the back revealing a diamond and platinum ring. "I was wondering if you'd do me the honor of marrying me?"

While Justin waited for Gino's reply to his marriage proposal, Keith found Michael in the crowd.

"There you are, Stormy," Michael said with a smile. "Where have you been?"

"I need to talk to you."

"Are you okay? You're trembling."

"There is just something important that I need to talk to you about."

"Okay."

All of a sudden, all the lights in the restaurant and club went out. In the darkness, some people began to scream and panic while others tried to calm those around them and wait for the lights to come back on. Max and Dustin tried to make their way toward the back of the club to head into the basement.

Suddenly, a huge burst of fiery flames shot out of the vents in the floor at the front of the club, blocking the windows and door. Window coverings and tablecloths immediately caught fire as people jumped back from the flames, which illuminated the room.

In the basement, Ben worked quickly. He opened the valves on the barrels that he had installed earlier so that when someone upstairs pulled the fire alarm, the flammable fluid spewed from the ceiling sprinklers in the club. Immediately catching fire as it emerged from the sprinklers, the liquid rained fire down on the guests as they chaotically rushed toward the back exits of the club, which Ben had locked from the outside.

Hearing the screams of the guests upstairs, Ben hurried to leave the basement. When he reached the door, it was stuck. He tried the handle, but the door wouldn't open. He pounded on it and tried to shove it open, but he was trapped. Looking down at the base of the door, he saw smoke entering the room. "Help me! Let me out of here!"

Ben's screams couldn't be heard over the loud yells of the guests upstairs. Fire spewing in every direction, guests scrambled to find a way out of the inferno Ben had created. Thick smoke filled the room, working its way up into the bedroom where Emmett's unconscious body lay on the floor.

From outside the building, flames could be seen and yells could be heard. In the distance, the sound of fire truck sirens gradually grew louder. As the club windows shattered, fire and smoke emerged, working their way up into the sky. The wind pushed the smoke across nearby blocks quickly and it soon passed over the area where Derek's bloody body rested on the ground. The moon hung high over the city of Chicago, casting its warm glow on everything beneath it.

Made in the USA
Middletown, DE
20 May 2015